SOME OTHER LIFE

E Farrier

authorHOUSE®

AuthorHouse™ UK Ltd.
500 Avebury Boulevard
Central Milton Keynes, MK9 2BE
www.authorhouse.co.uk
Phone: 08001974150

© 2010 E Farrier. All rights reserved.

No part of this book may be reproduced, stored in a retrieval system, or transmitted by any means without the written permission of the author.

First published by AuthorHouse   10/262010

ISBN: 978-1-4520-7752-9 (sc)

This book is printed on acid-free paper.

Chapter One

Tom Bernstein walked briskly down the bright corridors of St Margaret's Hospital anxious to get to his destination. He pushed his way through the throng of student nurses, oblivious to the admiring glances thrown his way. His latest case dominated his mind. He stood just over six foot, with dark wavy hair cut very short emphasising his dark blue eyes. He loosened his tie resisting the urge to open every window he could see to let the sultry Boston air waft over him.

This case troubled him and he felt sorry for the young girl lying in hospital day after day with no one to visit her. Her beautiful, battered face had haunted Tom from the first day he saw her. She looked so fragile, like a small child lying in a large bed surrounded by a maze of tubes, wires and bandages. He wanted to pick her hand up and squeeze it. Of course, he couldn't get emotionally involved and had to work hard to distance himself. It was the first time an assignment like this had affected him but Harry Fox, his boss, had warned that this would happen one day. He wouldn't rest until he had discovered her true identity. At least they'd found out her first name from a bit of her driving licence. They couldn't make out the rest of it because it had been damaged in the fire. It had been a few days since they found her lying unconscious next to a burning car. He felt that they were finally getting somewhere.

Dr Rosie Shaw and her team still monitored her very carefully. Until she woke up, they couldn't determine the level of brain damage she had sustained in the accident. The longer she stayed unconscious, the more concerned they became about how long it would take the patient to make a full recovery.

'Mel, how is she today?' Rosie asked, carefully scanning her notes.

'She's moving her eyes and is starting to whisper. She's showing no signs of consciousness yet but it's only a matter of time.'

Mel smiled at her friend; she noticed Rosie looked pale and tired. This patient was getting to Rosie but she wouldn't dare say anything, Rosie being a woman who didn't take advice, however well intentioned.

'Mel, let me see the CT scans please? Hmm - interesting, the swelling has gone down and everything looks normal, she should be waking up by now.'

Rosie's stomach growled again for the third time that day. She had a busy morning clinic so hadn't had a minute to grab some lunch.

'Page me if there are any changes. I'm going to get a coffee and a bagel before my afternoon clinic starts. Tom Bernstein is coming in to see me. Can you send him down to the canteen when he arrives?' Rosie almost collided with Tom as he walked in, giving Rosie a million- dollar smile. She smiled back wishing her heart wouldn't flutter every time he grinned at her.

'Rosie, we've had a breakthrough,' Tom said breathlessly. He had taken the stairs to the tenth floor, instead of the lift. He held the door open for Rosie to walk through. They were wandering through the crowded corridor heading towards Rosie's office.

'Have you found her family?' Rosie asked.

'Not yet, we know that she's Scottish and stayed with a family called the Emersons. We don't have an address for them yet. We have a team working through all the people with the name Emerson in Boston and the surrounding area. Give us a couple of days and hopefully we will be able to track down her family. How is she?' Tom asked as casually as he could.

'She's still having seizures but we're hoping that she'll wake up soon. Don't assume that she will be coherent because, as with anyone who's been in a coma for a long time; we'll have to take things very slowly,' Rosie warned as she hugged the file with Alison's notes close to her chest looking at Tom's intense gaze and wishing she wouldn't blush when he looked at her. Oh those piercing navy blue eyes; perfect for policing bored right into you. It was almost as if he could read your mind – don't be silly, she thought – you're just tired and hungry, wake up. Rosie cleared her throat and said:

'Look I'm starving; can we discuss this further down at the diner? I need to get some lunch before my afternoon appointments start arriving. There's something else you need to know before I carry out any further tests.'
'Sure, I haven't eaten myself – I need a caffeine fix anyway.'
Tom smiled down at Rosie; he liked her because she was straightforward and unassuming. He noticed there were dark circles under her large hazel eyes.

'It's good that we have a name for her at last, she may start responding to it but the thing that concerns me is the longer she stays unconscious, the more worried we become about her memory coming back. We've seen patients recover their memory quite quickly. It does vary from patient to patient. Alison is young and strong though,' Rosie pointed out and continued.

 'Also there's strong evidence that she was attacked before getting into the car.'
'You mean – was she beaten up?'

'Yes but there's also evidence of rape – there's bruising in certain areas of her body that are not consistent with a car accident and traces of recent sexual intercourse. However, I can't confirm this until she wakes up. She may not remember the attack or what happened to her in that car for quite some time.'

'Unless she confirms that she was attacked and makes a complaint then we won't be able to investigate any allegation of rape at the moment. Poor kid, I feel for her lying there day in day out with no one to visit her. I'm glad I'm not in her shoes.' Tom said thoughtfully with a distant look in his eyes.

'Sounds like you've got a crush on that beautiful girl lying up there - you're blushing Tom,' Rosie teased as they walked into the diner.

'Um, not at all, I'm just doing my job – Hmm that coffee smells good,' Tom said, annoyed with himself that Rosie could read his thoughts so easily and he couldn't afford to get personally involved in this case. She was a very intuitive woman.

Tom hastily picked up a tray, and grabbed a pastrami, cheese and salad baguette together with a mug of steaming coffee. Annoyed at himself for blushing, he could see a mischievous glint in Rosie's eyes. Rosie picked up a cream cheese and salmon bagel with salad and a generous chocolate fudge brownie. She smiled sheepishly at Tom – 'I need the energy today, so what the hell!'

'Don't worry Doctor – I'll just call the diet police later!'

Tom had a deep throaty laugh that was like a growl. They sat down at a small table by the grimy window. You could see most of the Boston skyline on a clear day, but it was rather hazy today.

'So, what's the long-term plan for Alison then?' Tom asked, looking out the window and sipping his coffee.

'Well when Alison wakes up and once she's stable, the best place for her would be The Boston Center for Head Injuries – it has a dedicated team of psychologists and physiotherapists. It's for people with all types of head injury. Some of them will be close to her age. I'll inform you when she is fit to move but at the moment she'll stay where she is."

Rosie took a final bite of her bagel but her pager went off. With a big sigh she frantically searched her pockets for it.

'It's the ward. Sorry Tom, I need to go. Look if there's any change in her condition. I'll let you know – okay? I'll send you a report on Alison in a couple of days.'

'Okay, thanks Rosie.'

Rosie stuffed the brownie in her pocket; she would eat it later and hurried out of the diner, her auburn ponytail swinging jauntily from side to side. Tom sat where he was, wondering what to do next. Rosie was surprised to see her young patient had her ventilation tubes removed. Mel had removed them from her throat to make her more comfortable.

'Hi, what is it Mel?' Rosie asked but before Mel could answer Alison spoke for the first time.

'Where am I? What's happened?' Alison croaked and blinked rapidly struggling to focus properly.

Finally Alison climbed out of the darkness that had dominated her mind. The intense pain that had gripped her for so long eased, dancing shadows of what looked like people, seemed to come and go. Her mind was a kaleidoscope of raw emotions, colours and smells. At times she thought that she'd died and was floating in another world, not quite in heaven or hell. Like a bird's feather in a breeze going in no particular direction.

'You're in hospital, you've had a nasty accident and you've been asleep for a long time,' Rosie explained.

'Accident? What accident? I can't remember having an accident? Who are you? Where am I?' Alison asked still groggy from being unconscious for so long.

I'm so thirsty, Alison thought but all she could focus on was the two large brown eyes that peered down at her and a faint smell of perfume filled her nostrils. It smelled familiar but she couldn't understand why.

Bloody hell – what's wrong with me – why can't I move or speak properly? Alison wanted to ask but the words failed to come out. She swallowed hard, her tongue stuck to the roof of her mouth so she tried to concentrate on the moving lips of the red headed woman in front of her. Where's the remote control – I want to turn the volume up? She smiled at that ludicrous thought. The mist was coming back to claim her but Alison didn't want to return to that strange and unreal world.

It was like being doped, only she had no control over it and neither did the shadowy beings that looked like hospital staff in front of her. Come on girl, concentrate on what they're saying, this is important, Alison thought and with a surge of determination she tried to concentrate on what was being said.

'Alison – you've been in a car accident and you've hurt your head. You're in hospital. You've been unconscious for a long time.' Rosie said patiently smiling down at the confused young girl before her.

'What? Why do you keep calling me Alison? It doesn't sound like my name? You don't know me and I don't know you! What accident. I don't remember having an accident.'

Oh my head, it hurts so much I can hardly stand it. I want to get off the roundabout. Am I going mad or am I dreaming? Where on earth am I? This is nuts – I must be dreaming surely? Either that or I've had too much vodka.

Alison tried to lift her head, but she was too weak and the room spun wildly. She could just make out the blurred faces of Mel and Rosie. They both looked at her with concern in their eyes but this only annoyed Alison. She couldn't remember a thing, every time they called her name, she didn't recognise it.

What on earth have I got on my head? Is this some kind of sick joke? I wish I could wake up. Alison noticed a drip on her right hand and it hurt when she moved it. Oh no, this isn't a dream, this is real, Oh my God! What the hell has happened to me?

'How long have I been here?' Alison whispered her throat was sore and dry; she kept swallowing to try and clear it. God – my head really hurts I can hardly stand it.

'A few weeks, we've been trying to contact your family. Can you remember anything about your family?' Rosie asked, holding her breath.

'But where am I?'

'You're in St Margaret's Hospital in Boston, North America. We think you came here for a holiday, Alison. You had a car accident and you've been asleep for a long time. Do you remember anything?'

'No and I wish you would stop calling me Alison, it doesn't sound like my name,' said Alison groggily.

'Do you know what your name might be?' Mel asked looking at Rosie, who was across the bed as Alison still tried to sit up but fell back onto the pillows.

'If I knew I would tell you? Why aren't you helping me? You're supposed to be a doctor – you have all the answers so why do you keep asking me the same questions when I don't know the answer!' Alison cried bewildered.

Why doesn't anything look familiar to me: even my own

name doesn't sound right? Alison is a name I don't like the sound of and they keep telling me that's my name but is it? I feel so weak I can't think straight, my limbs are like dead weights. I ache all over and my head feels like it's going to explode into a thousand tiny fragments. Where's Mum and Dad? Why can't I speak without slurring my words, my throat is so dry all I can do is gape at them. I'm trying to concentrate on their words but all I can see is their mouths moving in slow motion like a silent movie without the subtitles. They're so bloody patronising bending over me and talking at me like some village idiot. Everything is such a blur, I'm floating and it feels weird. Its does look like I'm in hospital; this is not good. I'm shattered, so tired I just can't fight the dark anymore. This time Alison welcomed oblivion; anything was better than the reality of her situation.

'We are trying to trace your family, Alison, but at the moment you need lots of rest,' Rosie said as Alison closed her eyes but she was sure Alison could still hear her and continued, 'You've had a very serious accident but the good news is that you're going to be okay. You will get your memory back but it'll take time and you need lots of rest.'

Rosie patted Alison's hand reassuringly and ushered Mel to the door. Alison's eyelids fluttered again before Rosie finished her last sentence, Rosie thought she was asleep but Alison listened to what was being said as she wasn't quite asleep yet.

'Are you thinking what I am thinking? It's worse than we thought. However it's early days yet. Reduce the amount of medication she is on and with a bit of luck, her memory might start returning when she is less groggy.'

'I'll let the rest of the team know and put it in her notes,' Mel said.

'I'm not staying here!' Alison opened her eyes and glared at Mel. She'd eventually found her voice, and had heard what they had been discussing. Wow, my vocal cords seem to work when it suits them! This is mad, I want to sleep but I'm afraid I'll never wake up again.

'Calm down Alison – you mustn't wear yourself out by shouting. I'm not going to hurt you,' Mel said soothingly. Alison struggled to stay awake after her outburst and had fallen asleep again. This time, she heard nothing.
'Thanks Mel, see you later, I'm late for clinic.'

Rosie hurried down the corridor, she would check on Alison before she went home. Rosie walked into her office and picked up the phone to call Tom.

'Hi Tom, Alison has just woken up. I'm afraid she doesn't recognise her name or where she's from. Don't worry; we've reduced her medication, and then we'll discuss when she is fit to interview. We just have to take it a day at a time. Look, I've got to go. I'll have patients breaking down my door if I don't get a move on.'

'Thanks, Rosie. I'll speak to you in a couple of days.' Tom headed back to his office with a heavy heart; he called Harry who was relieved that she had woken up at last. They just had to be patient after all; they had virtually nothing to investigate until they found out what exactly happened to her.

Chapter Two

Roz was in the middle of a tense meeting when the boardroom telephone sprung into action, making everyone jump.

'Lucy, I told you I didn't want any interruptions. What is it?' Roz said through gritted teeth as she picked up the cordless phone that was beside her handbag.

'Sorry it's an urgent call from Mrs Emerson in Boston, it's about Alison.'

'Put her through. Hi Amelia, is everything alright?'

'Oh Roz, I've been trying to reach you all morning, Alison never came home last night. I gave her a key but she hasn't come back,' Amelia said anxiously.

'Really?' Roz was concerned because Alison hadn't been in America long enough to stay overnight with anyone and muttered to herself, 'That's strange.'

'Yes, I thought so too and her mobile phone is switched off as well.' Amelia shrilled making Roz cringe; panic rose in her voice like a pneumatic drill.

"Look, you must calm down Amelia. I'm sure there's a reasonable explanation. Call me if she does appear. I'll contact David and Alex to see if she's been in touch with them and then I'll ring you back."

Roz paced up and down the boardroom aware that ten pairs of eyes watched her every move. She turned her back on the table and walked over to the window with the phone still attached to her ear; her burgundy fingernails drummed impatiently on the sill as she listened with growing impatience whilst Amelia twittered on.

'Don't do anything until I've contacted you, I'm really sorry, I have to go. I'm in the middle of a meeting, David's in Thailand so I can't reach him.'

'I hope she's alright, I don't know what to do for the best..........'

'Don't worry; I'll speak to you later, Bye'.

Roz hung up abruptly; damn I should have taken this call in my office. I don't want any gossip circulating around my staff about Alison's whereabouts. This is the last thing I need. She was uneasy; it was not like Alison to disappear. Amelia didn't feel any better after talking to Roz either.

Alison had been missing for fifteen hours but Roz knew she couldn't contact the police until at least twenty - four hours had elapsed. An ominous feeling was building within her that something was very wrong. Like most mothers she had a sixth sense about these things. Even then, Alison was twenty one, what could they do? Roz tried Alison's mobile phone again but all she got was a dead tone, which only heightened her anxiety further. She glanced at the telephone throughout the meeting, praying it would ring with more news.

Roz gave her management team an icy glare. They looked away hastily and some stared at the floor. Others focused on their projection figures for Christmas, playing with their pencils or ties. The youngest manager, Liz, chewed on her necklace whilst doodling on her shorthand pad.

'Liz! Stop chewing on your bloody necklace, it's unprofessional. The rest of you'd better pay attention when I'm talking to you or none of you'll have a shop to run by the end of the day. Do I make myself clear?' Roz roared.

This made Liz almost jump out of her seat, not knowing where to look.

'Sorry Roz', she stammered, bewildered at Roz's angry outburst. Roz smiled with great satisfaction when she saw the anxious faces peering at her around the boardroom table. That got their attention, she thought smugly.

'Right where were we?' Roz strode across the room to the overhead projector and started to plan the strategy for Christmas. Roz's business was struggling and she needed a miracle to keep it all going.

After the meeting the managers were despatched back to their shops like naughty school children. Roz contemplated how many would stay with the company when she stopped paying the Christmas bonuses. She hurried to her office, closed the door and slumped into the chair. After a few minutes she noticed the mountain of messages, e-mails and accounts figures on her desk. Roz felt her throat was tightening and her head ached. There were small beads of perspiration sticking her blond fringe to her forehead.

Her stomach churned producing a feeling of sickness. Momentarily the room spun. I can't afford to be ill now. There was a knock on the door and she raised her head thinking bloody hell, what now?

'Come in.'

It was Lucy, her PA, smiling nervously at Roz.

'I've managed to reach David's hotel and I've left him an urgent message. He's staying in the same place the last time he visited Thailand.'

'Thanks Lucy, you're a star. I'm going back to the house for the rest of the afternoon and if Alex calls, ask him to call me on my mobile.'

Roz smiled warmly at Lucy for the first time today. The girl was worth her weight in gold. I must give her a bonus to ensure she stays with me. As Lucy scurried out of the office Roz tried Alex's mobile, it was his voicemail again. She left a message and wondered where on earth Alison was? Who was she with and why hadn't she been in touch? The whole situation made Roz uncomfortable. How was she going to explain Alison's disappearance to the rest of the family?

Her mind drifted back to the business and how she was going to solve her cash-flow problem. Putting her head in her hands, she considered her option: I've got so much to do? Is it worth trying to keep this business I built up from scratch going?

The market is flooded with cheaper imports from the Far East. Can I be bothered to carry on? Roz sighed, I guess I have to, that's why I get up in the morning. This business is all I have – it's my legacy for Alex and Alison. I'm worrying myself sick and Alison's probably enjoying herself somewhere. She'll turn up eventually with some lame excuse.

Roz lifted her head and sighed as she took out her little pocket computer from her drawer, found David's number and tried to ring him again. No luck, he was still out.

Damn, where is he when I need him? Roz ground her teeth as she stared out of her office; it was only when she was really nervous that she lapsed into old habits that she had thought she'd conquered. She opened the drawer, took out two painkillers and swallowed them, leaning back in her chair because the room was still spinning like a wooden top. Oh God, this is the worst headache I've had in ages. She didn't feel any better. That's it I'm going home I need time to relax and stop my brain from going at a hundred miles an hour, she thought miserably. The last thing Roz needed was Alison going missing on top of everything else but there was little she could do about it at the moment.

Chapter Three

Rosie's shift was just about to finish; her legs ached and she hadn't eaten since breakfast. Her stomach rumbled, she'd missed lunch and dinner. The thought of home dominated Rosie's mind. I'll just check on Alison before I go, she should be more alert by now. Poor kid's just lying there day in, day out with no family to support her. I don't know what I'd do if it was my daughter in that condition, Rosie thought as she walked into the Intensive Care Unit. Melissa sat by Alison's bed cleaning her wounds and checking the mass of equipment that surrounded her. They sedated Alison to stop her from pulling out her drip and catheter again.

'Hi – how is she?' Rosie enquired.

'She's stable but the swelling in her brain has reduced though not enough to stop her causing me a few problems. It's early days though, I've got a gut feeling that she'll be up and moving around in a few weeks. This girl's a fighter for sure.'

'Where are the results of the CT scan we did yesterday?'

'They're down at the nurses' station. I've checked them again.' Mel pointed out.

'Good, I'll look at them on the way out. Has she woken up long enough to give us any more information on what happened to her?'

'No, but Tom's still trying to track down her folks. They really need to find them soon. I hope she's got travel insurance because they're going to get a hell of a shock when they get the bill.'

'I'm sure that will be the last thing they'll be thinking about,' Rosie retorted.

It annoyed Rosie intensely that Mel always went on about money; it was the least of Alison's worries at the moment. Rosie dreaded telling Alison's family of the bleak prognosis and possible side effects that are commonly associated with head injuries.

Her case was unusual because they didn't have any previous medical records to go by; it could take months for Alison to recover.

'Look I'd better be going, I'm dead beat and I've only got one day off this week. I'll see you on Wednesday if you're working.'

'I'm on a late shift. Try and get some rest – I know what you're like,' Mel smiled.

'Yeah – I wish!' Rosie stifled a yawn and wearily trudged out the door past the nurse's station where Alison's notes were lying along with the other patients that had crossed her path that day and headed out of the hospital. She'd forgotten to read Alison's notes.

The smell of freshly ground coffee drifted down the hospital car park from the local café. She bought herself a latte and sipped it on the way to the car, gazing at the numerous stars starting to appear one by one in the inky black sky. It's going to be cold tonight; poor Alison, I hope she remembers what happened to her soon. Then Tom can start investigating properly and hopefully they can catch the creep who attacked her. Rosie instinctively knew from experience the difference between *rough sex* and rape but you could never be absolutely sure either. Rosie thought of Alison again as she walked over to her little sports car; it was her pride and joy and the only luxury she'd allowed herself to have. Well at least she's woken up a bit, Rosie thought and started up the engine. She pushed Alison's dilemma out of her mind and started to think about her menagerie of animals waiting to be fed and watered at home and was anxious to get back to them.

****

Somewhere in the dark corner of her fragmented mind Alison dreamt of being back in Edinburgh, the city of her birth, the day after her graduation ball.

Alison dragged herself out of bed and groaned. Her head thumped and she had a sour taste in her mouth.

She only had half an hour to get dressed because today she started her new job as a junior manager in her mother's firm, 'Just Roz'. Alison had got her Business Degree and now her mother seemed to have Alison's life all mapped out for her. The telephone rang making her jump.

'Hello?' She whispered, hoping it was her friend but her mother's deafening voice rang out.

'Darling I was just checking that you were up and about. How was your graduation party last night?' Roz asked.

'It was fine – I really enjoyed it. The band was great and the champagne flowed. I didn't get in until two.' Alison stifled a yawn, and rubbed her throbbing temples with her other hand - Yuk. Why did her Mother have to shout down the phone or was it her imagination?

'Look I have a busy day ahead of me, so I thought we could go for coffee instead of Sunday lunch. I have to be in New York on Monday to look for new business premises. So we won't have much time to go through our plans for the Christmas collection.'

'Okay where do you want to meet?' Alison was relieved; her stomach lurched at the thought of any food let alone roast beef with all the trimmings.

'I'll see you at Harvey Nichols at one thirty – it'll give you more time to get over your hangover and Alison I need you to concentrate on what we're trying to achieve here. It's really important,' Roz pointed out.

'Yeah okay – see you then.'

Oh god, Alison thought. That's all I need. Why can't mum just stop thinking about the business for two minutes and relax? How am I going to tell her that I'm not sure about taking over her precious firm? I'm so sick of trying to please her and not getting anywhere. I'm being dragged into something that I don't even know I want to do. What's so wrong with studying Psychology anyway? It's not as if it isn't a worthwhile career. I don't know who I'm trying to convince me, or her.

Alison slumped onto the sofa and put her head in her hands. She didn't want to be part of the Just Roz fashion empire. Stuff it, I've only got one chance and I don't want to spend my life up to my neck in designer clothes that I have no interest in, models who behave like Divas and designers who have nervous breakdowns at the stupidest things! The whole industry is built on image and perfection and it drives me nuts. I'm not cut out for this job and mum is kidding herself if she thinks I am. I'd rather run away and join the circus; it would be easier trying to tame a lion than telling Roz that I don't want this job, Alison thought grimly. She didn't have the energy to battle with her. Not when Alison was feeling like death warmed up.

Roz's world was a constant stream of meetings, networking, parties, fashion shoots, and sourcing goods from eastern manufacturers. It was an endless battle with her competitors to keep one step ahead. The pressure was on Alison not only to succeed but to fulfil her mother's high expectations as well. Haute Couture was also an alien world and Alison didn't understand Roz's obsession to be the best at all costs.

Alison got up and staggered towards the bathroom – she'd better start getting ready, otherwise there'd be hell to pay if she was late again.

Roz sat in her office waiting for Lucy to get back to her about the travel arrangements for the New York trip and she bristled with anger after talking to Alison.

She didn't have a clue about what she was taking on and this vexed Roz. Her daughter was a mystery, always absent-minded and vague about her plans for the future. Alison didn't seem enthusiastic or excited at the prospect of taking over her empire; her baby.

Roz would have killed to be in Alison's position right now. She was so lucky that she didn't have to start from scratch like Roz had done 20 years ago.

Well she would have plenty to say to her when they met up and maybe a holiday was what Alison needed after all. Roz smiled as she opened her briefcase and looked at the flight tickets for Boston she'd recently bought as a graduation present and couldn't wait to see the look on Alison's face when she gave them to her. Alison could have a little holiday in Boston and then Roz would meet up with Alison before they left for New York together. Roz had made plans to keep Alison in New York with her for the duration of the project, once it was up and running. Maybe then, Alison would be more enthusiastic. The Big Apple was the most vibrant and exciting city in the world and Roz was determined to be at the top of her profession. Her New York collection was the best work she'd ever produced and she hoped that Alison would share her vision to move the company forward to global domination.

Chapter Four

It had been a few days since Rosie had been able to monitor Alison's progress and she had drifted in and out of consciousness on a daily basis. Finally, Alison was well enough to be moved out of intensive care. Tom visited twice a day but he was unable to ask her any questions regarding what had happened before the accident. His desk overflowed with reports that were more pressing to work on but this one was a priority because Alison had no one to visit her. Tom desperately wanted to find her family and was keen to investigate who had beaten and raped her and why? He grabbed his jacket and headed out of the office, he had two other witnesses to interview regarding a robbery that had gone wrong. Luckily, they'd both survived and were at the same hospital as Alison.

Alison was in a heavily sedated sleep and through the mist of pain and darkness, another vivid memory rolled out in front of her like a grainy black and white movie.

***

Alison jumped off the bus and rushed straight the doors of the elegant glass façade that was Harvey Nichols. She raced up the escalators two at a time, startling the well-heeled shoppers that stood side by side in twos like the animals going into Noah's ark.

'Excuse me! I'm sorry – I'm late for a business appointment!' Her long chestnut hair was tousled and her belted linen dress was slightly creased; it wasn't a good look. Especially since Alison was entering into the company as a junior fashion buyer setting an example to the rest of Roz's team.

Oh bugger! Alison thought. I've left my portfolio on the coffee table, I'm dead meat.

Alison had meant to pick it up before she hunted for her car keys but unfortunately, Alison was in such a hurry, the portfolio had been left on the table and the realisation only dawned on her now.

'Great – I'm probably going to get fired before I've even get started.' Alison muttered under her breath as she finally reached the top of the escalator and hurried across the immaculate white and glass restaurant with its magnificent view of St Andrew's Square spread out before her. She sailed past the waiter before he had a chance to open his mouth and went straight over to Roz who was sipping a latte, composed and elegant as always.

'Have you been waiting long?'

'No I've just sat down and you're only five minutes late so that's an improvement, isn't it?' Roz's eyes narrowed as she looked at Alison's messy hair and crumpled dress.

Alison grinned nervously, she could tell her mother wasn't amused and it was only going to get worse.

'Erm –so sorry but I've left my portfolio at home.'

'Oh for goodness sake, Alison! What did I tell you this morning, you need to focus on the job in hand? The Christmas season is the busiest time for Just Roz. We get more customers through our doors than at any other time of the year.' Roz rolled her eyes and a bead of sweat trickled down Alison's back. She shifted nervously in her seat.

'Look Mum, I really don't know what to say. I'm not sure if I'm cut out for this job.'

'What do you mean? Of course you are, you just need a firm hand and a bit more confidence and that will come with experience.'

'Right – okay. I'd better order that cappuccino then.'

This is going to be harder than I thought; Alison could see the steely glint in her mother's eyes when she spoke. It had always been hard to say no to Roz.

Roz was the type of woman for whom the word No wasn't in her vocabulary. Roz always got her own way and Alison had seen grown men crumple under her unyielding gaze.

She'd seen that cold look many times when Roz was in the boardroom striking deals and barking orders at her staff.

She didn't suffer fools gladly and Alison wasn't the only one who'd been on the sharp end of Roz's tongue.

Roz leaned back and let out an exasperated sigh and closed her eyes as if to block out how pathetic her daughter looked when she tried to wriggle her way out of an awkward situation. Instead of losing her temper, she would try a gentle approach. She opened her eyes and leant over the table lowering her voice.

'Look darling, I know you've been stressed recently so maybe you just need a break. Hopefully, you'll be a bit more enthusiastic about your role in the firm when you come back. I really want you to succeed Alison. I've worked flat out for twenty years and I'd like to hand over the business to you, eventually.'

'Look Mum – it's just…'

'I've got you a little present for getting a distinction. There you are darling.' Roz interrupted Alison and passed her the envelope beaming from ear to ear.

Alison tore it open, her hands shook.

'Wow - a trip to Boston and Cape Cod. It's fantastic! I don't know what to say; brilliant. Thank you so much.'

Alison got up from her seat and leaned over the table to give her mum a hug and Roz tensed a little; she never liked public displays of affection.

> 'Well – you've worked really hard and I thought a little holiday would do you the world of good. It's just as well I brought the Christmas portfolio along myself as we need to make some changes before next week. We need to go back to the office now to talk to the design team. This is the best collection I've ever produced and I have a feeling that its going to be a huge success. I can just *feel* it.'
>
> 'The dresses are really superb, Mum. You've surpassed yourself this time.' Alison said looking over them trying to still her hammering heart. They were as good as anything she'd seen in Milan and Paris but she felt she didn't have the same enthusiasm or drive as Roz. Oh Lord, there's no way I can back out of this now. Maybe I could do this for a couple of years and then discuss the possibility of a career change? I have to give this my best shot and then at least I've tried, it's the least I can do since Mum supported me through University. I've got my trip to look forward to, that'll buy me more time. I just have that sinking feeling that I'll never be able to study Psychology at the rate I'm going.

She watched Roz going through the collection, Alison tried hard to concentrate on what was going on but she couldn't. All Alison could think about was the dream of becoming a psychologist slip through her fingers.

***

Alison woke up and the memory of her first day at work vanished as quickly as it came.

'Alison – can you hear me?' Rosie asked.

'What? Is that you Doctor? What's your name again? Sorry I've forgotten it', Alison said sheepishly. It drove her mad when she couldn't remember people's names.

'Just call me Rosie – welcome back – I'd thought for a moment we'd lost you again.'

'Lost me where? Sorry – I still feel really bad. When will this awful headache go away? said Alison putting her hands gently on the bed and then slowly rolled over to face Rosie who was standing at the side of her bed.

'It's hard to say really – you should be up and about in a few days. We need to run some more tests and then we can start getting you mobile again. Do you remember anything about the accident or what happened before you got into the car?'

'No – nothing except for the odd dream about a woman who I think is my boss at work. I still can't remember anything about my family. Is that man coming back today?'

Rosie smiled, relieved to hear that Alison vaguely recalled Tom visiting her on a regular basis.

'Yes – Tom rang me and said he would pop in this evening. If you can – try and write down what you remember. It may help you to piece together a few things. You're doing well and healing nicely – it's just going to take time. We have to focus on getting you walking and talking properly as well as more independent with your bathing and so on. Once we can do that, then your memories will start coming back to you. Don't be surprised if you start getting flashbacks of the accident, it won't be pleasant but we're here to support you 24-7."

'Thank you Rosie – you've all been so patient with me', Alison said with tears streaming down her face and she was anxious to remember something, anything that would help Tom and Rosie find out who she was.

'Alison please try and rest – concentrate on taking things a step at a time. I want to focus on getting you well.'

'Okay', Alison suppressed another yawn and thought, everything is such an effort. I feel so slow and cumbersome, and I'm fed up of being tired all the time.

All I want to do is sleep – why can't I remember what happened? I don't know how much longer I can handle this.

'Rosie – has Tom managed to find out if anyone is looking for me?'

'No, not yet but I'm sure he'll come up with something soon.'

'I wish I could remember where I lived or what my favourite colour was. I don't even know what my Mum or Dad would look like if I saw them anyway. It's like a computer virus has wiped out all the memories in my head. It's so weird and I just feel so lonely and empty inside', Alison sighed and sank back onto the pillows. She couldn't see Rosie for the tears that swam in front of her eyes and the dull ache in her head that never left her.

Rosie's heart went out to Alison. It was bad enough having a serious illness but to try and cope without your loved ones was another matter. She really liked Alison because she was brave and determined to get well despite her ordeal.

However, Rosie was aware that she couldn't get emotionally involved; she had to keep a clear head when dealing with Alison's care and distance herself from the situation. It was becoming increasingly difficult because Alison had a similar outlook on life as Rosie did together with a wicked sense of humour, despite her condition. Rosie sat down on the side of the bed and took Alison's hand and said.

"We're going to keep you pretty busy in the next few weeks with physiotherapy and stuff which will start this afternoon. Once we get you up and about, your memories will start to come back to you. Alison, you had a very serious head injury and you've made a remarkable recovery. I'm not going to lie to you; it's going to take a long time before you'll be able to lead a normal life. It will happen and you are on track to make a full recovery. Just hang in there honey, you'll be fine.'

'It would help your recovery if we could locate your family but I'm confident that they'll turn up. In fact you can count on it,' Rosie said confidently but she made a mental note to chase Tom for more details later.

'Thanks Rosie – I don't know what I'd do without you. You're more like a friend than my doctor', Alison smiled weakly, and she felt better already. Rosie stood up and said 'I'll pop in later for a chat but I've got more patients to see this afternoon. Now rest because the physio team will be here after lunch.'

'Sure', Alison said sadly as she watched Rosie hurry out of her room into the busy corridor, wishing she didn't have to go.

Chapter Five

Tom walked into Alison's room and grinned sheepishly at the woman of his dreams, who was propped up in bed trying to chew a small piece of bread.

'It's good to see you up and about.'

Alison smiled and beckoned him to sit down by the bed.

'It makes a change from being in zombie mode all the time. I was beginning to wonder if I was ever going to feel normal again.'

She put the bread down slowly. Tom was conscious that her movements were uncoordinated and her speech was a little slow.

'That's understandable considering what you've been through. It must have been really tough.'

'Yeah – well as Rosie said I just have to take things a day at a time and not expect too much. It's hard though because every time I try and remember something my head spins and I get so confused.'

'It must be very frustrating.'

'Hmm – what brings you here then? It can't be my riveting company that's for sure,' laughed Alison bitterly.

'I thought I'd drop by to see how you are and if you'd managed to recall anything. I'm sorry to keep asking you but we have to try and find out what happened.'

'I dreamt about my boss, the other day. I was late for work and I ran up an escalator on the way to a coffee shop and then we started talking about clothes but I remember nothing else. I'm sorry Tom – I wish I could conjure up something that reminds me of my parents or where I'm from but I can't,' sighed Alison.

She felt tears spring behind her eyes but blinked rapidly. She wasn't going to do self-pity anymore but she was so shattered after all the physiotherapy she'd had that afternoon. Tom's heart melted every time he spoke to her and he hated to see the distress and confusion in her beautiful green eyes.

'I know it's tough at the moment but Rosie said you'll get your long-term memory back gradually; she's a great doctor who knows her stuff. I've worked with her before. Your boss - can you remember what she looked like or what kind of accent she had?'

'What?' Alison looked at Tom with a vacant expression on her face like she was just coming out of a deep sleep.

'Can you tell me what he or she was wearing or where you think it was?' Tom asked tentatively, hoping that he would get a straight answer. Alison frowned for a moment before answering.

'She had a blue dress on - we were in a large store in a city but I don't know which one.'

'At least you've remembered something Alison, you've made some progress and your speech is getting so much better.'

'Do you think so?' Alison grinned. Tom cleared his throat.

'Sure.'

Alison stifled a yawn and then beamed at him.

'Hi Tom – what brings you here?'

'Pardon?' Tom repeated noticing the vacant expression on Alison's face.

'I popped in to see you five minutes ago.' Tom said slightly confused that Alison hadn't remembered the conversation they'd just had. Alison shook her head and beamed at him.

'No – you've just arrived. Do you think we could get out of here and go for a coffee?' 'No one will notice – let's go,' Alison tried to get out of bed but Tom leaned over, and put his hands gently on her shoulders.

'Alison – you can't you're in hospital.'

'Come on Tom – no one will notice. Have you just arrived?'

Alison threw him off, stumbled out of bed and dashed towards the door. Before she reached it Tom grabbed her arm from behind.

'Tom – what are you doing?' Alison cried in alarm trying to break free from his grasp but Tom held her fast and gently sat her down on the bed.

'Alison – you're in hospital and you've hurt your head. You can't leave yet, not until Rosie says you're better.'

'Rosie? We can go out – she won't mind, do you want to go out for a coffee?'

'I'll go and get Rosie and she'll bring us coffee? Okay Alison?'

'It's nice to see you Tom, – have you just arrived?'

'I'll go and get her, you stay here.' He led Alison back to the chair next to her bed and quickly wrote a note to tell her that he would be back a couple of minutes, otherwise she would forget that he'd visited her at all. Tom walked out of the ward with a heavy heart; he could still hear Alison prattling to herself. He'd never felt so helpless in all his life, one minute Alison was fine, in a New York minute she would become confused and tearful. Rosie assured him this was perfectly normal for someone who had memory loss, and with the right help, Alison could make a full recovery. However, Tom was not so sure; he was under pressure to get a result. Rosie ambled down the corridor reading charts as she walked; she saw relief written all over Tom's face.

'Rosie – I was on my way to get you. Alison's trying to leave again.'

'Don't worry, she's due for some medication and she's exhausted from the physio she had this afternoon. She always puts quite a performance when you come to see her; she thinks it will convince us that she's ready to be discharged.'

Oh, so she does like me after all. I was beginning to wonder." Tom smiled.

"Oh – has she mentioned anything else about the crash or what happened to her before that? He asked.

'Nothing about the crash or the attack but she's starting to remember her life before the accident, where she worked. She worked in the fashion industry and has told me that her boss was a woman. Alison still has the odd seizure but we can't afford to over - stimulate her. Her short-term memory has completely gone therefore, she'll repeat herself over again not realising that she's asked the same questions already.'

"Will her memory return sometime soon? – I have to get a result, her story is hardly front page news and I'll end up working on other cases until she remembers what happened to her,' Tom said looking at Rosie earnestly; she heard the frustration in his voice.

'Tom – she's starting to have flashbacks but it'll be a while before she starts to remember any traumatic events. The trouble with a brain injury like this one is that every patient is different. Alison may make a full recovery or she may not. We are playing a waiting game; there is no set period for any recovery at this stage. We just have to wait and see. I know it's exasperating but I don't have answers. Patience and hope is all we have at the moment – I'm sorry.'

Rosie squeezed Tom's arm and turned to go into Alison's room but Tom stopped her and said.

'Rosie – I guess I'll have to work on this one alone as I've too many cases that are more pressing.'

'I know–I don't have a more positive prognosis at the moment.'

When Rosie and Tom walked into the room Alison sat motionless in the chair staring into space with a vacant look on her face.

'Alison – how are you this evening?' Rosie asked gently putting the charts on the bottom of Alison's bed and then talking her hand, waiting for her to reply but she looked past Rosie and called out to Tom.

'Hi Tom – you were away for ages – I didn't think you were coming back.'

Tom sighed as he'd not been away from Alison more than five minutes; he turned away and ran his hand through his dark hair. I can't stand this – I want to take her home and look after her. I'll have to stop thinking like this – it's crazy.

'Alison – look at me – Tom has been here for a while – don't you remember?'

'No – he's just arrived. We could go out for coffee – couldn't we?' Alison looked over at Tom smiling, hoping that he would stay longer but she didn't register the distress in his face as he looked out of the window and thought. Oh Alison – you've no idea how much I want that too. I can't turn around because if I do Rosie will see how crazy I am about this woman. I can't afford to show it – not now.

'Alison, I need to ask you a few questions.' Rosie interrupted. Alison looked straight at Rosie and concentrated as hard as she could.

"It's been sunny today and I noticed that there are sixteen red cars in the car park."

"Alison – do you know what day it is today?" Rosie asked gently.

"Erm – Tuesday I think but it could be Friday?"

'Alison do you know your full name and your date of birth? Where were you born?'

'Scotland and I think its Friday. See I'm getting better at remembering stuff, I know I am. I just need a minute to think. I'm tired you see.' Alison said sheepishly.

'It's okay Alison – it's Wednesday today. You did well, don't despair you'll get better, why don't you try and get some rest.'

'I am getting better – aren't I?' Alison said desperately fighting back the tears blurring her vision of Rosie's face. The persistent, dull headache was still there and Alison wished it would go away, even if it was just for a few hours.

"Tom can you stay here whilst I get her medication? Alison, get yourself into bed and I'll be back shortly."

'Sure Rosie.' Alison got back into the bed and looked over at Tom who was still looking out the window.

'I'm getting better, though I know I am.' Alison wasn't sure who she was trying to convince, Rosie or herself. Rosie picked up the charts and Tom walked across to the bed. Alison looked grey with exhaustion as she climbed between the cool sheets. It saddened Rosie to see Alison struggling to recover on her own; it would help her so much if she had her family with her. Alison needed them more than anything else at this time. Rosie was glad Tom came to visit on a regular basis. She knew he cared for Alison and she was relieved because he was the only visitor Alison had. She rubbed her bloodshot eyes and pressed on, only three more patients to see and then she could sit with Alison for a while before her twelve-hour shift finished.

Alison was almost asleep but before she drifted off she took Tom's hand; her long delicate fingers looked so small in his large brown hands. It feels so good when she touches me – I wish I could tell her how I feel. God, you are beautiful when you sleep, Tom thought, his heart thumping in his chest as he lifted her hand to his mouth and kissed it. Alison stirred but didn't wake up; it was the only time Tom could look at her without fear that his feelings would betray him. He let go of her hand and left a few minutes later.

***

Rosie realised that Rufus, her highland terrier, hadn't been walked properly for a days. She would have to take a few days off and spend some time at home. There was still so much to do at the hospital and she didn't want to leave Alison. On the other hand, if she didn't have a break, she would end up collapsing with exhaustion and then what use would she be to her patients? She rang her friend who looked after her dog whilst she worked away.

> 'Hi – I won't need you to look after Rufus for the rest of the week. Yeah, I'm taking a few days off. Thanks for looking after him and I'll see you tomorrow.'

She checked on Alison but to her surprise she was awake and watching the news on television.

> 'I thought you'd be asleep, Alison.'
> 'I was but I woke up with an awful headache.'
> 'You'll be able to get something for the pain in a couple of hours.'
> 'Rosie – don't you ever go home? You seem to be here all the time.'

Rosie laughed and blushed at how observant Alison was at times.

'Funnily enough – I was just going to leave a note for you. I'm taking a few days off but I'll be back for the weekend though.'
'Good – I'll miss you but I'll manage – Tom still visits me. You guys are the only friends I have at the moment.'
'I know but that will change – we're doing everything we can.'
'Oh it wasn't a criticism – can I ask you something?'
'That depends what it is?' laughed Rosie.
'Why aren't you married? I mean you're such a great person – I just wondered, that's all.'
'Lord, Alison – what a personal question – there was someone once. His name was John, we dated for a number of years but we split up. He wanted to settle down and have kids but I didn't. I'd just been promoted and I couldn't take time off. So he left and found someone else. I believe his partner is having their first baby and its due in the spring,' Rosie said wistfully. It pained her to talk about him and she was surprised at herself for being so open with Alison.
'I'm sorry to hear that Rosie – it seems to me that you're married to your job. It's not healthy you know.' Alison squeezed Rosie's hand and tears pricked the back of Rosie's eyes. She blinked rapidly and sighed, she was suddenly dog-tired.
'You're right; my job has become my life. I can't believe I'm sitting here listening to you giving me advice when you should be resting. You don't need me prattling on.' Rosie suddenly felt very guilty talking about her problems when Alison had her own to deal with.
'Don't be silly – we're just two friends chatting – that's all.'
Alison loved talking to Rosie she was the only one that understood what she went through every day.

'Well – it's been a long day for both of us. I'll see you in a couple of days.' Rosie stood up and the tone in her voice became brisk and business-like. For a moment she'd forgotten she was talking to a patient and that was becoming a bad habit. She needed to take a break for a couple of days.

'Rosie.'

'Yes?'

'Thanks for coming to see me – you're the only one that treats me like a friend instead of a patient.'

'Take care, Alison.'

'I will – I'm stronger than you think you know.' Alison stifled a yawn.

"I know but you've a long way to go. See you on Saturday."

Alison didn't answer so Rosie left a note by her bed because she knew Alison would forget that she was going away for a few days. For once Rosie was thankful that Alison wouldn't recall the conversation they'd had. She had a habit of telling Alison more than she'd meant to and that in itself was dangerous. Rosie had stepped over the mark of a doctor – patient relationship by volunteering personal information to Alison and Rosie knew she was on dangerous ground because she was getting too involved in Alison's life. Alison was so perceptive for one so young. It was like she had an old head on young shoulders which was no surprise considering what she had been through. Rosie would have to be a bit more cautious about what she said to Alison when she came back from her vacation.

Chapter Six

Rosie arrived back at the hospital full of enthusiasm ready to start her shift. It had been great to escape the pressures of her job for a few days but she was keen to see how Alison was progressing. However, before she got to Alison's room she was met by the hospital manager who walked down the corridor to greet her. Rosie could tell by her pinched expression, it wasn't going to be good news.

'I need to talk to you about Alison's care, when are you free?'

"I was just on my way to see her. What's up?' Rosie asked. She didn't like management interfering with her patients, especially when she had been away for a few days. This woman was particularly ruthless and it wasn't the first time Rosie had fought with her over the choices she'd made regarding patient care. The woman hesitated and said as quickly as she could.

'We've made arrangements to transfer Alison to another hospital.'

'Why wasn't I notified of this – when did this happen?'

'Oh didn't you read my email? I sent it yesterday.'

'No I've just come back today – I've been on vacation for a couple of days. Where's Alison going?'

'We thought she would be better off in Ashvale so the bus is picking her up this afternoon.' Anger rose in Rosie's throat but suppressed it.

'That's a mental hospital, Alison doesn't belong there. She's not mentally ill for goodness sake! Who authorised this because it certainly wasn't me.'

'I'm sorry Rosie but we need the bed and she's not insured – Ashvale is the best place for her at the moment.'

'If it's a case of money – I'll pay for her care – for crying out loud the kid has no one to look after her. You can't dump her in a place that is not suitable like some unwanted animal.'

'You can't do that – it's not ethical Rosie and you're getting emotionally involved with this patient. Think about it Rosie – it's not good for your career.' The woman retorted then regretted what she said as soon as she'd said it.

Rosie lost her temper and raised her voice.

'How dare you dictate to me what is good for my career. My patients are always my first concern. You've gone over my head and arranged for her to be transferred to a mental hospital without my permission. That's down right sneaky. Alison will not get better in a place like that; it will seriously affect her recovery. You know what those places are like; she has no family so I guess there's no one to fight for her best interests is there? How *convenient*.' Rosie's voice dripped with sarcasm which was not like her. The woman shrugged and said.' It's out of my hands; Susan Matthews agreed it was in Alison's best interests.'

'The hell it is – I'm going to see Susan right now!'

'I don't think it will do you any good – wait...' stuttered the woman.

Rosie stormed down the corridor and waited for the lift to take her to Susan's office. I don't believe this; who the hell does she think she is? Wait till I see her. This won't help Alison at all. What a start to the day. I'd better keep a level head because Susan won't listen to me if I'm angry, Rosie thought as she paced up and down. She pressed the button for the lift again. I'm not going to take this lying down – not without a fight.

***

Rosie knocked on the door and walked straight in without waiting for Susan to answer. Susan sat at her desk. She was taking a call from the department where Rosie worked.

Rosie just sat down for a brief meeting not caring if Susan could see her or not. Rosie knew right away that she was in trouble, so she braced herself.

Susan finished her call and leant back in her chair studying Rosie's face. She had anticipated that Rosie would turn up like this so she'd cleared her diary for the morning.

'I wanted to have a word with you in private about Alison. Why the hell didn't you contact me when you decided to transfer Alison two days ago? You're a doctor Susan you know the rules, she's my patient and my responsibility. I can't believe you didn't call me.' Rosie's voice shook with anger.

'I'm sorry I went over your head but there's a very good reason why I didn't ring you. I felt you were getting too emotionally involved with this patient and it's not healthy or professional.'

'You had no intention of ringing me so don't try and bullshit me, Susan– I can see right through you. Have you any idea what you've done? Alison was in a pitiful state when she arrived here and, yes I shouldn't have got emotionally involved, but that girl has no family, no one to support her, she's completely alone and she's just a kid.' Rosie exclaimed.

'We can't keep her here any longer – we need the bed and she has no insurance…'

'Yes as always, it's all about money isn't it. I could pay for her care but, no, that would be too simple wouldn't it? If her family finds out you've dumped her in a mental hospital they'll sue your ass.' Rosie said sarcastically. Now it was Susan's turn to be angry.

'Now just a minute – I have the whole department to run with hundreds of patients to think about. Do you realise how crazy you sound, what you gonna do? Pay for all patients that come in with no insurance? Wake up Rosie – talk some sense and think about what you're saying. It's not ethical for you to pay for Alison's care and you know it. You a damn good doctor and if you push for Alison to stay here I can't protect you from the boys upstairs. It's goodbye to your career. Do you want that?'

'Ashvale is a mental hospital – Alison is not mentally ill. She has a head injury and I don't want her progress to be hindered. I don't want her to think that I'm abandoning her. Alison was raped or have you forgotten that as well? She nearly died twice and she's gone through so much on her own already. I don't want her to regress and give up. I don't want that on my conscience either.' Rosie cried.

'You are so irresponsible Rosie, Alison is a person. She isn't some stray animal you can pick up and look after for a few weeks.'

"That was below the belt and you know it!"

Rosie was furious now; Susan had no right to bring her personal life into this. She genuinely cared about Alison.

"Alison will have the best of care - Tom Bernstein is still investigating her case. Her family are bound to turn up eventually. The boys upstairs are breathing down my neck, Rosie. Ashvale is the best option for her at the moment and that's the end of it. If I were you I would go back to your patients and keep your head down. You can argue all you like.' Susan was resolute and glared at Rosie, whose heart sank. This was one fight she was about to lose. Susan continued.

'Alison is going to Ashvale, end of story. Let me know how she progresses. I've made an appointment for you to see her in outpatients' two weeks from now. So you're not abandoning her – that's the best I can offer. Take it or leave it.' Susan added.

'Okay Susan – you win this time. Just don't highjack my patients again – do I make myself clear?'

'I'm sorry. I screwed up. I should have called you to let you know what was happening. Am I forgiven?' Susan asked calmly.

'Sure – see you in a few weeks.' Rosie sighed as she got up from her chair and shook Susan's hand. She was trying to keep her emotions in check; it had been a rough day.

'I apologise for barging in on you like this.' Rosie said through gritted teeth as she walked to the door and opened it. She was still angry but had to be professional, she couldn't afford to burn bridges just yet.

'See you both in clinic.' Susan said. She would need to monitor Rosie for a while.

'Rosie?'

'What.'

'Try and keep a low profile for a while. You're one of the best and most diligent doctors we have – it would be a shame to mess up now.'

'Yeah okay - I'm not happy but I'll go along with it.'

In spite of their heated argument, Susan liked Rosie and would be very sad to see her throw her career away on one patient when so many more would benefit from her expertise. Rosie had lost her fight over the issue, and it was too late to change the decision to move Alison, which was obviously set in stone. Rosie burned with resentment as she walked back to her department. Her mind was racing with ideas like a whirlpool.

There was always plan B; they couldn't prevent her visiting Alison in her spare time. Rosie decided that she would visit Alison once she was settled in. When Rosie got to her office, she rang Tom.

'Tom – its Rosie's there's been a development regarding Alison's care. She's being moved to Ashvale later on this afternoon. No I'm not happy about it at all, it's a mental hospital and she doesn't belong there. I'll email you the address, it's my first day back from vacation so it's a bit full on at the moment. Yeah – I'll be in touch. Can you visit her when she's settled in? Great – see you later." Rosie hung up and was pleased that Tom had agreed to continue visiting Alison and, hopefully, her family would find her soon and she wouldn't be left languishing in Ashvale for too long.

Chapter Seven

Later on that afternoon Alison was finally ready to leave St Margaret's Hospital. During her stay there, all the doctors and nurses had become like friends to her and Alison was apprehensive. She was excited about leaving because it had been so long since she'd been outside of a hospital environment but was anxious about settling into the new one. It was another step forward on her long journey to make a full recovery. When she was ready, she stood at the main door, feeling like a child who was going on her first camping trip away from home.

'They'll take good care of you at Ashvale so don't worry', Rosie said unconvincingly but Alison didn't pick the apprehension up in her voice as she put the last of Alison's medication in her travel bag. She didn't have the heart to tell Alison that she was going to a mental hospital because Rosie knew she wouldn't go if she knew. Rosie wondered if she was doing the right thing by keeping Alison in the dark but she had no choice.

'Thanks Rosie. It'll be weird not seeing you every day. I've gotten used to being here. You must be sick of the sight of me by now. I'm so sorry about all the trouble I gave you guys – you know, the shouting and stuff', Alison laughed.

"Not at all – you were a model patient, Alison. It was your head injury that made you behave that way, not you. It's great to see the progress you have made and don't you forget it!' Rosie scolded, hugging her at the same time.

'I'll be in touch when I get settled.'

'Take it easy and good luck. Remember your memories will return one day. It's just going to take time so don't be impatient – I know what you're like!'

Rosie's pager went for the third time, and this time she couldn't ignore it. She would see Alison in a couple of days. Alison got onto the hospital bus and watched Rosie hurry down the corridor and felt a twinge of sadness. She was the only person she felt safe with; she had given her unconditional care, above and beyond her duty.

She would never forget her or Tom Bernstein, who visited her every week to try and jog her memory. She felt very anxious and utterly alone. As the hospital bus drove off Alison hoped she would be happy in her new surroundings. She tried to convince herself that this was a new phase in her life as she continued to recover. A sense of foreboding washed over Alison as she looked out of the window watching the world go by for the first time since her accident.

The hospital bus took half an hour to drive her to Ashvale. As it turned down the narrow lane she was taken aback at how beautiful the woods were. There was every kind of tree imaginable; the colours of the leaves in the fall would be stunning, after all that was what New England was famous for.

Since it was November most of the leaves were gone but the grounds were beautifully kept. They included a large pond with reeds, lily pads and other assorted grasses. There were some heather flowerbeds and wild herbal plants next to the immaculate emerald green lawns. They had white iron wrought benches littered all over the grounds for people to sit on in the summertime. Even though it was a dull day, the gardens were magnificent. Winter shrubs and rich green bushes filled the flowerbeds. Their branches were bent over with red and yellow berries. Alison was very relieved to be in such a lovely place.

The house was a large, square brick Victorian structure. It was built by pioneering Doctor Jacob Abraham Dakin, who had founded the first mental health hospital in the Massachusetts area in 1900.

In 1975, the hospital was refurbished and a large glass conservatory was added. Then it became a mental health unit, employing the best medical staff in North America. The huge sash windows had been replaced by modern ones in 1996 and the lintels had been recently painted white making the red bricks really stand out.

It looked warm and welcoming, from the outside at least, Alison thought on her first impression of the place. She noticed patients in little groups with a nurse assigned to each group. She was relieved to see that they were allowed to roam freely around the grounds.

It wasn't too cold but everyone said it was going to snow early this year in time for Christmas. I wonder where I'll be in six weeks' time. Will anybody come for me? I'll probably still be here, she thought sadly. I've got no one to share Christmas with and where are my family? Do they miss me – I hope so? Is someone out there searching for me? I just hope the patients are friendly. It would be nice to have someone to talk to for a change. She had to cope with heartache, headaches and apprehension about the future. She pushed these melancholy thoughts out of her mind as she stepped off the bus, took a deep breath and smiled at the two men who had come out to greet her.

'Welcome to Ashvale - you must be Alison right?'

'That's me – it's good to be here.'

'Hi I'm Doctor Pierce Williams –I'll be treating you for your amnesia until you make a full recovery'.

'Do you know when that will be?'

'Until we have assessed you fully over the next couple of weeks I can't answer that at the moment. Let's get you settled in first.

My nursing team will go through all the details and will show you to your room.'

'My room?' Alison said. She thought the unit would be split into wards. Fantastic – life is looking up at last.

"Yes, you either have a room of your own or share it with another patient. You are sharing a room with Lisa Becker. She's a really nice girl and about your age. I'm pretty sure you two will get on well. If you have any problems just talk to me and we'll try and accommodate you – is that a deal?' Dr Williams replied smiling at this beautiful, amiable young woman in front of him.

Alison was immediately impressed by not only her surroundings but the staff seemed great as well. She felt she could talk to Doctor Williams; he was in his late forties, over six feet with broad shoulders and dark brown hair with grey streaks at each side. He had an air of authority about him yet he was seemingly laid back, like a father figure.

'I'll let you settle in and I'll see you at 3pm. Ben will show you to your room.'

'Thank you Dr Williams. I feel less anxious already.'

'You're welcome.'

The man called Ben stepped forward and said.

'Come on – I think Lisa's in her room. She's just as anxious about meeting her new room mate as you are. Can I carry your bag for you?' said Ben taking hold of Alison's bag. His hand brushed hers and she pulled it away.

'No thanks – there's not much in it – believe me', Alison said nervously.

'I'm sure you'll get along fine.' Ben pointed out.

Ben led Alison up the richly carpeted stairs into the reception area on the way to her room. The wooden floors in the corridors were so shiny, she could see her reflection. The hospital was bright and airy; it was like a guest house. The only giveaway was a small nurse's station at the end of each corridor.

Each room had been individually decorated, and as they walked past the rooms, some were open wide enough for Alison to notice that the patients had added their own personal touches. By the time they got to the second floor, Alison was quite tired. Lord, I feel so dizzy – it's ridiculous. I've only walked up to my room for goodness sake.

'Are you feeling okay?' Ben enquired; he noticed that the colour had drained from Alison's face as she walked up the stairs.

'I feel a bit dizzy and tired, its just relief I guess – you know, coming to a new place. It's a bit like your first day at school. You don't know what to expect.'

'Well, why don't you lie down before lunch? If you don't feel any better, just have a quiet afternoon and rest in your room', Ben said.

Alison wore a fitted red polo neck jumper under the black coat Rosie had given her which was open. Her black jeans were also given to Alison by Rosie, who had outgrown them. They were the only clothes she had. Her other clothes had been cut off her after the accident.

"Thanks – I think I will." Alison had learnt to listen to her body over the last few weeks because if she didn't she would start having seizures. She wanted more than anything to get better so that she could start looking for her family. Ben knocked on the fifth door along the corridor on the third floor. Alison was surprised to see a young blonde-haired girl in a wheelchair.

'I'm Lisa Becker.' She said stretching out her hand to shake Alison's.

'Hi Lisa – it's good to meet you.' Alison smiled awkwardly not knowing where to look. She was naturally shy and found meeting strangers, let alone sharing a room with one, a little daunting.

'Lisa – Alison is very tired after her journey. She is going to lie down before lunch, so don't tire her out.' Ben said a little too sharply.

'I'm okay – honestly. I need to unpack my stuff and then I'll lie down', Alison was embarrassed by Ben's change in attitude. Lisa was only trying to be friendly.

'Of course – just remember. Buzz if you need anything; it's located by your cabinet', he explained.

'Thanks Ben, see you later,' She turned around put her bag in the wardrobe and sat on the bed.

'See you later,' Ben left them to it. He was unhappy. He knew right away putting Lisa and Alison together was a mistake. His gut instinct was that she was going to be as much trouble as Lisa was.

'Don't worry about him; he's a bit of a pain, a control freak. He thinks he owns the place. I'm used to him trying to boss me around like he does the others." Lisa smiled.

'How long have you been here?' Alison asked.

'Just three weeks – I need a lot of psychotherapy and counselling, I must learn to get used to the chair. I dived into shallow water and got a neck injury, which partly paralysed me. It could have been worse, it's only my legs, the left side is worse than the other though', Lisa's voice quavered, trying to look on the bright side.

'I'm so sorry.'

'I was devastated at the time but I've got used to the idea of being in a chair now and I can still swim and get myself around.' Lisa said ruefully.

'I can see that. Well it's good to be here and I'm glad to have such a brave room mate', Alison said.

'Thanks - I'm not really. You should've seen me a few weeks ago. My family supported me and I couldn't have done it without them. What happened to you?' she asked with genuine interest.

Alison sank slowly onto her bed; she was at a loss for words. Every time someone mentioned the word "Family" it cut like a knife across her heart. What am I going to say? I don't want Lisa's pity. Lisa was concerned because the colour suddenly went from Alison's face and it worried her.

'I'm sorry I didn't mean to upset you – are you okay? Did I say the wrong thing? You don't have to tell me, I'm always putting my foot in it', Lisa said hastily. *Damn* she thought.

'I had a bad car crash and when I woke up I couldn't remember my name or where I'm from or who my family is. They say everything will come back in time but I'm not so sure', Alison sighed.

'Oh Alison – that must be so hard for you. I couldn't survive without my family. I'll introduce you to mine! Look I'm going downstairs to the library; I'll come up for you just before lunch – okay? Lisa replied.

'Thanks Lisa, it's good to meet you, I'll be more with it, when I've had a rest', Alison smiled weakly; she felt a headache coming on.

Lisa was happy with her new room mate. Alison seemed like a nice person but maybe a little fragile. No wonder, she thought, as she went down the corridor towards the lift. Alison lay down on the bed and pulled her coat around her shoulders. The room was slightly bigger than the others so that Lisa could manoeuvre her chair. It was painted pale blue with standard white shelves and both beds faced the large bay window. Alison could see the trees from her bed and she was happy. She loved lying down and watching the trees swaying in the wind. She fell asleep as soon as her head it the soft pillow. When Alison woke up she was surprised to find that it was already dark. She had been asleep for a long time and was annoyed with Ben for not waking her. How was she going to get to sleep tonight?

Her neck was stiff and someone had put a blanket over her and had hung up her coat. She was just about to put on the light, when Ben got there first.

He leant across the door with a small plastic pot in his hand with pills in it. Alison didn't like the way he looked her up and down, she couldn't quite work out what it was. There was something about Ben she didn't like. She didn't know why – he had been nothing but kind and attentive since she arrived.

"Hello sleepyhead, we thought you were never going to wake up. It's time for your medication."

'Oh, okay – um – where's the girl?' She felt groggy, disorientated and didn't quite catch what Ben had said as she swung her legs over the bed to stand up.

'She's still downstairs with the others, they're watching TV. It's nearly time for dinner. You must be starving, there's a jug of water over there', he said, walking over and giving her the cup. Again his hand brushed hers, it felt cold and clammy. She stepped back and nearly lost her balance on the edge of the bed.

"Steady - are you alright?"

Ben grabbed her by the waist to stop her falling over. He held her a bit too close for comfort and then let go. Ben was taller than her and she could feel his lean body next to hers. He was a little intimidating, but she just put it down to being not quite awake yet.

'Yes I'm fine – I just lost my balance – you were a bit too close to me that's all.'

'Really? I was just trying to stop you from falling backwards that's all. You should get something to eat and I'm sure you'll feel better', Ben said soothingly, like he was talking to a small child.

'I know', Alison replied sarcastically.

"Just have your medication Alison, and then I'll take you down to the dining room'.

Yep – you are a bit of a control freak. Lisa was right about you.

Alison took it like an obedient child and then followed Ben along the corridor and down the stairs. She was relieved to see Lisa with a group of friends already at the table.

The dining area was informal with a dozen square tables, with four chairs at each one. There was an archway leading through into the conservatory that took Alison's breath away. It was a large glass and wooden structure, in a long rectangular shape. It had double French doors at the end going out onto a gravelled path overlooking the magnificent pond. The floors were laminated in oak style and covering that were multi-coloured rugs with white wicker chairs and sofas. There were wicker coffee tables scattered around them, adding to the informal atmosphere. At the back of the dining room was a small library of books and magazines. Alison wished she could read the books but she still had difficulty with her memory, consequently, she stuck to magazines because they were easier to remember. When Lisa saw Alison, her face broke into a big, welcoming smile.

'Hi – I thought you were never going to wake up –Alison', Lisa laughed.

'Well – here I am at last and I'm really hungry, does anyone know what's for dinner?' Alison asked.

'I'll leave you to it – see you guys later', Ben said brightly and walked off. Lisa made a face.

'Not if I see you first, he's such a pain', she said under her breath. Alison sat between Lisa and a dark-haired girl who introduced herself as Ashleigh.

'I think – it's some sort of fish and then pecan pie for desert', one guy said. He spoke very slowly and precisely which Alison found unnerving because she used to speak the same way. Then he got up without saying a word to talk to a girl who had just entered the room.

'Yummy – I love pecan pie, it's my favourite', Alison replied.

'I'll introduce you to everyone; this is Ashleigh and Mary-Ann. Welcome to the Ashvale posse!' Lisa said and the red headed girl known as Mary-Ann smiled and they all shook her hand.

They all chatted easily amongst themselves over dinner. The food was particularly good and Alison really enjoyed herself. It was good to meet other people who had had similar experiences. Each person had their own story to tell and it was nine thirty in the evening before they went up to their rooms.

They were sympathetic to her situation but they didn't pity Alison; they understood what she was going through and that was such a relief. The only person Alison was uneasy about was Ben but she just told herself not to be so paranoid. Her short term-memory was improving every day, so she didn't repeat the same conversation over and over again like she had done in St Margaret's. She still kept her journal up-to-date but, deep down Alison knew that she was a long way from living independently just yet.

Chapter Eight

Alison tossed and turned in her sleep; she dreamed she was running to a car.

'Get off me! Get away from me!'

Fear pumped through her veins, someone was after her and she had to get away fast. After what seemed like an eternity, she reached the car and jumped in, the engine roared into life. The tyres screeched echoing through the underground car park, and Alison swerved to avoid a parked car as she turned right into a dark deserted street. She drove at top speed out of the city and ended up on a long, winding road. The rain battered the windscreen but Alison didn't slow down. The forest on her left looked dark and menacing tonight and this added to her anxiety to escape at all costs. She couldn't stop crying, she could feel the muscles in her upper arms ache as she drove. She'd had to fight hard to get away, to escape her tormentor. Her mobile phone rang incessantly; she grabbed it, switched it off turning to chuck it on the back seat. She turned back just as the car slammed into a large stag. It smashed the windscreen as its body flew over the roof of the car.

Its blood splattered across her face, she let out an ear piercing scream, the car crunched through the barrier and headed straight down a deep ravine. The car broke up whilst crashing through bushes and bounced off rocks. Alison's brown handbag flew out and landed in some thick bushes. Her head was being thrown backwards and forwards; the pain ricocheted down her spine. The car caught fire and Alison tried to jump out but the car hit a large rock projecting Alison through the broken windscreen. She hit the ground with such force it knocked her unconscious. Her broken body lay fifteen yards from the burning car which exploded on impact.

'No!' Alison screamed and sat bolt upright. The first person she saw was the stricken face of Lisa who had sat up in her bed.

'Alison – thank God you woke up. Are you alright?'
Before Alison could answer Ben switched the light on and said.

'I came as soon as I could – I heard you shouting down the corridor. It's okay Alison – you're safe here, you'll be alright.'

'I had a dream, I remember the crash. I was trying to get away from someone – they hurt me...' Alison's teeth chattered with fright, she shook uncontrollably.

"Calm down, Alison – this is important. You've had a major flashback, breathe deeply and start again', Ben said gently and mouthed she's okay to Lisa who sighed with relief.

Alison swallowed hard and looked imploringly at Lisa and Ben and blurted out breathlessly, 'I want to remember but I feel so afraid, something really bad happened to me. I know that now and I don't want to remember the awful stuff. I can't believe I survived that crash. Oh God, why can't I remember the happy times I had? What a nightmare, the whole hospital must have heard me?'

'Its okay, Alison – if you find it too painful to talk about it now, write it down in your journal and then we can go over it tomorrow. You're in shock and it's only natural; I promise you'll be fine', Ben said quietly, Alison realised he was genuinely concerned.

'Thanks – your right. I'll write it down and I'm so sorry I woke you all up', Alison said wiping away the tears that were streaming down her cheeks.

'You need to sleep – I'll get you some sleeping pills okay. They're quite strong so hopefully they will stop the nightmares', Ben said.

'I'm just glad you're not hurt Alison. That was a helluva scream you frightened me to death', Lisa said.

'I didn't mean to give you a heart attack. I bet you wish you had the room to yourself again',

'Don't be silly – I'm just glad you remembered something about the accident – it's good that you beginning to remember stuff again. Isn't it?'

'Yes I suppose so', Alison sighed.

Ben came back with the sleeping pills and a glass of water. Alison didn't want to have the same dream again so she was only too happy to take them.

***

Alison hadn't been in Ashvale for more than twenty - four hours when she realised that she'd been placed in a mental health hospital. Some of the floors were out of bounds to other patients and the staff who worked in those wards wore a uniform. The double security doors stopped the more seriously ill patients from trying to leave without an accompanying nurse.

Occasionally, she would hear the tortured screams of patients trying to leave those wards. More often than not they had to be dragged back by several members of staff for their own safety.

Lisa and Alison were in the library; Alison was still mortified that she'd been screaming her head off in the early hours of the morning.

'Oh Lisa – I hope I don't have another dream like that for a long time. It was so vivid and very frightening'.

'I know what you mean I've had a few nightmares myself but you mustn't be scared Alison. You're surrounded by friends here and if you can piece together what happened then maybe you'll start to remember who your family are.'

'I know something bad happened to me and I can't believe Rosie didn't tell me. She's supposed to be my friend and look what happened – she dumped me here', Alison said bitterly and thought, she's left me in a mental hospital when I'm not mentally ill.

How could you Rosie? Alison fought back the tears that sprung into her eyes and then looked at Lisa who said, 'She did her best for you – that's all she could do. I'm sure she'll come and see you.' Lisa went very pale; Alison turned around and looked out the window to see another police car speed up the drive of the hospital. Two heavily built police officers opened the car door and dragged a man kicking and shouting at the top of his voice.

'You can't leave me here – you animals – I'll kill you both when I get out of here.'

The man had blond greasy hair and was naked apart from a dirty pair of underpants; he was frothing at the mouth. When he yelled the spittle dripped onto his scrawny chest.

Lisa and Alison couldn't hear what the officers said to him because he let out another ear-splitting scream. Alison burst into tears and covered her ears to block out the din. Two male members of staff came out to them and one of them stuck a syringe into the man's arm, who promptly collapsed into their arms. They took him inside, peace was restored once more.

Lisa gave Alison a hug, until she stopped crying. As God is my witness – I've got to get out of here, this place will be the death of me, she thought desperately. Deep down Alison knew she would do whatever it took to get out of this hell hole.

'It's okay Alison – he's gone. I think we should go to our room. No one will bother us there.'

'You're right – let's go before someone else kicks off.'

Alison pushed Lisa through the dining room and into the hall where the lift was.

'Alison.'

A familiar voice called out to her when she turned around, Rosie stood in the doorway with a large bunch of flowers. Alison shook with anger and said through gritted teeth, 'What the hell are you doing here? You're the last person I want to see right now. How could you dump me in a place like this Rosie? What have I done to deserve this?'

As soon as the words flew out of her mouth Alison regretted it. Rosie stepped back with a hurt look on her face as if she'd been punched in the guts.

'Alison – I came here to explain what happened. I went away for a few days and the decision to transfer you was taken out of my hands. I let you down and I'm sorry. I came to see you today to try and get you out of here. I came as soon as I could.'

Alison shook her head fighting back the tears, feeling that she'd been betrayed by the one person she thought cared about her. Lisa interrupted.

'Alison – why don't you go back to the library with Rosie? At least hear what she has to say. You've got nothing to lose. I want to lie down for a bit – I'm bushed.'

'I'll talk to you later Lisa – take care.' Alison said as Lisa wheeled herself into the lift and the doors shut behind her leaving her and Rosie standing there awkwardly.

'I guess you'd better follow me then', Alison said coldly.

'I brought you these – I hope you like them', Rosie gave Alison the flowers and she accepted them out of respect for Rosie. However, what she really wanted to do was to chuck them in the nearest bin.

Alison led her through the dining area and seated herself on a window seat in the library, and discarded the flowers on the coffee table. There were books and magazines scattered everywhere.

Her long chestnut hair fell over her face, Rosie sat opposite her wishing she'd fought harder to keep Alison in St Margaret's and wondered if Alison still trusted Rosie because she looked like she hated her and it tore at her heart.

'I know you don't belong in a mental hospital Alison and I'm working hard to get you out of here. I don't blame you for being angry with me but I did try and stop them. They were sneaky – they waited until I went on vacation and made arrangements to transfer you without my knowledge or consent.'

'How're you going to get me out of here Rosie? I don't want to go back to hospital I want to lead a normal life, have my own space. I hate this place – I'm on edge the whole time because I don't know what's gonna happen next. I can hear people screaming at night – it's awful.'

'Are the nurses and doctors treating you well?'

'Yes – they're nice enough but it's the place – I don't think its helping me get better and I so want to remember my family. I hate being in limbo, every day I wake up hoping that today will be the day I remember a snippet of my past but I don't. You were the only one that treated me like a friend instead of a patient.'

'I am your friend Alison and so is Tom – he's coming to see you too. Don't give up, not yet. I have an idea but I need to talk to the doctor first – can you trust me again?'

Alison didn't answer because she realised that she was being unreasonable and felt guilty about the way she had spoken to Rosie when she arrived. Alison sank back into the easy chair and closed her eyes; she was beginning to get a headache again. Rosie was the last person Alison expected to hurt her but then she became aware it wasn't Rosie's fault.

She couldn't look at Rosie without betraying the hurt she felt at being abandoned in this place so she looked out the window instead blinking rapidly to fight back her tears.

> 'Alison – can you look at me please? I have to go back to the hospital soon and I need your co-operation before I can help you.'

When Alison looked up all she could see was a blurred face, the tears flowed down her face and splashed onto her hands, and she said quietly,

> 'Okay Rosie I'll listen and I'm sorry for being so rude.'

> 'I know you're hurting Alison but it's going to be alright I promise.'

> 'You're a good friend – thank you', Alison broke down for the second time that day and Rosie went over to her and hugged her as if she was comforting a small child. She'd made up her mind at that very moment; she needed to get Alison out of Ashvale. I could do with the company, Alison's right – I'm married to my job and I need to stop and take stock of my life before it's too late. I'm nearly forty and I don't have a lot to show for it, no husband, and no kids. She's coming home with me, people will think I've lost the plot but I don't give a damn. Sometimes you just have to take a risk, if I was in Alison's position I would want someone to stick my neck out for me too. Rosie let Alison go and said.

"I've made an appointment to see the doctor as soon as I could. So hang in there, you won't be here for long. Okay?"

'Rosie – you haven't told me where I'm going.'

'That's because you're coming home to live with me for a bit.'

'Wow – are you *serious*?' Alison asked incredulously.

'You bet – but as I said I have a lot to organise so be strong for me and stick this out.'

'I don't know what to say.'

'Don't say anything – I have to get going but I'll be in touch.'

'Thank you so much.'

'Don't thank me until you're out of here. I'm going to have a battle on my hands', Rosie said grimly and continued.

'I've got to go back to the hospital because my shift starts soon but leave it to me and I'll be in touch in a couple of days.' Rosie leant over and gave Alison a hug.

As Alison watched Rosie walk out, she felt a sense of relief. She was getting out of here and it couldn't come soon enough as far as she was concerned.

***

Rosie sat in Dr Williams' office holding onto the belief that she was doing the right thing. She clenched her teeth in determination when Dr Williams said,

'Dr Shaw *have* you really thought this through? Think of your career, you're highly respected in the field of head injuries and you seem to be throwing it all away for a patient.'

'Excuse me – a former patient', Rosie interrupted.

Dr Williams had to admire her courage even though he felt it was misguided. She was a striking woman with auburn hair and beautiful creamy skin and utterly captivating when she was angry. Dr Williams had trouble hiding his admiration and shifted uncomfortably in his seat. He clasped his hands on the desk and tried a different tack, but she was resolute.

'Okay, a former patient and someone you hardly know.'

'I don't care what your personal opinion is – I want to know if I can take Alison home to convalesce.'

'If you do – you will probably lose your job at St Margaret's. How are you going to support yourself then?'

'Look don't lecture me on what I'll do – I've applied for various jobs in teaching and research so mind your own business! It's up to me to worry about my future not you. I firmly believe it's in Alison's best interest to recover in a home environment', Rosie retorted, annoyed at him for bringing her personal life into the equation as if she were an irresponsible teenager.

'Okay – you've clearly made up your mind and if Alison agrees then I cannot stop you. If Alison is happy to go with you then I'll discharge her at the end of the week. However, I'll want her to attend regular appointments at the outpatients' department. Rosie looking after a patient at home is entirely different from a hospital environment', Dr Williams added quietly.

'Alison is no longer my patient. She is a friend, and yes, of course it will be different but I'm already emotionally involved with Alison and this is a very clear indication to me that its time to leave my job and move my career in a different direction. Thank you for your time Dr Williams. I'll pick up Alison on Friday.'

'I'll email you a date and time for Alison's first appointment. Good luck Rosie.'

Rosie smiled and shook Dr Williams' hand. She couldn't wait to get out of the office, as soon as she shut the door behind her; she let out a big sigh of relief. Rosie wondered if she should go and find Alison but decided she'd had enough excitement for one day. She had a lot to do at home now she was bringing Alison back to the cottage. She'd wait till the morning and call Alison then. As Rosie walked out of the hospital, she could hear a woman screaming. She had to get Alison out of there before it was too late. Deep down Rosie knew she was doing the right thing despite resistance from her friends as well as the hospital regarding the whole situation.

She decided not to tell Susan at St Margaret's that she was taking on Alison full time just yet. She would resign from her job first. She was taking quite a gamble with her career and her personal life was going to change.

Rosie had got used to living alone. For once, she could really make a permanent difference to someone's life instead of just patching people up and shipping them out for devastated relatives to look after.

Her job had become a conveyor belt of human misery as she moved from one patient to the next without really getting the chance to follow their recovery through to the end. That was always left to the outpatients' department. Rosie was lonely and she knew that she couldn't carry on with her life as it was. She had to change direction and live a little before it was too late. She wanted more to live for than just her work. Talking to Alison and watching Alison struggle to get well alone had made Rosie look hard at her own life. She had to change her career and in doing so, maybe, just maybe, she could have time to enjoy herself. As she left Ashvale Rosie knew there was no going back, her life would change but it would change for the better now she had Alison to look after.

Chapter Nine

Later that evening Alison went to bed early after an exhausting day of counselling and she dreamt that she was on a beach running after a little boy; the sun was bright and warm. He wore a blue t-shirt and white shorts and he kept running faster when she tried to catch him up.

'Come back, you're going too fast! Come here! It's not ready yet!' Alison giggled.

He was smaller than her, had dark brown hair and a wiry build. The sand was warm and powdery, and it sprayed up under his feet as he ran. She could hear the waves of the sea lapping against the shore. The gulls screeched and circled the sky looking for scraps of sandwiches that people had dropped on the beach; brightly coloured buckets and spades were scattered everywhere.

'I'm going to get there first!' said the boy.

'No you're not – you cheated! I've been trying to make this sandcastle all afternoon and you've just started yours', Alison laughed.

The tall blond woman with a large sun hat sat up in her deck chair and said, 'Alex McIntyre what are you up to now?'

'Now Roz don't go all bossy on me – you're not in the boardroom now you know.'

'You cheeky little monkey – wait till I get you, it's Mum to you.' She jumped off the sun lounger and started to chase after her son, shouting.

'Alison grab hold of his legs and we'll throw him in the sea.'

Alison woke up with a start and a huge grin on her face. She couldn't believe it, she had remembered something. *I'd better get write this down before I forget*, she thought happily.

She got her journal out of her bedroom drawer and wrote down the word – Alex and Roz McIntyre. Who was he? A friend? A brother or cousin? She didn't know but his name sounded familiar. She tried to remember as much as she could about her dream.

Roz McIntyre is my mum – I've dreamt of her before when I was in that shop. She's the woman I was talking to about clothes. Oh my God – I can't wait to tell Tom and Rosie. I can't doubt my dreams, not now.

Alison leapt out of bed and hurried into the corridor, the night staff were in a huddle talking in hushed whispers.

'Alison – what's up?' One of them asked.

'I've remembered who my mother is. I've remembered my name– It's Alison McIntyre and my mother's called Roz. I need to call Tom right away.'

'Alison – that's brilliant news but its 3am, you'll have to wait till the morning.'

'No – you don't understand – I need to call him now. He's been trying to find out who I am for weeks and we need to phone my mum as well…'

'Alison, you're getting worked up and that's understandable but Tom will probably be in bed at this time. You can call him first thing and that's a promise. Think about it –nothing will happen until the morning anyway. It's only a few hours away, go back to bed or you'll wear yourself out and then you'll be no use to anyone.'

'Yeah, I suppose your right but can't you see this is a huge thing for me?'

'Of course I do and I'm thrilled that you've remembered something. I'll write what you've remembered in your notes and I promise that we'll call Tom Bernstein in the morning.' The nurse started to walk towards her but Alison backed away holding her hands up in the air in frustration.

'Alright, I'm going', Alison sighed and walked slowly back to her room, frustrated that she couldn't phone Tom herself but accepted that there was no point, he did need his sleep as much as anyone else.

You've no idea how important this is but I as usual I'm getting nowhere with these people. My mum is probably going out of her mind with worry but if I can't remember her address or number then it's going to take a wee bit longer. I can't wait to tell Rosie at least she'll be thrilled for me, Alison thought, irritated at their unenthusiastic reaction until one of them called out.

'Alison – I know it's a big deal to you and it's great that you've finally remembered something, it really is, but we can't do anything until the morning.'

'Okay – you win as usual', Alison sighed and turned around to go back to bed. I probably won't sleep a wink anyway but I'll try. Alison drifted into an uneasy sleep, praying that she would recall more of her past life.

***

Tom managed to get hold of the local police very quickly after Alison called but he'd had a hunch that if she was in the fashion business then she must have a website. He put her name into a website search engine and up came the Just Roz fashion empire with an address in Edinburgh. He prayed that it was the same woman for Alison's sake and contacted the local police to check if it was the same family and if they had a daughter who was missing.

Chapter Ten

It was two o'clock in the afternoon when Roz was greeted by a rather white-faced Lucy who led two policewomen, through to her office. When Roz saw them, her heart lurched.

'I'm sorry, I'm going to have to call you later', Roz put the phone down and clasped her hands, trying to steady herself for the news to come. Oh please don't tell me she's dead. Please God – not now. The two detectives sat down and introduced themselves.

"Good afternoon Mrs McIntyre. I'm DC McClure and this is DC Andrews from Portobello CID. We've had some news from Hyannis Police Department regarding your daughter Alison McIntyre. I'm sorry to have to inform you that the car your daughter was driving exploded and caught fire. That's why it has taken us four weeks to discover what had happened to her', DC McClure sat down in front of Roz looking grim.

'What happened? I can't believe this?' Roz wept as Lucy put her arms around her. Roz held onto her waist and sobbed into her jumper; she held onto Lucy so tightly she could hardly breathe.

'The car was completely burnt out. She was probably unconscious before the final impact. The car hit a stag and it crashed through a metal barrier and went down a very steep ravine. She's in Ashvale Hospital in Cape Cod with a serious head injury but we've been informed that she's making good progress and will recover. Naturally, the hospital will hold all the information that you'll need. Here are the contact details and if we can be of further assistance please don't hesitate to contact us. We will send you a full report of the accident as soon as we get it, if you wish', DC Andrews added.

'I want to know what happened to her. Oh, I can't believe this – are you sure you have the right person?' Roz blurted out in a state of shock.

Lucy had never seen Roz so distressed, she could hardly string a sentence together. Her eyes were bright and the colour had drained from her face.

'We had a call from Tom Bernstein, a Boston detective who's been working on her case.'

'I'm so sorry this must be an awful shock for you', DC McClure said sympathetically.

'Thank you for taking the time to see me. If you don't mind I'd like to be alone for a few minutes. I need time to compose myself before I call the hospital.'

'Lucy can you send the car around for me – I need to collect Alex from school.'

'No problem Roz.'

'If you have any further questions, here is my direct number', DC McClure said giving Roz her business card.

'Thank you very much.'

Roz watched them go and as they opened the door, all she could see was a gaggle of anxious faces staring back at her. Oh God what am I going to say? I need to tell them the news but I don't know how I'm going to find the strength. I'm under enough pressure as it is without this as well, she thought as she closed her eyes and breathed deeply. She lifted her head, she had forgotten Lucy was still hovering. She couldn't forget what the police had said; the words were going around in her head like a spinning washing machine.

'Um – do you want some tea? Is there anything I can get for you?' Lucy asked awkwardly, not knowing what to do.

'Yes please, if Alex calls put him straight through, cancel all my meetings. I'm going to take time off so put all my business calls through to John – I'm sure he can manage without me for a few days.'

'No problem – I'm so sorry about Alison – it's unbelievable. Don't worry about anything – Ill take care of it', Lucy said looking at her boss with tears in her eyes.

'Lucy thanks for everything – I won't forget the help you have given me. You are an excellent PA, one of the best I've had actually. Now I'd like to be alone now.'

'Thanks Roz, that means a lot to me. I'll make sure you are not disturbed.'

Roz picked up the piece of paper that they'd given her and her hands shook as she rung the number for Ashvale. It rang for a long time and Roz was just about to hang up when they finally answered.

'Dr Pierce Williams, please. This is Roz McIntyre; I believe Alison McIntyre is a patient at your hospital. I want to find out how she is. I'm her mother and I'm calling from Scotland.'

Roz spun around on her chair after speaking to Dr Williams and looked out of her office window – Alison like a zombie? This is the last thing I expected. How on earth am I going to cope with Alison and the business? I'm not sure what the situation is regarding her will either. One thing I do know is that there'll be enough money there to save my neck. Oh what am I thinking? I never wanted this to happen. Poor Alex will be distraught, what a nightmare, I just can't take it in.

Lucy was stunned, she'd worked for Roz for over a year and she had never praised her, not once. Lucy had met Alison several times and she really liked her. She was much more approachable than Roz and would happily chat to other members of staff whilst she was waiting for her mother to finish her calls.

Lucy remembered joking and laughing with Alison about music, make-up and clothes. They were about the same age and had a lot in common. She was really looking forward to working with her if Alison decided to join the firm.

She made Roz her tea and headed back to her office dreading what state Roz was going to be in when she walked through the door. Surprisingly, Roz was on the phone but Lucy quickly realised she was talking to David, Alison's father.

'Oh David, thank God – I was hoping you'd call. Can you come straight to the office because I think we need to go to the school and tell Alex together. I don't know what to do; I just can't take anything in. When will you be here? – See you in fifteen minutes', Roz croaked, then smiled at Lucy.

'Here's your tea.'

'Thank you – tell the staff I'll be out in two minutes', Roz replied.

'Are you sure you don't want to wait until David arrives?' Lucy asked tentatively.
Roz looked up and glared at Lucy. 'No – you can go now.'

Lucy left quickly, she knew by the tone of Roz's voice that she was back in control. She hurried back to her office and shut the door. Then she set about re-organising Roz's hectic schedule. David arrived in the office just after three. He was absolutely shattered. Not only from the long flight but he couldn't take in the news that Alison was in hospital recovering from a serious head injury.

His beautiful, bright, fun-loving daughter was seriously ill and he didn't know how he was going to tell his son. He'd never felt so desolate and empty in his life, it was as if he was carrying a yoke of heartache on his shoulders that would never come off. He had just come out of the lift when he bumped into Lucy, looking tense and anxious.

'David, I'm so sorry to hear about Alison, it must have been an awful shock for you. Erm - I'll take you to see Roz', Lucy stuttered, blushing bright red.

'It's okay Lucy; I know the way and thank you for your kind words', he said patting her shoulder as he walked towards Roz's office, which was at the other end of the room.

Lucy was shocked by David's appearance when she bumped into him. What she saw was the shadow of a broken man, walking through the silent office to Roz's door. His face was white and his dark blue eyes were bloodshot and heavy, like he hadn't slept for months. It saddened Lucy to see him like this; he was a kind and gentle man. He lived for his children and took a close interest in everything they did. Roz and David had been divorced for many years but they were still close and kept in regular contact with each other. She headed back to her office ignoring the open curiosity of her colleagues. Roz jumped up and ran to David when he entered her office and broke down.

'Oh thank God you are here; I don't know what to do'. Roz started to cry again, her shoulders were shaking uncontrollably and David walked over to her and took her in his arms and whispered into her hair.

'Shh- it's alright. Look we'll have to go and get him – we have to be strong for his sake. School's nearly over and I've phoned the Headmaster. We'll face this together – okay?'

Roz nodded and looked up at the man who was once her husband. Her heart warmed to him, he was always there when she needed him.

'I need to inform the staff because I'm not going to be in for a few days. I'd like to go to the hospital and see Alison for myself.'

'We'll tell the staff together, you are too upset.'

'Let's get it over with.' replied Roz.

They both walked out of the office and you could hear a pin drop, the atmosphere was so tense and deathly quiet. Some people stood and others were rooted to their desks as if they were survivors of a shipwreck clinging onto their rafts for security.

'Can everyone please gather round? Don't worry about the phones just leave them.

> David and I have received some terrible news regarding our daughter, Alison. As you know, she went missing a while ago and…' Roz turned around and wept on David's shoulder.

The office was so quiet; you could hear the distant traffic filtering through the windows. The sea of shocked faces stared back at them, holding their breath waiting for the awful news that was about to come. Roz had never shown such emotion before.

> 'We've just found out that Alison was in a very serious car accident and is in hospital with a severe head injury. Roz and I will not be available for a few days as we need to make arrangements for her care. We're counting on all of you to support us through this difficult time. That's all we have to say for the time being', David explained.

Roz couldn't look at anyone. What the hell is wrong with me – I'm the strong one. I need to get a grip here. I'm mortified – blubbering like a bloody baby.

Roz could feel her mascara running down her cheeks and she didn't want her staff to see her looking so dishevelled. The shocking revelation stunned the staff and they were anxious to get back to work. It was quite late by the time David and Roz arrived at Alex's school. It was dark and the November wind cut through them; they shivered as they walked across the bleak school yard to the Headmaster's office. The school secretary greeted them and sent them straight in. Alex jumped up and his eyes widened when he saw his distraught parents.

'Oh God, it's Alison, they've found her haven't they? It's not good news is it?' He started to cry because he knew almost instinctively, just by looking at his parent's stricken faces, that his big sister was seriously ill or even worse – dead.

'Mr and Mrs McIntyre – would you like to sit down?' The Headmaster sat back in his chair, not wanting to witness the tragic scene unfolding before his eyes.

'Yes Darling, it's true – Alison had a serious car accident. She's in hospital,' Roz held onto her son as he wept. She hadn't held him so tightly since he was a child.

'Why didn't they tell us sooner mum – why? I don't understand why we've been waiting so long? It's been doing my head in not knowing what's happened to her.'

'The car she was in crashed down a ravine. It exploded sweetheart, there was only a shell left but she didn't feel any pain. The police said she was already unconscious before the impact and she'd lost her memory. That's why it took so long for them to find out who she was', Roz replied looking at David whose face was ashen.

'Oh my God – is she going to be alright? Alex asked.

'We don't know yet.' Roz said quietly.

'I'm so sorry this is appalling news. Please take Alex home and I don't expect him to be back in school until arrangements are made for her care. If we can be of any assistance don't hesitate to call us.' The Headmaster stuttered wishing he was somewhere else.

'Thank you, we'll be in touch in due course.' David said, ushering Roz and his devastated son out of the door.

As they made their way out of the school Roz said.

'David – can you stay at the house for a few days to support Alex? We need to stick together at a time like this', Roz asked.

'Of course – I don't want to go home to an empty house either. Come on son; let's go home. I'm not going anywhere until I've discovered how bad Alison is. Amelia has offered to fly over to Edinburgh if you want her too.'

'No, that won't be necessary – we need her over there just in case the Police find out more. It's nice of her to offer. Oh God David, this is a nightmare and I wish I could wake up!'

'I know – lets go home, it's freezing out here.'

David walked along with Roz and Alex by his side wishing that Alison was with them and worrying that she might never recover from her injuries.

***

Roz had been awake since five; she wondered how she was going to get through the long flight to Boston to see Alison for herself. Everything had been arranged jointly with David and Alex. It upset her to see Alex so distressed and he had become even less communicative than usual. What hurt Roz the most was that Alex chose to talk to his dad rather than share his feelings with her.

One thing she did know was her business would certainly be saved. She felt very guilty thinking about Alison's trust fund but Alison had done her a favour in the end. As a joint trustee, she was confident that David would let her have at least 2.5 million pounds for personal use so that she could take care of Alison and she could use that to pump some much needed cash into the business. She couldn't afford to go bust especially when she needed money for Alison's care. She might need

24-hour care for the rest of her life. Roz shuddered at that thought, she was rarely ill and hated hospitals. The rest would go to Alex until he was twenty-five.

It was in his best interest to keep her little empire going too. School fees still had to be paid and life had to go on. Alison would not have wanted her business to go to the wall just because she was too ill to handle her own affairs, Roz convinced herself. I should be sorting out Alison's care, not thinking about the money that's just sitting there. David's already paid St Margaret's so it's now up to me to pay for her respite care until she's well enough to fly home. The bank's still trying to shut me down, bloody vultures, so how the hell I'm going to manage without that money I just don't know. I can't fail now. I can't let my children down, especially Alison. I *need* that money more than ever.

Roz pushed her troubled thoughts out of her mind and as she got out of bed, she opened the curtains. The sea was calm today. It was like a mill pond, and the distant street lights in Fife were twinkling like diamonds at her across the sea. The moon could just be seen from her bedroom window, a dark cloud went across its full face, obscuring it. She sighed, she was just about to run a bath when Alex knocked and popped his head around the door.

'Mum?'

'Come in Darling, can't you sleep either?' She hugged him and sat him down on the bed with his hands in hers.

She couldn't believe how big they were compared to hers. When she looked into his blue eyes, they were full of pain as if he was searching for answers. Roz knew that he adored his big sister. Even when they fought like cat and dog, they were devoted to each other. She felt a pang of jealously when she realised how close they were.

'Oh, Mum, I don't know how I'm going to hold it together today. I still can't believe Alison's ill. I'm dreading going back to school.' Alex continued,

'I don't know what to say to people and my friends just avoid the subject if I mention Alison's name. It's horrible, it's like they've forgotten her already.'

'They haven't forgotten her; some people don't know what to say so they change the subject because they don't want upset you. They can see how devastated you are, but everybody has different ways of coping with tragedy. It's happened to me and your dad as well. If you want to talk to me about Alison, I'm always here.

You are so precious to me, Alex, and I love you very much. Come on let's go downstairs and I'll make you some scrambled egg and tea', Roz said gently but Alex shook his head and muttered.

'I'm not hungry.'

'It's going to be a long day and you'll need something to keep you going. Be strong; it's what Alison would have wanted and she wouldn't want you to pine for her or be unhappy. We'll get through this together. It's going to be a hard day but she'll be back sooner than you think. I promise I'll call you as soon as I get to the hospital.'

'Thanks Mum – I just feel the pain will never go; it just sits on my chest and its horrible', said Alex, his tears spilling onto the back of his hands.

'I know sweetheart but the pain will ease with time, that's what we all need, time to come to terms with what has happened', Roz replied gently stroking his hair and holding him tightly to her.

He looked so young even though he was a strapping lad of seventeen. He still needed her and she would always be there for him, no matter what happened. She loved Alex unconditionally. She felt bad for loving him more than Alison but he was her only son. David was in the kitchen when Roz and Alex came down the stairs. He sat hunched at the kitchen table staring out of the window into the garden as the watery sun was starting to rise through the clouds. He didn't notice them come in, spread out in front of him were two large photo albums and a large cardboard box with a pink ribbon around it.

'Hey Dad – you okay?' asked Alex who squeezed his father's shoulder as he sat down to join him.

'Hi Son – I'm fine I just couldn't sleep. I was looking at photos of you and your sister when you were babies. I had forgotten how small you guys were when you were young. Look, there's you and Alison on the beach, and you're Mum's on a sun lounge. You were never keen on sand were you – Roz.'

'Um – no I hated the stuff but I enjoyed watching you get dirty with the kids', Roz added.

Alex's face lit up when he saw the photos. It brought back happy memories of the times that he and Alison had spent together as children. They started going through all the photos and then Alex had an idea.

'Why don't we all pick favourite photos of Alison and each put them into a small album and then we can carry them around with us. Then the old Alison will always be with us in some way. I'm so scared that I'm going to forget what she was like before the accident', Alex replied. His eyes were welling up again.

'Oh Sweetheart – none of us will ever forget how Alison was. I think that's a fantastic idea – don't you David?' Roz said looking over at David. He just smiled.

'You can look out the photos and I'll make the breakfast.' Roz said getting the pans out of the cupboard.

I'm not looking forward to this one bit. I don't know if I can hold it together but if I start crying, I won't be able to stop, she thought desperately.

Nothing seems to matter to David anymore but Roz was the only one who had to keep going for all their sakes. If David was going to pieces then she needed to be strong for all of them. The only way I know how to be strong is to throw myself back into my work. I have to get that money, one way or another.

She'd promised to meet the manager at the bank when she came back from Boston. They'd been lenient with her so far but as her business lost more revenue each week they were becoming impatient.

Chapter Eleven

Roz relaxed in a hot bath after her long flight from Glasgow to Boston. She decided to ring Ashvale again in the morning; exhaustion and jet lag clouded her brain like fog. *I'm dreading this – I haven't a clue what to do or say. What if Alison doesn't recognise me? Then what am I going to do? It's just as well I packed some photos of Alison and Alex when they were children; hopefully it will jog her memory. I'd better ring Alex now before I forget.* She picked up her mobile; it rung for an age before Alex picked it up.

'I've not long arrived at the hotel darling. I've rung the hospital. Alison's been transferred to another hospital unit in Cape Cod. It's too late to call them tonight but as soon as I see Alison – I'll ring you and let you know how she is.'

After Roz hung up she looked up the Ashvale Hospital Mental Health on her laptop, wrote down the directions on how to get there and slumped, exhausted into bed. *There's nothing more I can do. I'll just have to play it by ear.*

***

Roz's fingers shook when she dialled the number for Ashvale. It rang out for a long time before someone answered. Dr Williams just happened to be passing the main desk when he picked up the telephone, irritated that the Receptionist always seemed to be away from her desk.

'Ashvale – Dr Williams speaking.'

'This is Roz McIntyre – I spoke to Dr Rosie Shaw at St Margaret's hospital regarding my daughter Alison. I was wondering when I'd be able to visit her.'

'You can visit her anytime Mam – there's no restriction for parents.'

'Right – I'll pop down this morning to see her. Can you tell me how she is?'

'She's making good progress but it's still early days yet. I'll inform the nursing team that you're coming so that they can have a chat with you once you've seen Alison.'

'Thank you, you've been really helpful.'

'No problem Mam.'

What a nice guy, Roz thought as she hung up. Dr Williams was curious; he wondered what Alison's mother looked like. He imagined her to be the image of Alison, tall with long chestnut hair and a fabulous figure. He couldn't wait to tell Alison that her mother was coming to visit. Hopefully, it will put him in her good books for a change. He hadn't forgotten about the conversation they had the other night regarding Rosie's kind offer to take care of her. He'd tried to play devil's advocate to make sure that it was what Alison really wanted and that she hadn't been coerced in any way. She was adamant that going to stay with Rosie was the ideal solution to her predicament. He would bide his time and have a little chat with her again once Roz had gone. At least they'd located her family and then they could decide what was best for Alison in the long run.

As Roz drove up the tree-lined avenue she was immediately taken with Ashvale. The winter garden had borders full of beautiful herbaceous plants, their branches laden with rich red and yellow berries.

Bloody hell – it's like a luxury health spa. I hope the care they give her is as good as the surroundings. Roz thought, as she parked outside the gravelled entrance and strode into the Reception area. She was greeted by a pretty, blond, toothy receptionist.

'Can I help you, Mam?'

'Yes – I'm Roz McIntyre, Alison's mother – she's expecting me', Oh please God that she recognises me – otherwise it's going to be a very long morning. It's just as well Alex insisted that I bring the photo albums. At least it will give me something to talk about, Roz thought wearily.

'I'll just ring Dr Williams for you. Please take a seat – he'll be with you in a moment.'

'Thank you.'

Roz smoothed down her navy cashmere dress for the third time and switched off her phone. The last thing she wanted was any interruptions from Alex, David or her office. Lucy had rung her twice on the way to Ashvale with final arrangements for the New York Launch. As Dr Williams walked into Reception, he was not disappointed when he saw Roz. She was tall, blonde and absolutely stunning – what surprised him was that she looked nothing like Alison.

'Mrs McIntyre – Welcome to Ashvale, I trust you had a good journey.' He smiled magnanimously, ushering her through the corridors to the conservatory where Alison was waiting.

'Yes thank you. You can call me Roz - no one calls me Mrs McIntyre – how is Alison?'

'She's making good progress but she's still having a couple of seizures a week. Her long-term memory is still quite poor but we're working on that.'

'Do you know when she'll be well to fly home?'

'Hmm – not for a few weeks yet. She'll need to be fully assessed before she can be discharged and we need to organise a care plan for when she goes home to Edinburgh. 'Here she is. Alison – your mother has come to see you.'

Alison sat quietly in the conservatory, with her back to the door. When she turned around, Roz gasped when she saw a blank expressionless face staring back at her.

'Hi'

'Do you remember me –darling? I've come all the way from Edinburgh to see you.' Roz spluttered taking Alison's hand but she immediately withdrew it as if she'd been scalded.

'I'll leave you to it. I'll be back later with your medication Alison – okay? If you need any more information just inform reception and I'll be happy to help.'

'Thanks Dr Williams.'

Damn! I thought he might've stayed for a bit, Roz thought as she stared in disbelief at the girl she had once known so well. Alison said nothing and just smiled. Roz tried again to engage Alison in conversation but she just looked at her like a child who was meeting a stranger for the first time. She quickly took out the photo albums that Alex had given her.

'I've got some photos of you and your brother when you were children – would you like to see them? I thought it might help jog some memories.'

'Okay. I just wish I could remember you but I can't! I'm so sorry', Alison blurted out looking sadly at this strange but beautiful woman claiming to be her mother in front of her.

'It's alright – it's to be expected after what you've been through. Your dad and I have been beside ourselves with worry. We're so glad that you're safe and sound – that's all that matters', Roz swallowed hard, her voice quavered.

'Oh my God – that's Alex!' Alison cried with glee.

'That's your brother – he'll be so pleased that you remembered him first.'

She's remembered something – this is a nightmare. It's like talking to a completely different person.

I can't put my finger on it but it's as if there's a steely determination in her that was never present before. I don't like it, not one bit. Roz rubbed the back of her neck, the room was stuffy and she could feel tiny beads of sweat trickle down her back. *Yuk!*

'I dreamt about him the other night, we were on a beach. That's all I can recall', Alison said wistfully.

'You and Alex were as thick as thieves when you were children. You two loved to play on the beach in the summertime.'

'Is there a beach in Edinburgh?'

'Yes darling – we live just down the road from the beach.'

'I see – when will I be going home? Have you come to take me back with you?'

There was a challenge in Alison's voice and Roz felt uncomfortable and shifted nervously in her seat.

'I don't know – we'll have to see. You're still under the care of Dr Williams. I'll let you know when I find out myself. I'm sure it'll be soon – though.'

'Okay – look I'm tired. I'd like to go to my room now. Will you come back tomorrow?'

'Yes of course. Do you want me to come with you?' Roz was momentarily stunned but quickly recovered herself.

I've only been here half an hour – I can't believe she wants me to go already. Maybe it's just as well – I'm at loss for words. I don't know what I'm going to tell Alex but that can wait. I'll talk to Dr Williams before I leave – he seems to know what he's doing because I don't. Alison shrugged and said 'No – I'll be fine. Can I keep the albums for the time being? It'll help me with my treatment and at least I have a physical record of my past', Alison held onto the albums as if her life depended on it.

'That's a good idea. I'll see you at the same time tomorrow?'

'Alright', Alison yawned and left without uttering another word. This annoyed Roz, it was like dealing with a petulant teenager all over again.

She had travelled all this way for a short visit. However, it would give her more time to work on the New York store and that was a bonus – after all. *Well* – I'm glad that's over but what will David and Alex make of the new Alison? Lord only knows. Now – where's Dr Williams?

Roz hurried down the long corridor, her eyes were blinded by tears and she angrily wiped them away. She almost collided with Dr Williams as he came out from his office.

'Roz – are you okay?' Dr Williams took her by the arm but to his surprise she leant on his chest and started to sob. Reluctantly, he put his arms around her and took in the scent of her soft hair.

> 'She's a completely different person. She doesn't know me and I didn't know what to say. I wasn't expecting to be dismissed so soon, it was as if she didn't want me to be there.'

Roz felt safe in Dr Williams' arms – it'd been a while since she'd been held so tightly. She let go feeling giddy; it must be jet lag or the shock of seeing Alison in such a state.

> 'She's asked me to come back tomorrow. I'd like to speak you if you are available?'

> 'Yes, I've got twenty minutes before my next appointment. Why don't we go for a coffee or would you prefer tea? I know how much you Scottish ladies love your tea.'

Roz laughed and said.

'Actually I prefer coffee most of the time – thanks Dr Williams – you've been great.'

'No problem – it's my job – shall we?' as he ushered Roz down the corridor.

Dr Williams wasn't sure how Roz was going to react when she found out that Alison was leaving to stay with Rosie Shaw whilst she recuperated. He hoped that Roz would understand it was what Alison wanted; he decided it would be easier if Alison talked to her mother and Rosie first. He would have to handle this very carefully indeed.

Chapter Twelve

Roz was in her New York office when she got the call from Alison who was still at Ashvale. Dr Williams let Alison use his office to make the call. She stood nervously at the desk chewing her lip.

'Yes Lucy any news?', Roz enquired.

'Mum – it's Alison.'

Roz sat down and held her breath, Alison sounded so distant and fragile. She was the last person Roz expected to hear from and drew in a breath.

'Are you alright darling? Are they keeping you in hospital?

Do you want me to pick you up?'

'Mum – please don't ask me too many questions. I can't cope with it at the moment. I'm going to stay with Rosie Shaw. She's a good friend who's offered to look after me until I'm strong enough to fly home.'

'Really?' Roz couldn't hide her irritation and continued. Alright – look darling I need her address and her telephone number so that I can come and see you.'

Roz was uneasy – who was this Rosie Shaw that Alison and Dr Williams spoke so highly of? And why is Alison so keen to stay away from me? I think I'll give Dr Williams a call to find out more about this woman.

Roz sighed. She knew she was in no position to argue; she wanted to keep Alison happy and the launch of the New York Store loomed ever closer. It would give her more time to get used to Alison's way of doing things. She was far too independent and she wasn't sure how to handle the new Alison.

'I'll get the details later when I go to Rosie's. I'll call you later Mum.'

'Look after yourself darling and I'll see you in a couple of days. Love you lots.'

'Love you too Mum.'

It was strange saying those words; Alison wasn't sure if she meant what she said but she didn't want to upset Roz further. After she finished her call Alison went back to the main reception and waited for Rosie to collect her.

***

When Rosie picked Alison up, she was exhausted; the strain of being in Ashvale for a couple of weeks had taken its toll. They drove to Rosie's cottage in silence and Alison was relieved that she didn't have to make small talk. The old wooden cottage couldn't be seen from the main road, as it was obscured by tall trees and thick bushes. It used to belong to the local carpenter and was a hundred years old.

It had a wide porch, with a small swing seat but it was homely and full of character. Rosie had spent years lovingly restoring it because the place had been pretty run down. Everyone thought Rosie was mad buying such a derelict property but she had fallen in love with it as soon as she had seen it. John had helped her with some of the repairs but they had split up after a five-year relationship. Rosie had thrown herself into her job with gusto to forget the heartache she'd felt at the time.

'Well here we are – home sweet home.'

'Rosie it's wonderful, thank you for bringing me here.'

'How are you with dogs? I have a westie called Rufus.'

'I love dogs so it's no problem.'

The outside door swung back and forward in the rain squeaking like a badly made wind chime. Rosie was glad she had put the fire on downstairs before she left. Alison shivered with the cold when she walked up the path. The warmth from the fire hit her face like an electric fan oven making her ears and face tingle.

Alison collapsed on the sofa and closed her eyes, the room was spinning wildly and when she opened her eyes she saw the concern in Rosie's hazel eyes.

'Do you want some tea before I take you upstairs?'

'Yes please.'

Rosie quickly made some tea and when she came back into the room Alison beamed at her.

'Thanks – you're spoiling me. I could get used to this.'

'It's good to have you here.'

Alison gingerly took the mug of steaming hot tea and sipped it, smiling weakly at this amazing woman in front of her. It was like a dream and if she hadn't pinched herself Alison wouldn't have believed this was real. Rufus, the West Highland Terrier, sat at his mistress's feet waiting patiently to be rubbed down with his ears prickled up, his large eyes full of curiosity.

'You looked shattered – come on – I'll show you your room.'

As Alison followed Rosie up the stairs she took in her surroundings for the first time. It was a bright and cosy cottage, typically New England in every way, with its whitewashed walls and an outside porch. Rosie had decorated it in warm colours, making it homely and welcoming. Alison's room was yellow; the colour reminded her of daffodils. The room had a large window overlooking the forest and on a clear day you would probably be able to see the ocean. Alison sat on the bed and felt overwhelmed.

'Rosie, this is a beautiful room, thank you.'

'The bathroom's at the end of the hall. Do you need anything else before I go to bed?'

'No – you're an angel.'

'I'm definitely not – I hope you'll be comfortable here. I'll leave you to it.'

Alison changed into her pyjamas and climbed into the old pine bed. Alison was already asleep when Rosie popped her head around the door. She watched Alison for a while to check that she was okay. Rosie knew her friends would think that she was crazy taking in a strange young girl for a little while.

Rosie was no ordinary woman; she rescued stray dogs and had a menagerie of animals in her back garden, birds with broken wings, stray cats and occasionally dogs. Rufus was very possessive and it was not convenient to have so many animals to look after; she made sure the dogs went to the local dog rescue centre. The cats were always easy to re-house anyway.

Rufus nuzzled into her, whining, his mucky fur rubbing against her calves. His paws were muddy from the walk they'd had together earlier in the day.

'Come on boy, let's get you rubbed down. I could do with a bath myself.'

Rosie walked into her cosy white kitchen. She picked up his towel and rubbed him down; Rufus went trotting to his basket and settled down for the night. She threw Rufus a treat, his tail wagged in appreciation. Rosie picked up the coffee pot and poured herself a drink, looking out of the window. Her thoughts turned to the weather outside. I hope Alison's going to be alright here.

The heavy rain hit the small window panes like millions of tears.

Her pale oval face stared back at her in the reflection of the window. Her auburn hair was cut into a neat bob, but the rain had left it wavy and unruly. *I think I'll have a long soak in the bathtub tonight,* she thought. When she checked on Alison, she was sleeping peacefully; *that's her for the night I should think. It'll take quite a few days before she'll be strong again. Then, with a bit of luck – I might find out what happened to her before the accident.* She put another log onto the fire and went wearily upstairs to run a hot bath.

****

Alison woke up feeling slightly disorientated. The pale yellow sunlight shone through the windows bathing the room in an ethereal light, adding to her confusion. *Where the hell am I?*

'Where am I?' She cried and looked around wildly.
Rosie dashed into the room and said,

> 'It's okay Alison – you're in my place – I brought you here yesterday remember?'

'Yes – of course, sorry, I forgot where I was for a moment.'
'Did you sleep well?'
'Yes I did – this bed is really comfortable.'
'Are you sure you want me to stay with you?' Alison asked anxiously. She still shouted out when she had flashbacks and she was keen not to disturb Rosie.
'I genuinely want to help you if you'll let me.'

Alison lent on Rosie's shoulder and burst into tears, her whole body shook uncontrollably. Rosie held her tightly and she could feel how scrawny Alison was under her pyjamas.

> 'Shh – it's all right sweetie, just let it out there, there. You have a good cry. It's okay: I'm going to take care of you till you're strong', Rosie whispered and held out her arms.

Rosie held Alison and stroked her hair like a mother soothing her only child. Alison let out all the emotion she had held in for so long. The confusion about her identity, the sheer loneliness and the desperation of her situation had taken its toll. She'd spent so many weeks wondering if she was ever going to find her family again. She had felt bitter disappointment when she'd met her mother for the first time in Ashvale as she didn't feel close to her at all.

'I'm so lonely, I just wanted to die at times because I don't know who I am, or where I come from – I remember nothing. Will I ever find out who I am? I feel like an empty shell because there is nothing there to fill me, no memories and it's unbearable.' Alison continued. 'I had a car accident and when I woke up – I was surrounded by strangers who kept telling me what had happened. I don't even know my own mother. Why can't I remember?' Alison cried, rocking back and forward in Rosie's arms. She felt secure with Rosie even though Alison had only known her for a short time. Rosie let Alison calm down and said quietly.

'It takes time and you need a safe environment to heal properly to come to terms with what's happened to you. You've been through so much already. You are a beautiful, determined young woman and life has not been kind to you. You'll remember who you are in good time. If you're stressed all the time, then your recovery will take longer. I've had many years of experience in dealing with head injuries and the research I am doing is in this field.'

'Really? Is that why you are helping me?' Alison asked. Rosie let her go and sat back.

'If I'm honest, that's part of the reason but I'm also a great believer in fate. I was meant to help you, but I want to be your friend. You can stay here and get better. If you can you help me with my research – great. If not, then don't worry about it."

'Of course I will – I..', Alison stammered.

'When we start doing everyday regular things, that's when the memories will start coming back. But I warn you, there is no rush; you'll be convalescing for a long time. Is that a deal? Let's shake hands on it. I'm trusting you Alison, don't let me down.'

'It sounds pretty good to me. You don't know what this means to me', Alison replied and grabbed Rosie's hand and squeezed it.

'No problem, I want to help you Alison because if I had a daughter who needed help – I'd hope someone out there would help her too.'

'Do you have children?' Alison asked then as soon as the words flew out of her mouth regretted it because Rosie looked away for a moment and cleared her throat.

'No, I love my research too much; sadly I had to choose – family life or my career. I chose my career because it is too important to give up', Rosie said with a distant look in her eyes.

'I'm sorry.'

'Don't be – it's my choice. Anyway, let's find you something to eat. Will muffins and scrambled eggs do?' Rosie stood up wanting to distance herself from the sadness that suddenly overwhelmed her when anyone mentioned something that was too close to home.

'Sounds good to me, I'm starving.'

The more Alison spoke to Rosie, the more she liked and trusted her. Rosie had come into her life when she was losing hope. At a time she felt the whole world was against her. Rosie was an angel as far as

Alison was concerned. Then she remembered Lisa and Roz. She must call Lisa in a couple of days to let her know that she was okay. She was far too exhausted to do it now. As for Roz, she felt more uneasy; she seemed quite a controlling woman. She didn't want to call her Mother yet and that was odd considering she was the only family Alison had contact with.

'Come on, I'll show you where everything is. We need to get you strong, lots of eating and rest. Come on let's get you fed and bathed.'

'Rosie, you make me sound like your dog!', Alison laughed; it was good to laugh again.

'Sorry – I think I've spent too much time on my own, it'll do me good to have some company for a change.' Rosie grinned and turned to go out of the door. Alison laughed and shook her head as she got up slowly to and wandered through to the shower.

***

All the floors in the house were wooden and highly polished; Rufus had slid a couple of times as he trotted behind Alison. After a lovely breakfast with Rosie, Alison wandered around the house freely, taking in her temporary new home and enjoying the space to just be alone.

Rosie had started a new shift at the hospital where she worked and promised to be back later in the evening. Her room was quite large and square in shape; there was a large antique pine wardrobe to the left of the double bed and a free-standing bookshelf. It was crammed with medical books, and old battered paperbacks of all kinds; thrillers, biographies and some literature classics.

There were photographs in various shapes and sizes by the bed. Black and white photos of Rosie and her brother, lovely colour photos of a little redheaded girl with her parents at the local zoo. Rosie with her friends at various birthday parties, the number of candles on the cake marking the age she was, five, ten, thirteen and her twenty-first birthday. In one photo, there were at least thirty people all crammed in, all peering into the lens of the camera. Alison felt really envious as she looked at those photos. Rosie had a record of her past, a family, a career and friends. She probably could tell Alison everything about each photo in great detail. Alison put the photos down on the table and brushed away a lonely tear. On the other side of the bed there was a small table and on it were two colour photos of a young gawky girl receiving her medical degree. Her laughing eyes were full of hope and expectation, with her proud parents standing behind her.

Alison felt guilty that she hadn't got in touch with Roz. Despair hung over her like a dark cloud as she sat on the bed; silent tears rained down her face. As dusk fell, she fell into a deep and peaceful sleep.

When Rosie arrived home she called out for Alison and went upstairs with a glass of orange juice and fruit; she found that Alison hadn't stirred. She covered her with a large quilted blanket and left. The queen-sized bed was against the wall next to the window, so when Alison woke up the next day she would hear the various animals in Rosie's back garden, scratching about. There was a small dressing table with a matching stool overlooking the back garden. She would see the garden and the menagerie of animals that Rosie kept.

There was a chicken coup, a rabbit hutch with two rather overweight rabbits in it, and a cute racoon with an injured paw. The summerhouse had been converted into a small animal rescue centre. There were smaller shelves with room for birds, and anything else that would live happily in that environment. Rosie woke Alison at lunchtime the following day and served her with a delicious home made chicken soup with bread and cheese.

'Did you sleep well?' Rosie asked.

'Yes, it was wonderful and I had no nightmares either.'

'Good, how's the pain in head?'

'Okay, better than yesterday, I'm still really tired. I'm not much company am I?' Alison smiled.

'It's not a problem, as I said before – you need lots of sleep. I'm going out this afternoon, if you are up to it – can you feed the animals?'

'Sure, I'd love to. I probably could do with some fresh air anyway.' Alison sat up in bed.

'By the way, you'll have to borrow some of my clothes till we get you some new ones. Luckily, I found some stuff that might fit you! It's just as well I don't throw anything away. There are at least two pairs of jeans that are too small for me, so help yourself', Rosie said popping her head out of the window.

'Thanks Rosie – you're an angel.'

"I wish you'd stop calling me that. Look I'm going to be late, so if you need anything, my mobile number is on the kitchen board okay?', Rosie called over her shoulder as she dashed down the stairs with an armful of files and an overloaded briefcase.

'Will you relax – I'll be fine – see you later.' Alison said.

Alison leant forward and tucked into her food, savouring each mouthful. When she put Rosie's jeans on they were still a bit big but they were a better fit than what she had. It was a lovely crisp afternoon and Alison fed the animals enjoying the sunshine caressing her face. The winter sun and fresh air gave her cheeks and nose a rosy glow. What a wonderful place – I wish I could stay here forever but I suppose I'd better phone Mum as I promised. I didn't get the impression she was too pleased that I'd prefer to stay at Rosie's. I'd better do it now before I forget. Alison went into the house and called Roz; thankfully, she was in a meeting so Alison left a message with Lucy. It bothered

Alison that she'd rather talk to anybody else but her own mother. It just didn't make any sense.

Chapter Thirteen

Rosie took Rufus out for a long walk. He'd been stuck in the cottage all afternoon. He seemed to accept that Alison was part of the family now and it was unusual for him to take to a stranger right away.

It gave Rosie time to think. It was two days before Thanksgiving and she had promised to go to her parents' house in Chatham. Well, they would have to set a place for an extra one. She couldn't leave Alison alone in the cottage. Rosie's mother was a local doctor and had set up various voluntary organisations to help the local community. Her father was a veterinary surgeon and that's where Rosie got her love of animals from. If she hadn't gone to medical school, she would have been a vet. Rosie had worked in her father's surgery one summer when she was a senior but she hadn't enjoyed it. After a long spell of deliberation; she studied to be a doctor, following in her mother's footsteps.

The sky was overcast tonight, and looking across the path towards the city, Rosie reckoned it was probably going to snow. She would have to make sure there was enough firewood in the shed to keep them going. Rosie suppressed a yawn; it had been a long day. She walked down the path towards the cottage; the first flakes of snow fell silently on the ground. She let Rufus into the cottage. Even though it was cold, she stood in the porch and watched the snow swirl down in flurries. She tried to figure out how to help Alison, a vulnerable young woman with no memory of her past. Rosie looked at her watch; it was nine thirty, enough time to call her mom. She went inside and picked up the phone.

'Mom, it's me. How are you and Dad? Yes I'm sorry I haven't been in touch about Thanksgiving. That's why I'm calling you; I'm bringing a guest over. No, it's not a man, it's a young girl called Alison. She's staying with me at the moment. She's recovering from a serious car accident, yes I know it's short notice…'

Rosie ended up on the phone for over an hour explaining to her parents Alison's story. Rosie was going to bring Alison home to meet her family for Thanksgiving. It was a great weight off her shoulders and she couldn't wait to tell Alison in the morning. It would give her something to look forward to. She went upstairs and as she passed Alison's room, she heard Alison crying. When she crept into the room, Alison was talking in her sleep.

'Alex – come here. I'm not finished with that yet. Roz, I mean, Mum tell him!...'

Rosie ran to her room and wrote down Alex on her notepad, from what she heard it was obvious to her that Alex could be Alison's brother. She would leave her sleeping and tell her the good news in the morning. It had been a long and tiring day but it had ended with a glimmer of hope. Slowly but surely, now that Alison knew she was settled, she would start to remember more. Rosie wasn't particularly religious but as she went to bed that night, she thanked God with all her heart.

When Alison woke up the next morning, she was thrilled to see that it had snowed overnight. She gazed out the window, all the trees where covered in white and it was as if someone had taken some white soap powder over night and sprinkled it everywhere. She put on her dressing gown and trotted downstairs as she could hear Rosie pottering about.

'Hi – Did you get some decent sleep last night?' Rosie inquired, dying to tell Alison what she had heard.

'Yes – Can you believe it's snowing? It's like a winter wonderland out there. I have this childish urge to build a snowman!'

'Um – so you don't remember anything about last night?' Rosie added pouring herself a large mug of coffee and sat down.

'No why? What is it?' Alison was alarmed and she sat down at the kitchen table. Rosie poured them both a coffee and sat opposite her.

'When I came to bed last night, I heard you talking in your sleep. Do you remember dreaming?'

'No - tell me what I said. What did I say?' Alison's face was flushed with anticipation, her hearting was hammering wildly; she took a sharp intake of breath.

'Does the name Alex or Roz mean anything to you? Before you answer, try and think before you speak. I think this is very significant', Rosie pointed out, watching Alison's face for any signs of recognition.

'Oh – I'm not sure. I've heard the name before. It does sound familiar but I don't know', Alison was perplexed and chewed her lip at the same time.

Rosie sat in silence to give Alison time to think, it was still early days yet. Then without warning, Alison jumped out of her chair almost falling over and squealed.

"I remember now, I've had a dream about a boy called Alex when I was at Ashvale. We were on a beach, it was summertime I think. I chased him and then we stopped and a tall blonde lady with a hat spoke to us. She shouted Alex first, but I woke up before she said anything else. The woman in the hat – it's Roz – I mean my mum."

'Alison – that's brilliant, I told you! Didn't I tell you? I knew that your memory would start coming back. That's real progress', Rosie stood up, walked over to Alison and gave her a hug.

Alison burst into tears. After months of not being able to remember anything, there was hope.

'Sorry – I'm so emotional all of a sudden; I seem to cry at the drop of a hat these days.'

'Honey – don't be silly. You have suffered so much, more than some people have been through in a lifetime. It's no wonder you're all over the place. It must be really hard, so stop beating yourself up for crying all the time Alison, you mustn't get stressed about it.'

'Oh Rosie you really are the best thing that's happened to me in a long, long time.'

'Come on, I've got work to do, so why don't you run yourself a bath. Oh by the way, I called my mom last night; we're going down to Chatham for Thanksgiving weekend.'

'Brilliant, I can't wait to meet them. I've heard so much about your family.'

'Well, it'll give you something to look forward to won't it? I think a vacation in sleepy Chatham will do you the world of good,'

'Yes and I can't wait to go with you.'

'You better call your mum to let her know where you are, just in case she calls and you're not here.'

'Sure. I'll call her after my bath.'

'Well that's settled then – well I've got a full clinic today so I'd better get a move on. See you later,' Rosie smiled as she put her cup in the sink, picked up her bulging briefcase and walked out the door.

As Alison ran her bath, happy thoughts swirled around her head. At last I'm starting to remember stuff. I just wish I could remember what day it is and what my date of birth is without being prompted, then life would definitely be so much easier to bear.

Chapter Fourteen

Alison and Rosie were looking forward to Thanksgiving weekend. They headed down to the Cape on Friday and Rosie told Alison all about the place where she had lived as a child. Rosie had grown up in the town of Chatham. It was a charming and quintessential New England town with an old colonial feel to it. Each building on the main street was painted a blueberry colour with white shutters. There were many individually owned shops and Rosie knew most of the townspeople very well.

   A beautiful European style church where she used to go to Sunday school dominated the main street. It was large, painted white and had dainty arches adjoining the church hall. The impressive spiral tower housed the church bell and it rose up into the sky for as far as the eye could see. The pristine white walls stood out like a white marble statue. Rosie told Alison there were many seals and dolphins in the area, and they became stranded on the south beach quite often. There was a dedicated organisation of volunteers who saved them. Rosie explained that Chatham was famous for its lucrative fishing and maritime history and the town was always busy in the spring, summer and the autumn.

      'Rosie, this town is so pretty. I've never seen such a lovely place. Mind you, I bet it's really cold this time of year because you're by the coast.'

   Alison sighed looking out of the window, as they drove towards the famous lighthouse. She couldn't stop smiling; she'd fallen in love with Chatham with its unusual shops, art galleries and craft stores. The streets were deserted, and she couldn't wait to wander around without people rushing around her.

The few people who were brave enough to be out in the icy wind waved to Rosie as she drove down the street. She pointed out to Alison who everyone was as she cruised by.

> 'Alison - You need to be well wrapped up at this time of year, you can get some pretty nasty storms coming off the ocean. I love it though; the wind makes you feel alive, somehow. The beaches are empty in winter, except for locals and dog owners. I can't wait for you to meet Jess; she works at the local bookstore. We used to spend hours in there as kids; it has some neat toys too!'

'I can't wait', Alison replied.

She brimmed with happiness, as they drove along towards the lighthouse. Rosie pulled into one of the narrow streets leading straight to the seashore just before it.

'Here we are, home sweet home.'

Alison's jaw dropped when she saw the large house in front of her, it was magnificent. The wooden walls were painted a pale grey colour and the shutters were white. It really stood out against the misty sunlight; she heard the crashing of the waves against the rocks. The ocean spray leapt into the air like Icelandic geysers. The long rectangular porch was painted white, and there were two swing seats facing the superb view. A large white summerhouse faced the sea at the left of the main porch in the immaculate back garden. The ocean spread out as far as the naked eye could see. A small fishing vessel bobbed up and down like a wine cork in an ice bucket. Alison didn't notice that Rosie had taken her bag out of the boot because she was mesmerised by the view in front of her.

'Ali – are you coming in? It's cold and I can smell freshly baked cookies – come on! I'm freezing my butt out here!' she laughed as she dragged Alison onto the porch.

'Sorry – I'm just taking in this view – it's awesome. You're right, it's cold. I bet you never get tired of this view though. I love the sea and I would like to some spend time walking along the beach,' Alison said wistfully.

'Well you can enjoy the view from the inside as well; you'll catch your death out here!'

'Okay mom!'

'Watch it!' Rosie laughed.

Rosie's parents were in the hall to greet them; Alison felt a pang of sadness as she watched Rosie give her parents a tight hug. They were so pleased to see her, and she suddenly felt as if she shouldn't be here until Rosie's mom spoke first.

'You must be Alison; I'm so pleased to meet you. Rosie's told me all about you. It's lovely to meet you at last', the older woman smiled at Alison; she was a little taller than Rosie and she had the same auburn hair.

'Thank you for inviting me to your home, it's lovely to be here', Alison said. Her face went red and then Rosie's father spoke.

'You're welcome here, just make yourself at home, Rosie always does!'

'Thanks Dad.'

Rosie's father was a tall man with short silver hair and very piercing blue eyes. They were inquisitive but kind eyes and Alison suddenly felt safe with this man. She hadn't felt this comfortable with anyone and she felt relaxed even though she'd only just met him. She could see how much he adored his daughter and she felt a pang of heartache, wishing her own father was here to share these special moments too.

'I'll let Rosie take you to the guest room and I'll make some hot chocolate – would you like some Alison?'

'Oh yes please - that would be lovely – thanks.'

'Good choice – mom's hot chocolate is great, I'll probably put on 10lb because her cookies and chocolate cake are heavenly. I can't stop stuffing my face when I'm at home, so be prepared!' Rosie said as Alison followed her towards the stairs.

'It's beautiful here, thanks for bringing me, it's wonderful just to relax and your parents are great.'

'Yep – they are pretty special and as I get older, they are more precious to me than anything in the world', Rosie added.

Alison's eyes filled up as she looked out of the arched window at the top of the stairs, taking in the magnificent view of the ocean, wondering what her parents were doing right now.

'Here we are – I hope you like this room – it used to be mine', said Rosie opening the door to her old room.

'Oh Rosie – it's gorgeous, a four poster bed. You're really spoiling me! I love the quilted cover, did you make this?'

'No – my Grandma made it for me when I was ten, she's passed away now but I will always cherish it', Rosie remarked sadly.

'Oh – are you sure you don't want to sleep here? It's your room after all. You've done so much for me already', Alison exclaimed, suddenly feeling very guilty.

'No not at all, I like the other room, it's slightly bigger. I prefer facing the front garden anyway. The sound of the sea sometimes drives me crazy!'

'Rosie you are funny – you've lived by the sea all your life.'

'Exactly – that's why I like the other side of the house. It's a different view and I can see what's going on in the neighbourhood', Rosie said with a mischievous grin on her face.

'You're incorrigible!' Alison scolded.

Alison sat on the large double bed, and was in awe staring out at the long winding bay that stretched all the way down the Cape. Chatham was surrounded by water and there were lots of little ponds dotted around the area.

The sky was overcast with black clouds, it looked like a storm was coming tonight but Alison didn't mind. She would be safe and warm in this wonderful house; she suppressed a yawn. Rosie watched her out of the corner of her eye; Alison still looked pale and drawn. Rosie wondered if she was thinking about her brother Alex; she had that distant, far away look in her eyes.

'You okay?' Rosie asked.

'Yes – I may have lived by the sea before. I'm not sure but my gut instinct tells me I've been somewhere similar to this place. It's weird.'

'Well, all you can do is write down what you think you remember in your journal and then go through it at a later date. Maybe you'll be able to piece together some of the information you have', Rosie said.

"You know, that's a great idea. There's no harm in trying, is there?"

"No – come on let's go downstairs and be sociable."

Alison closed the door and trotted down the stairs, knowing that she was in for a treat. The smell of cookies filled her nostrils and suddenly she felt really hungry.

***

They had a wonderful turkey dinner later that evening. Alison really relaxed and enjoyed herself. Rosie's mom was a great cook, and she made the most wonderful pumpkin pie, of which Alison had two slices. Rosie's dad entertained them by telling Alison all the things Rosie used to get up to when she was younger, much to her dismay. Alison hadn't laughed so much in a long time.

She even managed to forget her problems for a while. She said good night and got ready for bed. She decided to keep the curtains open so that she could wake up and see the ocean in the morning. Alison leaned against the window brushing her teeth, it was pitch black. The only thing that she could see was the white froth of the waves crashing against the rocks. The sound of thunder rumbled in the distance. She looked at the little bedside clock, it was 22:30. She fell asleep as soon as her head hit the pillow. Alison dreamt again.

She was at a dressing table in a large magnolia bedroom; there was a large bay window with small square window panes. The top of the window was open because the cream voile curtains were billowing in the gentle breeze. She could smell the sea, and Alison could just make out the sound of the waves lapping gently on the shore. She was sitting on a pine chair with a rich cream and peach cushion attached to the bottom. There was a large-three way mirror and in the reflection, a little girl was trying to put on lipstick. She had curly chestnut hair that tumbled onto her shoulder and wore a pink Barbie top with matching white shorts. She picked up one of the many dainty crystal perfume bottles to smell its fragrance.

The bottle tipped over, and it went all over the lace cover. She picked up the tissue box that was at the left hand side and tried to clean it up.

'Alison! – What have I told you? Do not to come into my room and mess about. Look what you have done, you naughty girl, you have ruined my lipstick and my table. Get to your room now! I'll deal with you later!' All Alison saw was an angry face and cold blue eyes. She felt afraid and as she walked past the blond woman without warning she hit Alison across the back of the legs, making her yelp with pain. It was Roz; her beautiful face twisted into an ugly sneer.

'I'm sorry Mummy, I won't do it again,' she sobbed.

'Get out of my sight!' Roz screeched.

As she ran down the corridor, it got darker. The house changed into an office corridor, she flew down it as fast as her legs would carry her. There was someone behind her, trying to catch hold of her. When Alison turned around to see who it was in her dream, it was a blond man with a nasty sneer on his face. She let out a piercing scream, shouting.

"No! Get away from me! Leave me alone!"

Suddenly, in her dream, a hand went over her mouth making her jump out of her skin. She realised as she stared, wide-eyed in terror, that someone had clamped their hand across her mouth from behind. The familiar scent of soap and aftershave hit her nostrils. She started to struggle, but he was too strong.

'Don't scream or I'll cut your pretty face so badly that no other man will look at you again!' he whispered in her ear. She could feel a cold steel blade against her cheek. His narrowed blue eyes could just be seen glinting in the darkness.

'Remember what I've said so you'd better behave yourself! I'm going to take my hand away and then you and I are going for a little walk.'

He grabbed her roughly by the arm; she nearly fell on top of him as he had pulled her up with such brute force it made her wince. His clammy fingers dug into her arms. Alison nodded vigorously; the tears streamed down her face. Alison had never felt so scared in all her life, she felt sick in the pit of her stomach, and shook uncontrollably. He pushed her out into the office corridor; confident no one would disturb them at this time of night.

Alison's bare feet were making gentle slapping noises on the vinyl floor. Her mind raced, trying to think with clarity, but her hammering heart wouldn't let her.

The blood whooshed around her ears, making them throb. She daren't anticipate what he was going to do her, as he silently pushed her down the stairs. She could feel his hot breath on her cheek, and she nearly fell a couple of times because they were moving so fast.

'Please, please don't hurt me – I'm so sorry– for.'

'Shut up and do as you are told,' his tone had changed to a deathly quiet whisper.

This terrified Alison even more: Please God – *don't* let me die at the hands of this monster not now. She gasped for air, as her lungs were working to full capacity at the speed at which he dragged her down the cold dark stairs. They were surrounded by grey grimy walls and there was a faint smell of oil and damp stone. He let go her arm as they got to the bottom, which led into a dark corridor stretching both ways. It was long and narrow; there were endless streams of long white pipes of all shapes and sizes above their heads. The corridor was barely lit: right she thought, I have to time this very carefully and run when I get the opportunity. She began counting the rivets in each pipe to try and judge the way back to the stairs. They turned a corner; a small dark green door was just ahead. Just as he bent down to turn the key she took her chance and smacked him in the stomach with all her strength.

'Oh! – you bitch you'll pay for that,' he said, through clenched teeth, bent double with the wind temporarily knocked out of him.

Alison ran as fast as she could without looking round. She screamed; she could hear his heavy footsteps behind her and he was almost on top of her. Before she got to the stairs, he grabbed a handful of her hair. Alison yelped with pain as she could feel her hair being pulled out at the roots, giving her a headache. Then he pushed her forward, ripping her evening dress in the struggle to catch her. She lunged forward again and just reached the stairs, when he grabbed her ankle in a vice-like grip.

'LET ME GO – GET OFF ME – GET OFF ME,' She yelled as her chin bounced off the bottom step. She tried to get up, but he grabbed her ankle and dragged her back.

'Aargh! Alison screamed with pain as he pulled her up by her hair on to her feet. Her face contorted with pain. She felt dizzy and her legs were like jelly.

'LITTLE WHORE! – Boy *are* you going to get it now,' he muttered, slapping her across the face making her teeth rattle. She could feel the stinging hand print on her face. He leered, as her evening gown had slipped down exposing her breast. She gulped for air, as if she was drowning. He grabbed her breast roughly, and then ripped the rest of her dress off. He threw it on the floor; he'd collect it on the way back.

'You won't be needing this where I'm taking you,' he snarled looking at her like a hungry animal about to devour her flesh. At that point, the bile rose in her throat and she was violently sick. Even though she was bent double, retching, the man still had her by the hair. He grabbed the top and threw it at her.

'You're disgusting, now clean it up.'

'I couldn't help it, please don't hurt me anymore I promise I'll be good – I…'

Alison sobbed, trying to catch her breath, and knew it was futile to fight. He was too strong and she knew what she had to do, keep calm. The reality of the situation hit her hard. She would co-operate fully because her life depended on it. The acid was still in her throat and in her nostrils and she kept coughing.

Her head ached and her breasts were tender from being scratched, her left side was grazed from being dragged down the stairs. He took her hand and whispered, making her cringe.

> 'Oh I know you will, sweetheart, you'll do exactly as I say, won't you,' He said triumphantly giving her bottom a tight squeeze; her skin crawled every time he touched her.

She nodded and meekly followed him down the corridor, trying to steady her breathing and praying that she would get through this. Something inside her told she could block anything out, just as long as she survived. Alison walked through the green door into a dark, airless room and stopped dead in her tracks.

There was a mattress on the floor, it was filthy and the air was rancid with sweat and dried blood. A grey metal box sat next to the bed and in it was a red tie, a white tube of gel, a needle with liquid in it and a packet of condoms. Oh my god, she thought he's done this before. The tools of his despicable trade were laid out before her eyes.

He pushed her under the light in the middle of the room. Her heart lurched, as he locked the door behind them. She bent her head down, breathing deeply. To survive this ordeal she would have to concentrate, and block out what was about to happen to her. She looked up again, something caught her eye; she saw a spider's web. She sympathised with the fly as it was struggling to break free, she watched it intently. He walked up behind her, he pulled her hair back gently, murmuring how soft it was, stroking her back and he whispered.

> 'Why don't you like me Alison? It would have been so much easier if you'd co-operated in the first place. You are so beautiful, and we could've had so much fun together,' he whispered as he turned her around, cupping her face. She stared at him in

bewilderment. It was like he was talking to a lover rather than a woman he'd just met. You're the one that's sick in the head – not me! His small sapphire blue eyes were boring right into her as he hardened his grip on her head.

'I'm sorry – please can I have something to drink, my throat is still sore – please?' she begged hoarsely, her muscles in her body so tense that she ached all over.

He let her go, and she shivered as his eyes lingered over her body. Her thumping heart had slowed down, but her stomach was in knots.

'Of course, brandy?'

'Brandy?' she asked incredulously.

'Do you want some or not?' he yelled.

Alison nodded and stretched out her hand to take the bottle that he had taken out of his black bag. 'No – I'll hold it and you drink!'

'But..'

'Will you do as you are told!' he said, grabbing her chin with his fingers digging into her jaw. She yelped like a frightened dog, and took a couple of sips. The hot liquid seared her throat and her stomach, but at least she couldn't taste her vomit anymore. She felt a little light-headed. Then without warning, his other hand pulled down her lacy pants. This made her jump and she felt really cold and humiliated, standing there naked with a man she loathed.

'Step out of them and turn around in a circle – slowly - I want to see you in this light. Keep your arms by your side and lift your head up – I want to see your face,' he barked.

He had a grin on his face, like a wolf that was about to close in on his prey. She did what he asked; she shook so much she could hardly turn around. The man stood a few feet away, watching her with his arms folded and nodded like he was accessing a prize-winning mare. That's all she was to him, a piece of meat, something to be chewed up.

She thought frantically, be strong you can do this, just think of something else - the spider's web and the fly. The pungent smell of the brandy was making her ill. Concentrate on the web and nothing else she thought, clearing her throat and focusing on the corner of the room.

'I've waited for this moment for a long time. Do you appreciate the trouble I have gone to Alison? You think I'm not good enough for you? Don't you?' He said coming up behind her, pulling her hair so that she had to arch her back to stop it from being yanked out again. Ouch – I'm not going to have any hair left if he doesn't stop pulling it. Oh God, please don't let me die in this stinking hell hole.

'No, not at all,' she stammered.

'Liar – you're a lying whore like all the rest of them – aren't you? Aren't you!' he yelled as he walked her over to the mattress. He let go of her hair and she fell onto her back.

'Spread your legs, you whore!' I'm going to die – shit he's going to rape me. I need him to stop – anything but this. Alison thought frantically as he pushed her roughly towards the mattress and she fell awkwardly onto her back. The smell of the damn mattress nearly made her sick again. It was damp and clammy.

'Don't to do this me. If you really care about me – you won't do this!' she pleaded, closing her legs as tightly as she could.

'You're too late. You've made me wait long enough.' the man let out a harsh laugh.

She couldn't stop shaking; her chest was so tight with stress. Every muscle in her body went rigid. He had unzipped his trousers to lie on top of her, but she pulled her knees up. No – oh god no! I want to scream! You bastard - I fucking hate you! There were so many thoughts racing through her head, Alison couldn't get the words out, her mouth opened and shut again, time seemed to slow down.

They died in her throat from sheer terror. He pulled her legs down and threw himself on her. The weight of him temporarily knocked the wind out of Alison. She started to hit him, but this made him even angrier.

'Open your legs or I'll cut you!' he said angrily as he dug his fingers into her thighs, and prised them apart.

'No – please don't do this,' Alison begged as she desperately fought him off, she couldn't help it anything to stop him from hurting her.

Alison sobbed as he belted her across the face and she nearly blacked out. His hands were all over her, *I want to die* – when is this ever going to end? He leaned over and tied her hands above her head with the red tie, and took the tube of gel and put it onto the tips of his fingers. Alison reeled from being hit again, and was just focusing when he roughly shoved his fingers up her vagina. She screamed, she thought it was in her head but it wasn't – it hurts - oh god I'm going to be split in two.

'Oh please stop!' she whined like a wounded dog.

'Shut up – you've teased me long enough and lie still,' he said, biting her breasts making them bleed; Alison screwed her eyes shut, as he thrust himself in and out. He was licking her face and trying to kiss her.

The pain was so bad she thought I'm not going to be able to walk again! This can't be happening – I want to wake up now! It was like being rubbed raw with sandpaper over and over again.

Finally, after what seemed like an eternity, he shuddered and relaxed. Then he untied her, all she could see was his grinning face as he released her hands. A sudden surge of hatred went through her like lightning. 'You evil, sick bastard!' Alison finally found her voice and with all the strength she could muster, she smacked him squarely on the nose, throwing his head backwards. Her knuckles cracked as she had hit him. 'Oh! that bloody hurt! he yelled and the blood from his nose spurted out all over them both. He looked totally shocked and his face contorted with rage. She threw him off her and ran to the door. Her fingers were shaking as she unlocked the door, throwing it open and running for all she was worth. Her knuckles were raw and bleeding but she didn't care, she was determined to escape from her attacker at all costs.

'Aargh! Come here, come back! You're fucking dead Alison – wait till I catch you – you've broken my nose.'

Alison picked up her dress as she fled along the corridor to the stairs and ran up them two at a time. She knew he was close behind because she could hear him breathing heavily on the steps just below her. She spun round and kicked him squarely on the chest with both feet, and he fell backwards. He nearly caught her leg but she managed to break free. Her legs were wobbly and she was tiring pretty fast…

'Noooo!'

Alison sat bold upright in bed, hyper-ventilating. She could hear footsteps coming down the hallway. She was sweating and shaking and her mouth was dry. Rosie came in first, closely followed by her mom.

'Alison – are you okay? I came as soon as I heard you screaming.' Rosie said, sitting gingerly on the bed and she switched the bedside lamp on.

'Oh Rosie – I'm so sorry. I was dreaming about a little girl then I was running down a corridor. He was chasing me. A man – he attacked me. He took me down to a basement and he raped me. I was raped Rosie before the accident, some bastard raped me. I remember now and I don't want to, why would anyone do that to me – why? I was back in that corridor running and running……,'Alison shook so much she couldn't stop her teeth from chattering.

'Alison – slow down. You're not making any sense,' Rosie said as she sat on the edge of the bed and took both of Alison's hands in hers.

The thunder outside rumbled, as if it was right above the house. The noise shook the walls and this only added to her anxiety.

'What was that noise? – I need to tell Tom what happened. We need to get him – he had blond hair and blue eyes, cold eyes! I kept asking him to stop hurting me but he wouldn't, he just kept going and wouldn't stop. It was so real as if he was right here in the room with me. I could smell his aftershave and it makes me sick just thinking about it. He's still out there Rosie and I've got a horrible feeling he'll come back and get me.'

Alison stared at the door waiting for the man who attacked her to come through it but Rosie cut in, worried that her distress would bring on a seizure.

'Alison. Look at me and hold onto my hands. Concentrate on your breathing, breathe in through your nose and out through your mouth slowly. We need to concentrate on calming you down." Rosie continued, 'Shhh – you're safe here, Alison. Come on, I'll make you some tea once you've calmed down. Mom, could you make us some tea please,' Rosie said, her mom hovered at the door, looking as pale as Alison.

'Of course I will, its okay sweetheart. Don't worry about disturbing us; we're your family now,' Jane said observing the shivering, terrified girl.

Rosie turned back to Alison and gave her a tight hug. Alison cried until she couldn't cry anymore. When Jane came back with the tea, Alison felt better and she had washed her face.

'Thank you – I'm really sorry. I didn't mean to wake you all up. I still get vivid dreams now and then but nothing as bad as this."

'Don't be silly, just drink your tea and we'll see you in the morning. Rosie try and get some rest as well. I'm sure Alison will be okay now,' Jane smiled sadly.

Pour soul, she thought. No wonder Rosie wanted to help her, she was a lovely girl, polite and well-spoken and Jane sensed that Alison came from a good family. Her manners were impeccable. Jane and her husband, Stuart, had travelled to Scotland a few times over the years and she recognised that Alison had a Scottish accent. As she got back to her room, Stuart said.   'Is she okay? My God that was some scream she let out. It sounded like she was absolutely terrified of something or someone.'

'Yes, she'll be okay. She's suffering from post traumatic stress and has just remembered something important. It's only natural after the ordeal she's been through. It's healthy though, it's a good coping mechanism. Rosie will take care of her, she's in excellent hands,' Jane said as she climbed into back into bed.

'We've done a great job raising our girl,' Stuart smiled and cuddled into Jane. They fell asleep quickly. The rain had just started and the thunder storm had passed as quickly as it had begun.

Rosie went back to her room, Alison was settled again. She hoped that Alison wouldn't have any more nightmares tonight. Rosie needed to rest herself; she yawned and shooed her parent's dog out of her room and slept.

***

After breakfast Alison and Rosie walked down the main road towards the centre of the little town. Thankfully, no one had mentioned Alison's nightmare.

Rosie's parents had carried on as if nothing had happened. Alison was mortified that she had screamed her head off in the middle of the night considering she had only been there for five minutes.

I don't want to remember the rape – how did that happen? I don't recall meeting any blond man and my last boyfriend wasn't blond either. It doesn't add up and why didn't Rosie mention it before? She must've realised what had happened to me when they cut my dress off at the hospital. I don't want to think about it but I can't help it.

The shock of what had happened to Alison shook her to the core of her being. Whoever he was, she never wanted to see him again. She didn't want to talk about it or recall the horrific details of what had happened to her on that dreadful night with anyone let alone Rosie or Tom Bernstein. Alison couldn't distinguish between what had really happened to her. The lines of reality were blurred and her memories were still fuzzy and incomplete, as if an old reel of film had unravelled without warning, distorting the images in her head. Rosie's cheery voice cut through her thoughts and brought her back to the present.

> 'We're going into the bookstore first to see Jess. Then we're going to stuff our faces with muffins and coffee at Kara's Deli on the main street.'

'Great, we're all set then,' said Alison half heartedly.

Alison had been looking forward to her first free afternoon shopping and mulling around with Rosie since she had first found out that she was going to Chatham for Thanksgiving. However, one nagging thought that was going to dominate her mind the whole time she stayed in Chatham - who had raped her and why?

Chapter Fifteen

Rosie and Alison enjoyed a sumptuous dinner at the local seafood restaurant. They savoured every mouthful of the clam chowder and the lobster was delicious. Alison had never eaten so much in her life as she had done in Chatham. Rosie had noticed she wasn't as scrawny as she used to be. She'd met all of Rosie's old friends and they got on really well. She'd laughed till she'd cried at some of the antics they used to get up to when they were kids. Alison had thought Rosie was quiet and studious but her opinion of Rosie had changed overnight and she'd seen a whole new fun-loving Rosie emerge.

Rosie and Alison wandered back down the road after her friends had dropped them off at the top of the street where Rosie's parents lived. There was a cold wind coming off the ocean and Alison shivered as it whipped the strands of her hair around her face making her cheeks sting. She could hardly see in the darkness.

'You know, I've managed to forget all my problems tonight for the first time. It's been a brilliant weekend,' Alison said, as she walked into the porch, relieved to get out of the cold.

'I'm glad you enjoyed yourself, it's been great having you here.'

'I've been thinking, maybe it's about time I found myself a little part time job.'

Do you think you're ready for that? There's no rush to leave my place,' Rosie watched Alison carefully and thought maybe she's ready to stand on her own two feet.

'I'd like to see if I can cope living alone, it's important to me. I've got you and mum to fall back on if I need any help. I'll have to move out eventually and now is as good a time as any.' Alison said thoughtfully, shivering in the porch and staring out to the sea. The waves crashed against the rocks, adding to the eerie atmosphere on this dark and windy night.

'I think that's a good idea but there's something more important that you have to do first. You must call Tom tomorrow about what you remembered the other night.' Alison sighed and said nothing. Rosie flinched when she saw the haunted look in Alison's emerald eyes. Rosie didn't want to remind Alison about her attack but she plunged in anyway.

'It's very important – we need to catch this guy.'

'Why didn't you tell me that I'd been raped – you must have known about it because you were the doctor on duty the night I was brought in. How could you keep that from me? I thought you were my friend', Alison said and Rosie detected a defensive tone in her voice.

'Alison you nearly died – yes there was strong evidence of rape but you were in such a fragile state that I wouldn't let Tom interview you until you remembered the attack yourself. I didn't want to put words in your mouth and from an ethical point of view I couldn't tell you. It was in your best interest as a patient. I've had to wait until you recalled it. Sometimes when a series of traumatic events happen to you, the human brain can block that memory out completely. Do you understand why I didn't say anything?' Rosie said firmly and grabbed her friend by the shoulders and continued.

'I'm still your friend Alison, you have to trust me. I may get things wrong but I'm on your side – no matter what.'

Rosie had been dreading this moment but she'd prepared in her mind how she was going to defend her actions.

The anger in Alison died. She felt guilty because she knew she was being unreasonable. The anger she felt bubbled up from her guts and spewed out of her like a severed artery. She couldn't help it.

'I don't want any more secrets between us – ever!'

'Alison I wanted to tell you but I couldn't. I'm sorry if you feel that way but

I would have to do it again not just for your sake but for the wellbeing of all my patients.

It's wasn't a personal decision, it was a professional one.'

Rosie's right, Alison thought, she was keeping things from me but I know she wouldn't do that unless she had to. I'm dreading this but I have to do this not only for me but for anybody else this creep has raped. It makes me shudder to think about it.

'Come on, you're shivering. Let's go inside,' Rosie said quietly cutting through Alison's thoughts. Alison suddenly felt awful for tearing a strip off her friend, who after all, had tried to do the right thing.

'Rosie – thanks for everything you've done for me. You have cared for me like a sister and I'll never forget it – ever. I get so mad sometimes and I don't know why? You're right about letting Tom know. I'll call him first thing tomorrow. I don't know what I would I have done without you.'

'Aw forget about it – I'm blushing. It's been a great evening but I need my beauty sleep, especially since we're going home tomorrow. You'll be okay Alison – you know that don't you?' Rosie was desperate to change the subject to lighten the mood.

'I hope so – there are some moments I really don't want to remember. I know something positive will come back to me someday – but please don't mention the attack to my mum. I'm not ready to tell her about it yet.'

'Sure – anything you say to me is strictly confidential. Oh Lord, I've got work tomorrow and I'm not prepared as usual.'

'You just need to be a bit more organised,' Alison laughed hugging her friend as they went into the house.

'Oh really?'

They crept up the stairs, the old grandfather clocked chimed twelve times, and as Alison settled into her bed, she kept thinking about her evening. I can't rely on Rosie forever. Oh God – I'll need to phone Roz again, that'll be fun. I wonder what's she doing in New York? I don't have much time left in the States, so I may as well make the most of it. I haven't a clue what I'm going to tell Tom, I must try and remember what this creep looked like. The trouble is I'd give anything to forget what happened to me. I don't want to go there but I have to for my own sanity. Alison yawned and snuggled down for the night, praying that she would have no more vivid nightmares.

***

Harry Fox had been at his desk since seven, it was eleven o'clock and he was already tired. He rubbed his grey eyes with his chubby hands, squinting from the sunlight streaming through the grimy windows of his office and then started on the latest case that had landed on his overflowing desk. Case number 45077 really bothered him; he struggled with rape cases as they were never straightforward at the best of times. This one was no exception. He'd not had a case where the patient had amnesia before, and it was a real challenge to get a result. On the other hand, they had was a strong DNA sample, so it was only a matter of time before the perpetrator was caught. Alison's evidence wouldn't be deemed as reliable because of her confused state of mind.

He was furious when his partner and protégé Tom Bernstein had reported that the car rental company had mislaid the paperwork for Alison's car; which meant they couldn't track its whereabouts on the CCTV cameras that were dotted around the city. He was under pressure to get a result; the immigration department were breathing down his neck too.

They were keen to send Alison back to the country she had come from. Poor kid, that's if she remembers what happened to her. Dr Shaw had warned Harry that Alison may not remember anything about herself or the attack for quite some time.

Dr Shaw didn't know when Alison's memory would return either, nothing was certain. There were too many unsolved cases this month and he wasn't going to make his departmental targets again.

His thoughts were rudely interrupted; Tom popped his dark head round the door.

'Harry, we've had a breakthrough on Alison McIntyre,' his face was flushed with excitement. This amused Harry because Tom was still keen and it reminded him of a time when he had felt the same.

'Thank god, well has she remembered anything?'

'Yes – I got a call from her this morning. She remembers being raped and beaten by a man before she got into the car. She tried to escape and that's when she came off the road. Dr Shaw confirmed that there was strong physical evidence that wasn't consistent with a car accident when Alison was admitted.

'Do we have a description of this guy?' Harry asked.

'Not yet – I'm going to her place to get a full statement from her later on this afternoon, but it's only a matter of time before we find out who he is. I've got a team of people working on it now –we're going through the usual suspects just in case we get a match.' Tom sighed and continued. 'I'm hoping to interview her mother; she's over here on business but she's based in New York at the moment.'

'Tom, go and take a statement now, try and find out as much as you can and we'll take it from there, good work, keep it up.'

'Thanks Harry, see you later.'

Harry watched Tom walking through the maze of open plan stations with a computer at each desk. It looked more like a call centre rather than a Police Department. Harry hated computers and struggled to keep up with the new methods of policing.

He was one of the old cops who strongly believed in good old-fashioned detective work, officers on the streets of Boston. He would prefer to be organising teams of men sifting through evidence, statements and liaising with other departments face to face, rather through impersonal e-mails and databases. Harry's computer was still in the corner of his office collecting dust and usually Tom had to collect his e-mails several times a day; as he still couldn't get to grips with it. This exasperated his boss but he had huge respect for Harry because he was so good at his job.

During his thirty-year career, he had won three awards for bravery in the line of duty and was passionate about protecting his team. He felt like an old dinosaur at times, as he watched the ambitious bright young things come in and out the force moving up the career ladder. No one seemed to stay very long but he had to move with the times. He had never felt completely comfortable with mission statements or performance appraisals. The telephone pierced the silence of his office, he picked it up.

'No I haven't checked my bloody emails John – just send me a memo!' he slammed the phone down, muttering to himself. 'As if I haven't got enough to do.'

He sighed, smoothed down his creased shirt and continued going through his file changing number 45077 to Alison McIntyre – Rape Allegation. He would ask Tom to update his files and circulate the latest information around the rest of the office when he came back.

Chapter Sixteen

Tom picked up the phone to call Alison who was at Rosie's quiet cottage.

'Alison – Tom here. I'm on my way to see you now. Is Rosie with you? It might be a good idea if she's there to support you too. Okay – see you in forty minutes, Take care.' Take care! Why did I say that – I'm going soft. I need to get out more, he thought as he grabbed his coat and headed out of the building on the way to Rosie's house. Tom couldn't wait to catch the slimy little scumbag and he was confident they would. He wished sometimes he could take a drug that would eliminate his strong desire to love and protect Alison. He thought of her every day and just seeing her smile made his day. His radio buzzed and the gruff voice of Harry came over the airwaves.

'Tom, I'm passing Rosie's place so I thought I would sit in with you on this one. I'm five minutes away.'

'Okay Harry, see ya there.'

Alison lay on the couch watching daytime TV when she heard a resounding knock on the door. She knew from Rosie's note that she was not due back for a couple of hours. Rufus had already trotted down the hall to see who it was and had started barking.

'Rufus – calm down you silly dog!' Alison put him in the kitchen and froze when she saw who was at the door. She could just make out the stocky figure of Harry Fox through the screen door.

'Oh no! Who the hell is that?' she muttered under her breath, and crouched down, hoping Harry hadn't seen her.

She could see Harry trying to peer through the glass door to see if anyone was home. He knew Alison was there because Tom had called Rosie at the hospital; she was on her way home. Harry was hoping Rosie wasn't going to be too long.

'Alison – It's Harry Fox from the Boston Police Department – we're not going to harm you. We just want to talk to you about what happened to you before the accident. Rosie's on her way back from work. We just want to help you but we have to take a statement if you want to take this further.'

'I want to see your badge – if you really are a policeman,' Alison sat on the floor and chewed her nails wondering what to do. Why can't I remember him? I'm sure I've never seen him before. She thought wildly.

'No problem I'll show it to you when you open the door. We'd like to catch the man who did this to you. If he's done this before and if you speak out against him, others might come forward.'

'I don't trust you, how can I? I've never even met you,' Alison cried.

'You can trust me Alison, can't you? It's Tom here, Harry's my boss, he was passing – we didn't mean to frighten you.'

Harry hadn't noticed Tom had arrived because he was too engrossed in trying to coax Alison to the door and stepped back to let Tom take over. Tom's face was flushed and he looked harassed which was not like him. Just at that moment, Rosie came screeching down the driveway in a cloud of dust. She jumped out of her car, and stormed past a startled Harry and Tom.

She went straight into the porch only to find that Alison was leaning on door. Curled up like a sulking toddler on the floor, she could make out her shivering frame through the screen door.

'What are you playing at? She'll be terrified; you should've waited for me to come home before you waded in with your big size nines! Alison still suffers from short-term memory loss. Alison sweetheart, its Rosie, let me in and we'll talk.'

'Rosie – I'm so glad you're home. I feel safe here; I don't want to go anywhere. I'm scared about what I'm about to remember because all I want to do is forget! I've never seen that man before and I got such a fright. I thought Tom was coming, not anyone else.' Alison wailed.

'It's alright Alison, the police want to see this creep put away for a long time. They just want to help you; you're not going to face the man who attacked you except in a court of law. I promise you I won't let that happen. Tom and Harry are the good guys, they have been trying to find your family for weeks, and they've got your best interests at heart. Are you going to let us in? It's pretty cold out here and we could all do with a hot cup of coffee. What do you say?' Rosie looked imploringly through the screen.

'Okay.'

Alison got up and let Rosie in. She clung to her and they went into the small sitting room. The fire was dying so Rosie threw another log onto it and it crackled and sprang to life again. Tom and Harry followed them into the room. Harry sat on the rocking chair looking sheepish and Tom sat on the floor between Alison and the fire. Alison recognised him from the early days in St Margaret's and he'd visited her at Ashvale when he was off duty and smiled. His eyes were as wide as saucers and he kept fidgeting with his notepad. He was much more approachable than Harry and Alison felt more comfortable with Tom, but didn't quite know why.

'I'll make a fresh pot of coffee but first I want to be here when you start taking a statement from Alison. Tom, I'll get you a chair from the kitchen. Alison - are you up to this?' Rosie asked, giving Harry a meaningful stare.

'Yes but I'm not saying anything till you get back,' Alison said mustering as much concentration as she could.

'I'll just be a second – don't panic.'

Rosie left the room and let Rufus out of the kitchen who was whining like mad to get out. Once he got out, he settled himself on the sofa next to Alison like a lion protecting its cub. Tom stood up as Rosie came back into the room with a chair; Harry watched Tom out of the corner of his eye. He didn't like what he saw because it was obvious that Tom was head over heels in love with this mysterious, fragile girl in front of him. He couldn't blame him; she was beautiful with delicate features and had the most hypnotic green eyes. She seemed unaware of her beauty which surprised Harry but then she had been through hell. It was no wonder she had no confidence. He would have a chat with Tom later.

'Alison – we need to go back to the beginning before you were attacked. Can you remember what happened to you before the accident?'

'Yes – I think so but I can't remember all of it because I was terrified. It's the one thing I want to forget– I still have nightmares,' Alison was holding on to Rosie's hand.

Rosie sat next to her and looked directly at Harry and Tom praying that they wouldn't go into too much detail. Alison was still a bit unstable emotionally and Rosie worried that she might have another seizure.

'Can you tell us what happened before the accident? Take your time and try and remember as much as you can.' Harry asked, Alison went really pale and the colour from her cheeks just drained.

'I'll try,' her voice was barely audible. She tightened her hand around Rosie's. 'I remember being held by the upper arms and being taken down a corridor, I think it was an office corridor, but I'm not sure.'

'Where did he take you? What did he say?' Tom asked her this time and she couldn't look at him, wishing she didn't have to talk about something so personal, especially with Harry and Tom.

Alison looked at Rosie and then at the floor; she didn't want to remember what had happened to her. She tried to steady her voice and her beating heart. She took a deep breath and continued.

'If I didn't co-operate he would cut my pretty face up so badly no man would ever look at me again. I knew then as I went down stairs to a basement that I needed to keep calm to stay alive. He stripped my evening dress off me and I was sick on the floor, then he took me along a corridor with white pipes above our heads. He took me to a room, it had a filthy mattress in it and I can't remember what it was like and then he stripped my pants off me, pushed me on the mattress and raped me. The pain was so bad I thought I was going to be split in two. I had no choice, I begged him to stop but he wouldn't.'

Alison choked back a sob and Rosie held her tightly. Anger pumped through her like a piston on a steam train but she gritted her teeth, and kept quiet.

'You did the right thing, Alison. Did you get a look at his face? Do you know who he is?' Tom asked calmly but inside he fought to control his emotions. He loosened the knot in his tie whilst he waited for Alison to answer.

'I can't remember but I guess I must know him from somewhere but I can't tell you. I remember he was taller than me, muscular and had pale blue eyes. He became sarcastic and nasty when I told him I wasn't interested. He kept asking me why I didn't want to go out with him. I knew that something wasn't right but I never imagined that he would rape me. Not for a minute.' Alison shook her head sadly and continued.

'Please I can't tell you anymore – I have a headache and I feel sick,' Alison started to cry and Tom reached out for her other hand and patted it.

'One more question Alison – How did you escape?'

'Um after he stopped raping me I punched him as hard as I could in the face. He accused me of breaking his nose. There was blood everywhere.'

'Good for you girl,' Rosie interrupted and Tom glared at her.

'Thank you Alison – can we come back tomorrow when you are stronger? So this guy will definitely have bruising on his face although it's probably healed by now. However, we can check hospital records to see if anyone came in with a swollen or broken nose the night you were brought in. We'll see you tomorrow,' Tom added, looking at Harry who had a face like thunder. He went bright red and stared at the floor; he knew that was Harry's decision, not his. Before Harry could say anything Alison spat out.

'I want you to get this man – I want justice for what he did to me. I hope to God you catch him because I want him to suffer like I have!'

'It's okay Alison – we have good DNA evidence – we can get this guy. Others may come forward, thanks to your statement– you never know.'

'Tom's right – we'll continue to go through the rest your

statement tomorrow. Is there anything else you can tell us?' Harry added, giving Tom a withering stare.

'No, I can't tell you anything else.'

'You may have to go for another examination by a doctor.'

'Is that necessary Harry? – hasn't she been through enough? She's barely recovered; it's too much for her,' Rosie protested.

'Its okay – I'll go as long as you go with me Rosie. You won't leave me on my own will you?' Alison stuttered hanging onto Rosie like a limpet.

'Of course I won't. I'm coming with you – don't worry Harry and Tom are right. I think that's enough now guys – don't you?'

'Thank you for coming,' Alison said quietly and sank back into the sofa and closed her eyes to try and steady her hammering heart. She felt very tired, drained of every ounce of energy and found it frustrating as her head started to throb once again.

'See you tomorrow. I'll be here as well.' Rosie explained standing up, trying to show them out of the room as quickly as possible. She stole a quick glance at Alison who kept her eyes shut, she looked very white.

'Thanks Rosie.'

'We'll show ourselves out – you concentrate on taking care of Alison,' Harry said.

It pained Tom to see her distressed and he hurried to his car but before he got in, Harry shouted.

'Tom, come here! I want a word with you before we go to the station. Don't you ever go over my head again – I decide when to call it a day, not you. Also I've noticed you're are starting to get emotionally involved and that concerns me. I may have to take you off this case.'

'But..,' Tom protested.

'I'm not going to say this again – you're a damn good officer and I don't want you ruining your career – just be careful. I don't want to have this conversation again? Do I make myself clear?'

"Crystal!" Tom said and slammed his car door shut.

Harry watched him drive down the road and shook his head. He was not convinced that Tom would be able to stay emotionally unattached as far as Alison McIntyre was concerned.

He hadn't been able to take his eyes off Alison the whole time she was speaking and Harry hadn't liked it one bit when he'd touched her hand. It wasn't professional, but maybe Tom just needed a vacation? He would order him to take a vacation whether he wanted to go or not. Harry got into his car and followed him down to the station to file Alison's statement. He had a feeling it was going to be a long afternoon.

Tom drove down the road, hoping that Harry was right. He would love to nail the man that had raped and beaten Alison. However, Tom would love to dish out his own form of justice but he dismissed those thoughts as he rushed back to the station. He was keen to check the DNA database to try and match the vague description that Alison had given them. It was a start and it was obvious that Alison knew her attacker but they still had a long way to go.

Chapter Seventeen

Rosie had just got her last patient out the door when her pager went off. She groaned and reached into her pockets, when she took her hand out. She found a mashed up piece of fudge brownie she had put in her coat earlier in the day. Her hands were covered in brown goo and so was her coat. She'd had a morning clinic but was going to take the afternoon off to help Alison through her ordeal.

'Oh great – damn thing, will you stop buzzing,' she said to herself just as her clinic nurse popped her head around the door.

'Rosie – Susan wants to see you before you go home. She'd like to see you now when you're ready.'

'Thanks – tell her I'll be there in five minutes.'

The nurse suppressed a smile as she could clearly see the remains of the fudge brownie in Rosie's pocket, poor Rosie. It wasn't her day; by the way Susan had spoken to her, Rosie was in big trouble again. Rosie cleaned up her hands and ambled down the corridor, she knew almost right away what Susan was going to say so she didn't hurry. Well I guess I'd better get this over with. I just hope that this meeting doesn't take too long. Rosie sighed, she was exhausted and she knew she couldn't continue working crazy hours and look out for Alison as well.

Anger suddenly rose in Susan's throat when she saw Rosie stroll into her office. She couldn't believe that Rosie had not returned Alison to the hospital for the check up or even called her to let her know that Alison was okay.

'I wanted to have a word with you in private about Alison. Why the hell didn't you contact me when you took Alison out of Ashvale? You promised me you would bring her here for a check up. You're a doctor Rosie, you know the rules. I can't believe you didn't call me; the Administration Board will have my butt in a sling if this happens again!' Susan raged and sat bold upright in her chair. She could've happily strangled Rosie when she found out what she'd done. She couldn't believe it at first because Rosie was normally such a level-headed, professional doctor and wondered what on earth had got into her.

'I'm really, sorry. There's a very good reason why I didn't bring her back right away…'

'You had no intention of bringing her back at all – don't try and bullshit me Rosie – I can see right through you. Have you any idea what I have been through? I sent that girl to Ashvale thinking she would be well taken care off! Then I find out from Pierce Williams that you've taken her home. I've a daughter of my own, don't you forget? What the hell were you thinking? Are you hell bent on ruining your career? Well?' Susan paused and waited for an answer.

'She was in a pitiful state, and yes, I should've brought her back here but when I saw how she'd deteriorated I was going to give her a couple of days to recover. I decided to take her away to my parents for Thanksgiving and it slipped my mind. Whilst we were there, Alison remembered that she'd been raped so we called Tom Bernstein and Harry Fox to take her statement,' Rosie explained.

'What? Did you say that Alison remembers being attacked?' Susan said in amazement. She couldn't believe what she was hearing and continued.

'That's not the point Rosie – I've got no choice but to formally suspend you from your job starting immediately. You're damn lucky you won't get struck off for doing this – you may not get another job in medicine again. Why have you thrown your career away on one patient – you've been here for fifteen years.'

'There's no need Susan – I quit. I can't go back to my old job now and someone needs to take care of Alison since she has nobody else.'

'You're quitting? – just like that which is another thing you didn't tell me,' Susan was incredulous; she was prepared to fight for Rosie. She was one of the best doctors in the hospital.

'Yes – I've been thinking about it for some time. I want to go into research again. I've applied for jobs already. There's one in Sandwich that could be a possibility. I'm sick of the hassle and the long hours, I'm getting too old to do this anymore.'

'Rosie, are you sure? You are one of my best doctors.'

'I'm sorry Susan – Alison has made me realise I need to get a life outside these walls. I'm nearly forty and I've no family, no kids. I have to get balance in my life again. I'm sorry that I screwed up and made you look bad. I should have involved you in my plans but I knew you would try and talk me out of it. Am I forgiven?' Rosie asked.

'Do I have a choice? Sure you don't want a couple of days to think it over? There's no rush,' Susan added praying that Rosie would change her mind but looking at her determined face, Rosie was resolute and Susan knew she was not gong to change her mind.

'I've made up my mind and I've thought about nothing else for the past few days.' Rosie sighed, and suddenly she felt a big weight being lifted off her shoulders.

'Rosie, St Margaret's is going to be a boring place without you. You know I'll have to keep the boys upstairs happy so this isn't over. There'll be an internal investigation but for what its worth – it's been a blast working with you. Hospital life has never been dull when you're around.' Susan had to admire her courage even though Rosie had caused her a lot of grief.

'It's been interesting working with you too. I will miss this place but I won't miss the politics or the long hours.'

Susan sighed as she got up from her desk and shook Rosie's hand. She was trying to keep her emotions in check; it had been a rough day.

'Let me know how Alison progresses. I've made an appointment to see her in outpatients' two weeks from now. Can you make sure she comes? Do I have your word this time, Rosie Shaw,' Susan scolded but her eyes were smiling.

'Yes, you have my word – see you in a few weeks. I'm sorry but I had to do what I believed was right at the time. Take care Susan and good luck,' Rosie said as she walked to the door and opened it.

'You too – see you both in clinic.'

'Rosie?'

'What.'

'I'm glad it's you that's taking care of Alison. She's a great kid but she needs stability now. So keep me informed.'

'Of course I will, I owe you a lot Susan, you're the best.'

'Just go before you cause me any more trouble,' growled Susan looking at the floor, embarrassed by Rosie's open admiration of her.

Susan swivelled round in her chair and looked out of the window across the hospital grounds.

A few minutes after she'd be gone Susan knew Rosie Shaw would be impossible to replace, she would miss the spats with her as she was a maverick, a one off. Alison McIntyre had a home that she could call her own. Susan knew she had to let go of this brilliant doctor now and move on.

Chapter Eighteen

It was two weeks since Rosie and Alison had arrived back from Chatham after visiting Rosie's parents. Rosie had started a new research contract with a local surgery in the historic town of Sandwich, home of the famous Sandwich Glass Museum. Alison got a job in a coffee shop. It wasn't long before she found out there was a small one bedroom apartment for rent above the shop. She worked there every day until 4pm. She settled into her little apartment and she fell in love with the wooden shutters and creaky floors. Rosie drove to Sandwich every day and Alison loved the sleepy little town. It was a very popular tourist town in the summer with many attractions and the architecture was very old. The beautiful white Wren Church dominated the main street.

At the other end of the town were the stunning grounds of the Heritage Plantation. Sandwich had everything you could possibly want from the spectacular beaches to wandering through the mystical woods of Christopher Hollows. There were quaint and unusual stores and intimate coffee shops which were similar to those in Chatham.

Alison got to know the local people very quickly. They loved her unusual accent and she settled into her job as if she had been there all her life. She was glad to get out and meet people every day and she enjoyed supporting herself for the first time since the accident. She'd never been so settled in a long time, her life had got back to some sort of normality. It was just a pity her memories were still sketchy. The café owners, Joe and Andy, were friendly and they always clucked around Alison like mother hens, much to her amusement. She had mixed feelings about Christmas. She wondered if her father and brother missed her and wished with all her heart that she could remember who they were.

'A penny for your thoughts?' Rosie asked when she popped in for lunch one day. She found Alison sitting on a chair staring out the window lost in her own thoughts.

She was troubled because as Christmas was drawing nearer, she realised that Alison was becoming a bit more subdued as each day passed.

'Oh – I was just wondering about my family. I see families come into the shop and the children are excited about Santa coming. My Christmas wish is to find out who I am. I haven't had any recollections for weeks,' Alison said ruefully, admiring the pristine wooden houses with their pretty Christmas decorations adorning the doors and windows across the street.

'I know it's tough but you have to be positive; at least you know you have a brother whom you are close to, and living parents - that's something. As I've said before, it takes time; you had the accident at the end of August. You're doing very well,' Rosie replied, trying to sound positive.

'I still have nightmares about that monster who attacked me and snippets of vague memories but nothing that I can piece together. It's weird, I have fragments of events in my mind but I still can't remember people like my father, it's so strange.'

'It'll come in time; you mustn't give up, and keep your journal up to date. In fact, we'll go through it tonight if you like when we go for a drink later.'

'Sure that would be great – thanks,' Alison felt apprehensive; the memories of the night she was raped still haunted her and as much as she tried she couldn't forget what happened to her.

Alison went about her duties as normal, it was Monday and she knew they would be busy with Christmas shoppers and the odd tourist staying with relatives for the festive season. She had just served her first café latte and muffin when she felt that she was being watched. As she turned around, Tom was leaning on the counter with a large bunch of flowers.

'Hello stranger, I was just passing and I thought I'd drop in and say hi.'

'Tom! How are you? What are you doing here?' Alison asked, surprised and very pleased to see Tom turn up out of the blue.

He looked different in faded jeans and a black polo neck jumper showing off his muscular body. He had a leather jacket and cowboy boots on, he looked much more relaxed than all the times she had seen him when he was at work.

'I'm on vacation so I thought I would pop in and see how you are. Oh, these are for you.' He grinned at her sheepishly giving her a bouquet of white roses.

'Thanks Tom – they're beautiful, sit down and I'll get you a coffee.'

He watched her as she moved across the shop, greeting her regular customers and put her roses in a vase. His heart felt like it was going to jump out of his chest; she genuinely seemed pleased to see him. She came back with black coffee and he was amazed that she remembered what kind of coffee he drank.

'Have you got time for a quick chat? How was Thanksgiving?' he asked, aware that he was being watched by Andy and Joe who were serving customers at the counter.

'Oh it was great – I had the best time. We went to Rosie's parents in Chatham. I have never eaten or drunk so much in my life!'

'Good – I'm glad you had a good time Alison. You look really well,' Tom replied looking at her as she sat down, grinning at him. He noticed there was something different about Alison, her cheeks were flushed and she said.

'Tom – I've got something to tell you.'

'What? Have you started to remember stuff?'

'Will you stop asking me so many questions?' Alison giggled like a teenager, wriggling in her seat.

'Sorry,' he said and put his hands on the table and clasped them waiting for her news with great interest. He could hardly concentrate when he looked into those magnetic green eyes.

'I've dreamt about my brother several times and I also remember living by the sea. Rosie has heard me talking in my sleep.'

'Alison, that's great news! I'm so pleased for you; living with Rosie obviously suits you,' Tom said grabbing Alison's hand and squeezing it.

'Oh I'm not living with Rosie anymore, I've moved into a little place above the shop. I'm leaving for Edinburgh after Christmas I've got the all clear from the Doctor's to fly home.'

'That's brilliant Alison.' Tom said a little too brightly, disguising his despair at realising he was too late to tell Alison how he really felt about her. He cleared his throat and continued to listen to Alison.

'Look – I'm meeting Rosie and Jess tonight after work. Maybe you could come too? Rosie would love to see you again.'

'Oh well – we'll have to see. I'm pretty busy at work and I'm not sure I'd have the time,' Tom said sadly, wishing he was somewhere else.

'Tom – you've hardly touched your muffin. Look, I've got customers to serve, I'd better go. Call me in a few days and we'll have a proper chat. Maybe you could drop by my apartment next week? Anyway, see you later and enjoy your vacation. Thanks for the flowers, they're lovely.' She leaned over the table and kissed him on the cheek, failing to notice the anguish in his dark blue eyes.

'Bye – Ali. Take care and be happy in Edinburgh,' he said pensively.

He didn't have the heart to tell her about they'd drawn a blank on searching for the man who'd raped her. He would bide his time and it would give him another excuse to see her again before she left for good.

The coffee had left a bitter taste in his mouth. He realised she had no idea that he was hopelessly in love with her. It broke his heart when he realised that she would never love him the way he loved her. He stumbled as he got up from the chair to leave; she turned around and gave him a dazzling smile. Then she carried on serving customers unaware that was the last time she would see Tom for a very long time. Joe watched Tom leave; he turned to Alison and said.

'Ali – you are the silliest girl I've ever met. Can't you see that man is totally and utterly mad about you?" He rolled his eyes and looked at Andy who smiled knowingly.

'Joe – Don't be ridiculous, Tom is a good friend and has been for a long time!'

'Yeah and he buys you the most expensive roses in town and hangs on your every word, you're blind girl!' Andy agreed nodding his head.

'Oh dear – I'm really fond of Tom. Lord what am I going to say the next time I see him?' Alison felt awful, Tom had been such a good friend and she didn't want to lose his friendship.

The cold, crisp air hit Tom's face as he walked across the road to the pond by the little mill. The water wheel was turning round, making splashing and gurgling noises. He sat down on the nearest bench, put his head in his hands and wept. He didn't care what passers-by thought; he had lost the love of his life. Tom had stayed with Alison since she was in hospital; he used to sit by her bed for hours. Tom had watched her heal, struggle with physiotherapy, heartbreak and loneliness. He had rehearsed in his head what he was going to say to her so many times. Now he had left it too late. He sat on the bench for a long time, he had no choice.

He would have to put her out of his mind; otherwise he would drive himself mad. He decided he wouldn't call round to see her after all. He walked down the road with a heavy heart and as he went past the window of the coffee shop, he took one last look at Alison then got into the car and left.

Alison finished her shift a little later than usual, and she took a walk down the main street to the local hotel. It was her favourite meeting place as it was warm and welcoming. She loved to watch the log fire roaring in the grate. The fireplace was huge, with a large oak beam that served as a mantelpiece; it looked like it had come from a tall clipper ship. The grate and surround was made of jet black iron, making the flames come to life as if they were going to leap out at you at any time. There were old wooden booths on each side of the long rectangular bar with brass candle lanterns on each table.

The walnut floor shone and it was so clean, Alison could almost see her own reflection. The walls were lined with dark oak panels and it added to the nautical feel of the place. Her black boots clickety-clicked on the floor and she broke into a huge grin when she saw Jess and Rosie by the fire. Jess was visiting them for a few days before she went back to Chatham.

'Hi – how are you? Wow – what gorgeous flowers – who gave you those?' asked Rosie.

'You'll never guess who came into the shop today.'

'Try me.'

'Tom Bernstein –he just popped in to see me.'

'Alison – these flowers are heavenly and it's a long way from Boston just to be dropping by,' Rosie glanced at Jess, giving her a wink.

'Is he a potential boyfriend? It's about time you started dating. You have half the population of Cape Cod chasing you Alison,' Jess laughed.

'No – he's just a friend; I met him when I was in hospital. He's a detective; he worked on my case for a long time. Andy and Joe are convinced he has a thing for me but – honestly – you know what they're like, they're always trying to marry me off.' Alison replied.

'Well to be honest I think they're probably right, these are very expensive flowers. Ali – that guy has been in love with you the day he met you – it' so obvious. I've noticed the way he looks at you. The big question is – do you like him?' Rosie said, secretly pleased that Tom finally showed Alison how he felt.

'Of course I do but I've never looked at Tom in that way before. He looked pretty good in casual clothes and he is attractive – oh I don't know. Mm – maybe your right, he left very quickly after I told him I was leaving for Edinburgh. God I don't know - are you girls going to buy me drink or am I going to die of thirst?' Alison asked

'I'll go - what do you want?' Jess said.

'A white wine, please.'

Whilst Jess hurried over to the bar, Rosie leaned across the table and looked at Alison earnestly.

'Tom is a great guy – you could do a lot worse.'

'Yes but I'm leaving for Edinburgh soon and I just don't know if I'm ready to give my heart to anyone until I find out who I am and what I want out of my life.'

'Alison – this guy could be the man of your dreams. He spent months visiting you, worked flat out trying to find your family. He's doing everything he can to catch that creep for what he did to you. I think he would move heaven and earth to be with you if he could. Give him a chance if you're interested, that's all I'm saying.'

'Okay – I'll give it some thought,' Maybe Rosie's right – we get on so well and I feel comfortable and safe when I'm with Tom. Nothing ventured, nothing gained, so they say.'

'Good – I don't want you to get hurt either but some things are worth a try. When will you see Tom again?'

'He said he'll call me next week.'

'Okay guys – what have I missed? Do we have a date for Alison or not?' Jess looked at them quizzically.

'Yes – maybe,' Alison said but her mind was working overtime. She cared for Tom a great deal but could it turn to love? She honestly didn't know the answer to that question.

Whilst the girls began to plan the rest of the evening, Alison started to think about all the times she was with Tom and how she felt about him. He was handsome, especially when he laughed. She enjoyed his company and he'd never let her down; maybe Rosie was right, he could be the man of her dreams and he had been right under her nose all along.

Chapter Nineteen

Roz McIntyre was in New York refurbishing two of her shops with the money she had stolen from Alison's travel insurance. She raided Alison's trust fund money regularly to achieve her dream. The store on 5th Avenue was an innovative design and the New York fashion world buzzed with excitement about the small fortune she'd spent decorating it to her taste. She aimed high and had taken a huge gamble, hoping that she would eventually make a profit, even though the rent was phenomenal and so was the advertising. Then she could put the money back in before anyone noticed.

She didn't have time to feel guilty because she knew that Alison wasn't stable enough to handle her own affairs. She needed the money for Alex's future; the only thing that kept her awake at night was the fact that she hadn't heard from Adam Wilkes since they'd met at his offices in Boston. He didn't return her text messages or calls. He was a major investor in her business and she was desperate to keep him happy. She was becoming increasingly anxious about Alison's new found independence because she still wanted Alison to join the firm.

It was for her future and Alex's, she kept telling herself. Alison would also benefit when she took over the business. She couldn't wait to see the look on Alison's face when Roz showed her New York store. She'd felt very relieved when Alison had rung to say that she'd be away for Christmas, it gave her more than enough time to finish the arrangements for the grand opening. Then she'd had an idea, she could rope Alison into helping her with the arrangements for the celebrity fashion show. This could be her big chance to go global and reap the financial rewards.

She would visit Alison in Chatham after Christmas and persuade her to join the business in New York and then she'd be away from that interfering doctor and her family. She picked up her phone and dialled Alison's number.

'Darling – how are you?' asked Roz chewing on her lip waiting for Alison to reply.

Alison nearly dropped off her chair when she heard her mother's brisk voice. She'd not rung for weeks but she'd emailed her regularly.

'I'm fine,' Alison said brightly. Oh Lord, what does she want?

'I thought I would come and visit you on Boxing Day at Rosie's. If that's okay with her family.'

'You're coming to visit me in Chatham?'

'Yes – I hope they won't mind – if they do then I'll meet you at the local hotel. I thought we could talk properly then.'

'I'll have to check with Rosie's parents but I'm sure it'll be okay.'

'Have a lovely Christmas and we'll have a chat about your future then. Lots of love darling.'

Roz hung up before Alison had a chance to ask what she meant. Her heart sank; she'd a horrible feeling that her mother would bulldoze her into the business again. Great, that's all I need, she thought as she got ready for another busy shift at the coffee shop.

***

Alison and Rosie had gone to Chatham for the festive season. The town was decorated with little fairy lights hanging over the main street in a zigzag pattern. The magnificent church had a lovely Norwegian Christmas tree outside and a traditional nativity scene outside for all to see. The children went to see Santa in his grotto at the bookstore.

Alison popped into town to get some last minute Christmas shopping. Rosie and Alison were meeting Rosie's friends. They hadn't seen them for a while so she was looking forward to their evening out. Rosie wanted Alison to be happy, she wished her memories would return and it worried her that Alison still struggled to remember her past.

Alison looked out the window of Kara's Deli; she had finished her shopping and was waiting for Rosie. She watched a family of four people at a table nearby out of the corner of her eye and she didn't like the tone of the mother's voice.

> 'Ruby-May! Will you stop fidgeting at the table? Finish your muffin and be careful you're spilling your soda everywhere!'
>
> 'Sorry Mummy – it won't happen again,' The little girl said quietly, her big blue eyes filled with tears.

Alison felt for the little girl; she was only about four or five and her small hands struggled to hold the large chocolate muffin. When she tried to eat it, the muffin hit the floor and the crumbs scattered everywhere.

> 'You stupid child! What did I tell you? Just look what you've done.' The woman said crossly and let out an exasperated sigh.

The little girl burst into tears and Alison's heart melted because she was trying so hard to please this awful woman.

> 'Maggie – what have I said before? Don't call Ruby-May stupid, she may not be your child but she's mine and I won't tolerate you speaking to her like that!'
>
> 'Andrew doesn't make a mess like she does,' Maggie replied irritably.
>
> 'Yes because Andrew is ten years old, she's only five for God's sake!'

Ruby-May had climbed up into her daddy's lap and clung to him.

Alison gasped; she remembered that she had been in a large department store at Christmas. She was being dragged down one of the aisles by her arm; a tartan scarf hit her face. She was a child because her feet were barely touching the floor; it was an old-fashioned store but beautifully decorated.

'Hurry up Alison – we're going to be late for your father. Trust you to get your hands dirty playing in the toy department. What have I told you? Don't play with toys that are on the floor. But no as usual, you do your own thing – you silly girl!'

'Sorry Mummy – you're hurting me, can you let go?'

'I'm not hurting you – you're exaggerating. Come here and wash your hands!'

Alison started to cry because her mother was being so rough with her, she felt sad. Alison heard a strange noise in the distance, it sounded like a high pitched haunting sound that echoed. bagpipes! That's it, she thought that's what I remember – bagpipes. How strange? Why can't I remember my father?

'Alison – you scared me, are you okay?' Rosie asked gently touching her shoulder. Alison had a puzzled look that settled across her face when she desperately tried to remember her childhood.

'Yes – I think I remembered something. I was in a department store with tartan and bagpipes, being dragged upstairs to the restrooms by Mum. Every time I remember her, something bad is happening. Maybe that's why she's not that keen to have me back home." Alison's voice broke and a large tear slid down her face which she angrily brushed away with the back of her hand.

'Oh sweetheart – sometimes the strongest memories are happy or sad. I'm sure that's not true; just write down what you think you've remembered on this napkin.'

'Sorry I didn't notice you come in. I was miles away.'

'Don't worry, at least you remembered something. Can I have a cappuccino please and Alison? Do you want another hot chocolate?' Rosie said to the waitress who had come over to serve her.

'Yes please,' Alison wished with all her heart that she could recall memories of her father, even if it was just his face but nothing would come and it really frustrated her.

She hadn't felt so depressed for a long time. It was Christmas Eve and she still couldn't remember much; anyway at least she had Rosie and her family. She was really afraid that she would have a nasty flashback or a seizure. Oh well, I'll have to cross that bridge when I come to it, she thought. Rosie broke their comfortable silence.

'Why don't you invite your mother over to our place over the festive season? It might break the ice and you may feel better about going home if you spend a few days with her on neutral ground.' Rosie suggested.

'Funnily enough – Mum phoned me yesterday asking if she could come over on Boxing Day but I don't want to impose on your parents, Rosie.'

'They won't mind – I think they'd like to meet the wicked witch of the East.'

Alison laughed, she had become very close to Rosie's parents, and they treated her like another daughter. She could just picture Stuart giving Roz the third degree. It was such a shame that she wasn't as close to her own mother. Maybe I need to spend more time with her, we're like strangers and I suppose it can't be easy for her either.

***

When Alison and Rosie woke up on Boxing Day, there wasn't a cloud in the sky and the moon was still in the sky. The insipid wintry sun streamed through the window of Alison's bedroom; Rufus had sneaked into her room during the night and had settled at the bottom of her bed.

He slept at Alison's feet every time she visited Chatham since the night she had had that awful nightmare. She got out of bed and walked over to the window, there were people walking along the beach already. They took advantage of the sunshine and walked their dogs and she could see a few children playing with kites. The multi-coloured streamers of the kites danced in the air, as they whooshed backwards and forwards in the wind. If the weather held, she hoped they could go for a leisurely walk along the beach.

She glanced over at the lovely gifts she'd been given for Christmas. Tom had sent her a beautiful bunch of roses on Christmas Eve and she was thrilled. She also received a delicate silver bracelet from Tom in this morning's post which surprised her. It was beautiful and he had sent a little note saying that he would be in touch sometime in the New Year. She missed Tom and he was quite entertaining when he wasn't talking about work. He hadn't been in contact with her since the day he had come into the coffee shop. I must ring him and thank him for the presents. She showered, got dressed and went down stairs to be greeted by Stuart and Jane who were sitting at the large dining room table in their cosy kitchen.

'Hi – how's the head?' Stuart asked with a coffee pot in his hand.

'Not bad – I had a wonderful time yesterday, thank you so much.'

'I'm glad you and Rosie enjoyed yourselves. You are officially part of the Shaw family so you'll have to join us every year!' Jane said.

'Is Rosie up yet?' Alison enquired as she sat down next to them.

'No – she drank more wine than you so I don't think she'll surface for a while,' Stuart replied.

He studied Alison whilst she talked to Jane, she looked so much better than when he'd first met her. She had put on weight, was more communicative and he could see that living independently did her the world of good.

'Stuart?'

'Sorry – what have I missed?'

'Alison and I are going for a walk with Rufus. Do you want to come?' Jane asked with a bemused look on her face because her husband wasn't listening to them.

'I can't - I'm on call today for emergencies at the surgery. I'm going to read my book in the study and stuff my face with your delicious Christmas cake.'

'Don't eat all of it – Roz is coming this afternoon and I'd like to save some for her.'

'Oh she won't be interested she hardly eats anything as it is,' Alison retorted. How on earth did I know that?

'Still it would be nice to offer her some. Is that something else you've remembered Alison?' Jane said.

'It just came out without me thinking about it.'

'Okay I won't touch any of it but if Alison's right then there will be more for me to devour later,' Stuart grinned and patted his ever growing stomach.

'Anyone would think you'd never been fed, honey,' Jane said drily.

Alison laughed as Stuart winked at her and went into his study.

Alison and Jane took Rufus down the beach. As they walked along the yellow sand they greeted the neighbours as they walked past.

The wind had ceased and the ocean looked flat and lifeless. There were a few birds skimming the water looking for fish to catch. Alison loved Jane's wit and they started to talk about what she'd remembered yesterday.

'Alison – Rosie and I had a chat last night about what you remembered the other day. I think it's good that you are spending a few days with your mother.'

'I know – every time she mentions Edinburgh – it's like an alien world to me. I still can't remember my father, which is really odd because Mum's always saying how close we were. I just can't remember a thing about him. She's got an album that Dad gave her but I just hope something will trigger at least one memory – it's not much to ask is it? My brain seems to draw a blank every time I try and think of him.'

'Alison – bad memories always register more strongly than good ones. Maybe when you actually meet your father, events may return to you. It's bitterly cold; I think we'll head back to the house. Roz will be here in a couple of hours.'

Alison shivered. It'll be interesting to see what they think. Once they meet her, they might understand why I feel so uneasy about going home. Jane put her arm around her shoulders and said. 'Whatever happens – we'll support you. You know that don't you?'

'Yes and words can't express how much that means to me.'

They walked arm in arm up the beach back to the house; it was nearly lunchtime. Alison was happy in her new apartment and she liked her job; she was starting to remember more about her past life. Maybe the New Year would bring some closure and she could put her horrific experiences behind her when she returned to Edinburgh. The trouble was she didn't want to go back to the UK. She preferred to stay in America for the time being at least.

Chapter Twenty

The sun sank over the horizon adding to the mystical atmosphere. It was as if someone had painted the sand a rustic brown colour and the indigo sky was littered with stars.

Alison waited in the lounge for Roz to arrive; she kept fidgeting, uncrossing her legs and then smoothing down her wool trousers with her hands. She tried to read the local paper that she picked up from the table to calm her palpitating heart. Instead she caught Rosie's eye and they grinned at each other like jittery schoolgirls. The door went and Jane got up to answer it, Stuart stood by the fireplace. This amused Rosie because he had worn the same serious expression when she first brought John, her ex-boyfriend, to the house.

Roz steeled herself for the occasion, praying that Alison wouldn't play up like she had the last time. The quicker I get her back home – the better. I'll be able to keep a closer eye on her and without her friends around her; she'll be a bit more amenable to my plans for her future. I hope I'll see the last of her interfering little friend once Alison's back where she belongs, with me. If she becomes unreasonable, she'll just have to stay with her father back in Edinburgh for a bit. Jane was surprised to see a stunning blond woman standing in her porch. She was expecting Alison to look like Roz; there was no trace of Alison at all in this woman.

'Do come in – I'm Jane, please make yourself at home in the lounge. You did well to find us first time.'

'I've got sat nav in the car so it wasn't a problem. How's Alison been – thank you so much for all you've done for her. I must repay you for your kindness. I've been working flat out in the New York store since I arrived in the States. Did you see the local news? – we managed to make it onto primetime television.'

'No – we don't have time to watch much TV around here. Alison did mention it though. It's been a pleasure having Alison around. I hope your new venture goes well.'

'Thank you. You're very kind.'

Jane gritted her teeth, smiled and led Roz to the lounge. She didn't like this woman at all; there was no warmth in her. She was almost like a robot, logical and totally obsessed with her business.

'Alison – darling how are you?' Roz rushed over before Alison could get up and gave her a tight hug, knocking Alison back into the sofa.

'I'm fine thanks. This is Stuart, and of course you know Rosie,' Alison's voice quivered slightly, Rosie picked this up right away.

'Please make yourself at home – Roz,' Stuart shook hands with Roz and ushered her to a seat. She was beautiful but something in the way her eyes narrowed when they shook hands; she looked straight through him in a hard, unyielding way. Before anyone could utter another word, Roz said.

'Darling – I've got loads to tell you about the business, the refurbishment of the new store is going really well and I've done interviews with two of the city's finest fashion magazines. Tell me – what have you been up to since I've been away? Did you get the gifts and cards your father and I sent you? You know she hardly ever calls her poor old mum.'

Roz laughed nervously whilst playing with her gold and diamond necklace.

'Erm – yes thanks. I loved the cashmere jacket, and the silver earrings you gave me.

Look, why don't we go to the English Hotel in town, they do great coffee and it'll give us a chance to catch up. You're welcome to come with us Rosie,' Alison looked imploringly at Rosie whose heart went out to Alison.

'No – you go with your mum. I'll be here when you come back,' Rosie said giving Alison a meaningful stare.

'Okay – maybe in a little while. I've brought some more photo albums for you to look through,' Roz cut in.

'Oh right – do we need to look at them now?' Alison asked.

'I thought you'd like to see some recent pictures I took of the house and Alex has sent me over a photo album to try and jog your memory but we don't have to do it now. It's not a problem.'

I've come all this way, cancelled all my meetings and she doesn't even appreciate it. Unbelievable, what do I have to do to make her realise that I can't just drop everything on a whim? I don't like the way Jane's looking at me; it's like they have some sort of hold on Alison. Well, I'll soon change that. Roz forced a smile, looked directly at Jane and said.

'I'd like to freshen up – it's been a long journey. Would you mind showing me where the bathroom is please?'

'Of course. I'll show you where your room is and we'll leave you and Alison to it,' Jane said.

'Oh, there's no need to go out your way on my account. I don't want to be a nuisance.'

'Stuart and I are on call today and Rosie is going out with friends, so it's no problem, Jane replied casually.'

Roz squeezed Alison's hand, got up and followed Jane to her room.

'You have a beautiful home Jane – how long have you lived here?' Roz asked, as they went up the stairs, Roz eyed up the expensive antique furniture and drapes. Leaving Rosie and Alison in the lounge, Alison let out a big sigh and shook her head in dismay at Rosie.

'You okay?' Rosie whispered as she leant across the coffee table in case the others overheard.

'She is so overpowering. If she thinks I'm going to sit there and let her call all the shots – then she can think again. She doesn't seem to grasp how difficult it's been for me to bond with her. She's always talking about the business – she never talks about Dad or Alex. I need to choose my time to talk to her and when you guys go out I'll have a word with her then,' Alison said.

'You're right – you need to tell her how you feel before you leave for Edinburgh. She's a woman who's used to getting her own way – maybe she doesn't realise that she's treating her own daughter just like an employee. It must be her way – I guess.' Rosie replied.

'Look I'll talk to you tonight when she's gone to bed. See you later. Wish me luck. I think I'm going to need it. She's driving me mad already and she's only been five minutes,' Alison whispered.

'Good luck – I'm sure you'll be fine,' Rosie didn't have confidence in what she was saying because she was concerned about her friend.

Alison waited for her mother to come back into the room. She could hear the distant waves lapping gently on the shore and wished with all her heart she was on the beach right now. Instead she was spending the afternoon with her mother to try and sort out her future. Alison sighed and sank back into the sofa, trying to remember all the positive things Rosie had just said but she couldn't remember anything.

***

Alison and Roz drank cocktails in the local hotel bar. Alison decided it would be best if they went out for a bit, she sensed Roz was just as nervous. They were uneasy with each other at first and the conversation was a bit stilted. Roz felt a little more relaxed once she had a few drinks and Alison opened up a bit filling her in on her life back in Sandwich.

The place was busy, full of people who had come down to the Cape from Boston to enjoy the festive season. Everyone in the room was aware of the two beautiful women at the bar but they seemed to be oblivious to anyone else.

'Well this is nice – isn't it?' Roz eyed her daughter cautiously as if she was eyeing up a competitor in a boardroom meeting.

'Yes – we come here quite a lot when Rosie's not working. Have you heard from Dad in the last few days? I was just wondering how he is?'

'He's fine darling – when you come back to Edinburgh – Alex and your father will be meeting you at the airport. He's been away on business but when you come home he'll take two weeks off work to spend time with you. He's really looking forward to it and so is Alex.'

'Mum – can I ask you a direct question?'

What is she going to come out with next? Roz braced herself and played with her glass, waiting for Alison to speak.

'Why hasn't Dad contacted me?'

'Erm – I thought it was best that since you'll be living with me that I would handle all the arrangements. Your father loves you deeply and he can't wait to see you again. He calls me every day – but we were advised by the hospital that only one member of the family comes out to see you. It's been very difficult for your father too, you know.'

'Oh I see – I can understand that I guess.'

'I've got some letters for you from your father and brother. They're in my room at Rosie's house so I'll give to them to you later. Look Alison – I know it's been difficult for both of us but I was wondering what to do about you going to Edinburgh. You seem very settled here and I'm staying in New York for the next six weeks. Would you like to come to New York with me? – I need another pair of hands to help me with the launch party and fashion show. I thought if we spent more time together then we can get to know each other a bit better. What do you say?'

Please say yes – come on Alison don't let me down. Roz thought. Alison was stunned momentarily and just stared at her blankly. Roz could tell this wasn't what she'd expected and hoped that she would agree.

'Gosh – I'd thought we'd go to back to Edinburgh and that would be that. I'd never thought about going to New York. That would be great but Mum – I can't work full time yet – I still get very tired and muddled sometimes. I've never been to New York, - I'd love to go.'

Roz breathed a sigh of relief and said.

'Good that's settled then. I'll give you a week to get organised and then I'll arrange the flights and pick you up from the airport. I can't wait to show you the store – it's fabulous. I've flown in the architects from London to oversee the project and we have a celebrity interior designer endorsing the store. There's been a buzz in the press already – it's all going well so far. Let's make a toast to Wealth, Health and Happiness into the New Year.'

'It'll be lovely to spend time with you Mum. I just hope I'm ready for the challenge of a new job.'

'You'll be fine – honestly. All my staff and clients are lovely. The job is very straightforward; I'll show you the ropes and most of the hard work is done. We've booked the models, photographers and the collection is ready. All you need to do is shadow me and make sure everything goes smoothly. The guest list and the invitations are ready to be posted out and we're getting enquiries already.'

That's if I can persuade Adam Wilkes to invest more cash – I'll set up a meeting with Alison and Adam after the fashion show. I've got an appointment with the bank in Edinburgh in a few weeks' time so I'll leave Alison in charge whilst I'm away. It won't be too taxing for her – I'll make sure my PA is around to help her, Roz thought.

'Sounds great – Mum can we talk about Dad and Alex now. Shall we go back and look at the photo albums you brought with you? I'd love to see them,' Alison asked, anxious to stick to trying to remember the rest of her family.

'Oh alright then – sorry I keep talking about the business – you must think I'm a dreadful bore.'

'Not at all, it's just that I'd like to spend some time talking about Alex and Dad because I still struggle to remember that part of my life.'

"I know Darling – I'm sorry. We'll settle the bill and leave. Feel free to ask me anything about your father. Although we live separate lives we still get on well and keep in regular contact. We both want to help you as much as we can."

Well that went better than I thought. At least I can keep a closer eye on her and she's a lot better than the last time I saw her in that awful hospital. Rosie was right to take her out of there; it's done her the world of good, Roz thought as they drove back to Rosie's house. She was suddenly feeling very optimistic about Alison's future and was relieved that Alison was genuinely glad to be going to New York to stay with her. Things were looking up after all.

'We used to go on some lovely beach holidays when you were little…' She wasn't aware that Alison was anxious and wasn't really listening to the conversation.

All she could think about was being away from the people she felt comfortable with. Her mum didn't seem to understand the seriousness of her head injury. There were days when she could hardly remember her own name let alone get to grips with a new job as well as a new city. How am I going to manage without Rosie, Jane or Stuart or the people who've helped me through this nightmare? I'll have to take a day at a time and pray that Mum will understand although, looking at her, I bet she's never had a day's illness in her whole life, Alison thought ruefully as Roz prattled on. Alison had a thumping headache already and she'd not been in her company for a whole day yet. Her mind wandered back to Tom; she wondered where he was and what he was doing. Alison had thought about him a lot since the day he came into the cafe with the flowers before Christmas. She missed him and each day and the longing to see him again grew stronger, but did he feel the same? She hoped so.

Chapter Twenty One

Tom Bernstein had spent Christmas with his family in Boston. He had gone out with his friends for a few drinks over the festive period. His dark, swarthy looks attracted women, and he was tempted to go out with his sister's friend Alicia. She was tall, blond and a successful graphic designer. He had taken her out once but she was the opposite of Alison and he found her uninteresting.

Harry had been in touch to keep him up to date with the case. Tom had decided to do some digging himself. He was going back to the scene of the accident to look for anything they might have missed. He had a hunch that they hadn't found all the evidence because of the chaos that ensued after Alison was airlifted to hospital. Although Harry assured Tom many times that the area had been thoroughly checked, he wasn't so sure; they hadn't gone down to the bottom of the ravine for safety reasons. Tom had done some climbing when he was at high school; he had scaled a few mountains when he was on holiday in the Alps so he still had his climbing equipment. He checked all his climbing equipment before he left; his parents lived in the Beacon Hill district of Boston which is situated near Boston Park.

'Tom are you going climbing again, I thought you gave that up years ago?' His mother asked anxiously, chewing her lip.

Tom had had an accident a few years before and he had ended up in hospital with a broken leg and a dislocated shoulder. He couldn't blame his mother for being concerned about it.

'No Mom, I'm going to check another crime scene and it's down a steep hill. I'm just taking these ropes as a precaution, so don't worry,' he said reassuringly giving his Mom a hug.

'Good – you call your mother when you get back to your apartment okay? Promise me you won't forget!' She scolded jokingly.

'I will. Stop fussing will you. I'll be okay – I know what I'm doing. I'll call you when I get back,' Tom said reassuringly as he got into the car and headed off down the busy Boston street.

***

It was mid morning by the time Tom got to the scene of the accident. The barrier had been repaired and the tyre marks were long gone. It took Tom a while to find the right bend since the bushes had grown back with the passage of time. Tom eventually located the sharp bend when he stopped the car; some debris shone in the winter sunlight and it caught his eye. As he stepped over the barrier, he lost his balance on the shingle and slipped down the hill.

'Ouch – oh shit!' he muttered and he could feel his jeans being torn with the speed at which he descended. He tried to grab onto the coarse bushes but he couldn't get a decent grip.

'Dammit!' he barked as he stopped by a large rock. Tom had hit the same boulder as Alison had. He got up and dusted himself down. His knee bled profusely and he was covered in mud. He was just about to go up to the top to get his equipment when something caught his eye further down the slope.

Tom climbed gingerly to the bottom of the ravine and he couldn't believe his eyes: there was a brown leather handbag under the bracken. The contents had spilled onto the rocks below and at the bottom of the bag were old photos. Tom took the two photos of Alison out of her bag and caressed them. He felt he knew her so well. Her image jumped out at him. The first photo was a full length shot, her dancing green eyes and lovely wide smile seemingly captured her easygoing personality. She was leaning on a tall, dark haired gangly lad with her arm hanging lazily on his shoulder. Her hair fell loosely around her oval face and she seemed totally at ease with the camera.

The other photo was of Alison sitting on the lawn with her long tanned legs crossed on a picnic rug, with a pillar box red rhodendron almost enveloping her.

In her hand was a glass of wine and she was dressed in a simple white vest and faded denim shorts. She would've been at home on the cover of Vogue magazine, Tom thought as he looked at her brilliant smile and long, lean body. As Tom looked around he spotted the mobile phone lying on the ground next to various lipsticks and pens. He picked it up and looked at it carefully.

The phone was still in one piece – hopefully the information on it would help Alison remember what had happened to her just before the accident. He smiled-the obstacles he thought he would never overcome in trying to solve this case were melting away bit by bit.

I knew it. I knew they'd neglected this area- maybe this will lead us to the man who attacked Alison? I'd better bag this stuff and take it back to the station. It'll be a couple of days before I can contact Alison but it's a breakthrough at last. I hope she's happy wherever she is.

Tom gathered all of Alison's stuff and put it back in the brown leather handbag. He scrambled up the hill and went to the car and dialled Harry's number.

'Harry – it's Tom. I've found some new evidence on the McIntyre case. I'm at the scene of the car crash. I've found Alison's handbag and a mobile phone. I think the information from the SIM card will give us a better idea of who Alison was with before the attack. It may jog her memory. See you later with an update – I'll send it off as soon as I get back.'

'Alright Tom. We'll update the rest of the team when you get back.'

As Tom drove back to Boston, his mind raced with all sorts of possibilities. He'd have to sift through the information from the phone very carefully.

He had had a hunch for a long time that Alison knew her attacker when he sifted through her statements. He sensed that she knew him but was too scared to remember who had raped her and left her half dead.

Maybe there was a link with someone in the fashion business? Alison was adamant that she'd not had a boyfriend at the time of the attack and her mother had confirmed this. He would question her mother later; she was a hard woman to reach, always in meetings or travelling between Europe and the States.

Roz was keen to keep him at arms length and Tom's experience suggested she had something to hide - but what? Why wasn't she doing everything in her power to help him catch the brute that had attacked her daughter? He had to get a list of all her business associates and all the other people Alison had been in contact with when she started at Just Roz. He was determined to get to the guy who had done this to Alison before it happened again. Tom was uneasy; this guy is cunning and clever and that makes him very dangerous indeed. He may strike again. Tom's gut instinct was never wrong.

His mind drifted back to Alison, there wasn't a day that went by that he didn't think about her or wonder how she was. Tom hadn't contacted her since she stood in the coffee shop giving him that million dollar smile. She'd looked stunning and that was the image he carried of her in his head.

Tom wasn't sure if Harry would allow him back on the case but he'd seemed happy enough to let Tom take the cell phone to the forensics team for analysis. Hopefully, it would not take too long to compile a list of numbers. Then the real work would begin. It would bring them one step closer to finding out who'd attacked Alison. Tom's thoughts were interrupted by the shrill ring of his cell phone. When he glanced down, he recognised the number; it was Harry but he just let it go straight to voicemail.

Chapter Twenty Two

It was six am on a dull and damp January morning; Adam Wilkes was already awake before the high-pitched sound of the alarm clock sprang into action. Next to the king size bed there was a bedside cabinet. There was a glass of water on the carved oak cabinet and a book about the History of American Presidents and nothing else. His immaculately pressed Armani Suit and Ralph Lauren shirt were laid across the chair.

There were no personal photographs, paintings or other books except The History of US Presidents in the bedroom. It was like an empty cell. If Adam moved out tomorrow there would be no trace of the man who used to live there. The room was dust free and even the furniture was sparse, a large oak bed, two oak bedside cabinets and an exercise bench with weights by the large sash window. The room was painted white and had grey metallic blinds. On one wall the doors of the built-in wardrobes were oak and glass; a throwback from the 1990s when oak furniture was in vogue.

Adam got out of bed, stretched out his long wiry body and positioned himself in a sitting position. He laid his upper body on the floor and put his hands behind his head ready to go ahead with his daily exercises. He started each day with a hundred sit-ups followed by seventy press-ups; Adam followed the same routine in the evening just before he went to bed, seven days a week without fail.

He got up and went into the luxurious Italian marble bathroom to shower and shave. He rubbed the condensation off the mirror and looked at his reflection. He had a high forehead and a long, lean face with a large hawk-like nose. His blond hair was very short and receding. He had cold turquoise eyes, like those of a dead fish. There was no softness or compassion in his face at all. He smiled a malicious smile and started to shave meticulously and slowly, like a teenage boy shaving for the first time.

The bathroom was also sparse with just the basics in the cabinet. In it was one bottle of aftershave, a toothbrush and toothpaste, a razor and shaving cream and a comb. There were two small white bottles, painkillers and another smaller unlabelled bottle with liquid in it.

Once he had shaved, he smiled back at his reflection. It was booking day today. They were expecting two new female models and one male model from the agency. He always enjoyed meeting new models, especially the women. In his line of work, they always seemed to be so insecure and desperate to make it in the fashion world. It was pretty easy to detect their weaknesses, likes and dislikes early on. Adam was very good at assessing who would be a future supermodel very quickly, usually within the first few hours of meeting them. That's why he was at the top of his profession. He was highly skilled at creating the right look for his fashion magazine and as soon as it hit the shelves that look would be instantly copied around the world. He was always in great demand. As he hurried down the stairs, a door creaked quietly shut. It annoyed him that his neighbour spied on everyone who came in and of out of his penthouse.

'Good morning Mrs Kaplinski,' he shouted as he walked past her door so that she would know he had seen her. As soon as he spoke, she threw open the door instantly. Her little beady eyes lit up like a viper waiting to pounce.

'Oh Good Morning Adam – I didn't see you there. How are you?'

'I'm fine. Sorry, I have to go. See you later!' Adam said through gritted teeth as he rushed to his car. Nothing changes, he thought, no matter how quiet or quick I am she's always there. Maybe it was time to move, he thought as he drove down the Highway. His Blackberry buzzed incessantly but Adam just ignored it, he knew who it was and he decided he would make them sweat just a bit longer before he got back to them.

I am a God in the world of fashion, that's why I love my job. He smirked, turned up the music and drove his black Aston Martin down the busy highway to the airport where his private helicopter awaited; it would take him to New York in style and kept any unwelcome Press attention at a distance.

Chapter Twenty Three

Alison was up before dawn and stared out the window of her little apartment. She felt sad today because she was jetting off to New York to meet her mother. It would the last time she'd stare out onto the quiet main street of Sandwich. The trees that lined the street were bare, stripped of their luscious green leaves, and the landscape looked grey and bleak. Alison let her thoughts drift. As bleak as I feel inside, I'm going to miss living here. Everything has ended too quickly but I've got a strange feeling I'll be coming back and I don't understand why. I've got an exciting and rewarding job waiting for me in New York. I should be happy but I feel so flat. It must be nerves, I don't like going to new strange new places. I'm terrified I'll see the man who raped me. It's weird because I can't even remember where the attack took place – Boston? The Cape? Who knows? The phone interrupted Alison's train of thought and she let the answering machine pick it up. It was Mum probably making sure that she was up and about.

'Alison – I was hoping to catch you before you left for the airport…' Tom's rich, deep voice swept across the room and Alison dashed around the battered sofa and picked up the receiver.

'I'm here - I was just about to drag myself out of bed.'
She grimaced at that little white lie. That sounded so pathetic – get a grip girl!

'Is it a good time to talk?' Tom asked.

'Yes, don't worry, my taxi's not due to arrive for a few minutes yet.'

'Alison – I've found your mobile phone and handbag hidden in some bushes. I decided to go back to where you had your accident to make sure that we'd picked everything up.

'It was so chaotic when you left in the chopper, the wind must have blown your stuff down the ravine and into the bushes. There's quite a lot of numbers on the phone and I'm going to read out some men's names out to you. Do Matt, Richard, Adam, Alex or Luke mean anything to you? Take your time Alison,' Tom paused waiting for her to answer.

'The only name that means anything to me is Alex, he's my brother. I'm sorry Tom, that's the only one that's familiar to me.'

'It's okay we'll contact everybody that's in the phone anyway to see if they can tell me anything about your movements before the accident.'

'Well, if you think it will help. Haven't you spoken to my mum yet?'

'No, I've not been able to get hold of her. I'm going to speak to Harry and ask him if I can come up to New York to interview your mum. She's a very difficult lady to get hold of. Can you tell her I really need to talk to her when you get to New York? It would really help if you told her what happened to you. I understand that it's your call but maybe she'll get back to me sooner if she knew how important it was to the case.'

'I know and I'm sorry Tom if it's holding you back. I'll tell her soon. I'm just waiting for the right moment but it's really difficult. She's not an easy woman to open your heart to,' Alison said sadly and Tom's heart lurched in sympathy and replied.

'I know. Have a safe trip, Alison and I'll be in touch when I've spoken to everyone.'

'Thanks Tom, you're a great friend and I don't know what I would do without you.' Tom cleared his throat and replied hesitantly.

'No problem – I'm just doing my job. Look after yourself Alison and I'll be in touch when you get settled in New York.'

'I will - that's my taxi. I've got to go now.' Alison hung up, and picked up her bags as she took a last look around her apartment, sighed and left.

Once Alison had settled herself in the cab she was irritated that Roz hadn't got back to Tom; he had enough to do as it was without having to chase after her. Although, in her defence, Roz didn't know that she had been beaten and raped.

Alison realised that she was going to have to tell her sooner or later. The flashbacks were getting worse and Roz might find out anyway when she started yelling in her sleep. Every time Alison was stressed or in a new place, it usually intensified. Harry and Tom were keen to interview everyone at Just Roz as they were convinced Alison knew him. That's what terrified Alison the most about going to New York, she could come face to face with him and not even realise. What if it was her fault? What if she had led him on? Someone must know something about what happened. Maybe somebody at the party had seen her leave. All these names that Tom had read out, they seemed alien to her. Nothing, not a flicker of recognition, they were just names. Except for the name Alex, he'd been in touch with her a couple of times over the last few weeks but even he still sounded like a stranger. She closed her eyes and shook her head. She just didn't want to think about it, not today, and she was getting a headache already.

When the cab pulled up at the airport, they were already late. Alison paid the driver and swore under her breath that he was the slowest cab driver in the whole of Boston. As Alison walked into the departure area her senses were assaulted by the bright neon lights and flickering screens making her squint against the glare of the shiny floors. God, how on earth am I going to find out what gate my flight leaves from? Alison thought, as she stopped in front of the check-in area which seemed to be the size of several football pitches.

To add to her confusion, people kept bumping into to her every time she stopped to search for the flight information she needed.

A couple of young girls giggled behind her and their shrieking laughter reminded Alison of a couple of seagulls. She turned around and glared at them.

Her head throbbed. The noise of the crowds and the flight announcements were relentless. She mustn't miss this flight or Roz wouldn't be amused. Eventually, she found the right check-in area and ran as fast as she could to the desk praying that she wouldn't be too late. When she arrived at the desk, Alison was relieved to see there was no one in front of her.

'Good morning Mam, can I see your passport?' the dark hair woman asked in a matter-of-fact tone. Alison stopped to catch her breath as she felt lightheaded and there was a dull throbbing coming from the back of her eyes. She squeezed her eyes shut and rubbed her forehead to stop the room from swimming in front of her. I don't want to faint, not here, not now of all places, she thought frantically.

'You okay Mam?' the woman asked. Alison opened her eyes again and tried to focus on the woman's face.

'Yes of course,' Alison smiled weakly and handed the documents over to the woman and just behind Alison a luggage trolley screeched making her teeth rattle and she took a sharp intake of breath.

She was back in the car, it was raining and surrounded by a dark and menacing forest. Her phone rang incessantly and as she picked it up to switch it off, the back end of the car skidded as it went around a tight corner. A large deer stood in the middle of the road. Its big sinewy brown bulk quivered with fear and the huge antlers gleamed in the darkness casting a ghoulish shadow over the car. Alison tried to swerve to avoid it, too late. She hit the deer and the animal howled in pain, its blood splattered across the windscreen like mud.

The car hit a water pocket and aquaplaned off the road. Alison yelled as it lurched forward at a terrifying speed. She couldn't hear her cries of terror as the car crunched through the barrier.

The squealing of the brakes sounded like sharp nails going down a blackboard. The car tore through bushes and bounced off rocks. Alison's brown handbag flew out and bounced down the ravine landing into some thick bushes.

The branches crashed through the windows like gnarled fingers trying to grab her, scratching her delicate skin. Her head was being thrown backwards and forwards, the pain ricocheted down her spine.

It was the longest ten seconds of Alison's life, her whole world flashed before her in glorious technicolour. The car caught fire and Alison released her seatbelt to try and jump out. Suddenly, without warning the car hit a large rock propelling Alison through the broken windscreen as she hit the ground. she was knocked unconscious. Her broken body lay fifteen yards from the leaking car which exploded on impact. The upholstery lit up like a burning furnace. The echo of brakes screeching to a halt at the top of the ravine went around the forest. Several cars had stopped because they had seen the black smoke and the broken, twisted metal barrier. The mangled body of the deer lay by the side of the road.

Alison gripped the counter and tried to stay on her feet. Her mind was working overtime as she tried to process what she was seeing in her head.

'Mam, are you alright? Can I get you a doctor?' the woman sat beside her holding her hand and started to call for a medic followed by a huddle of other anxious passengers.

Alison had slid to the floor, beads of perspiration littered her forehead, her mouth dry. She blinked rapidly and smiled weakly. A sea of curious and concerned faces swam before her eyes. She got up slowly and said.

'No I'm fine – honestly I just felt a bit dizzy. I've not eaten since this morning, she lied; she had to get on that plane at all costs. Roz would be furious if she wasn't there to meet her.

'I can't let you fly until you see a doctor.'

'I'll be fine once I've had something to eat. I have to get on that flight; my family will be at the airport to meet me.'

The woman was not convinced and was already on the phone asking for the doctor on duty to come and check that Alison was okay. Alison was apprehensive; her flashbacks were getting more frequent and all too real. She couldn't hide the truth from her mother for much longer. She sighed and waited patiently for the doctor to arrive; with any luck she'd be able to board the flight without any further fuss. Thankfully, by the time he arrived, she had recovered sufficiently to convince him that she was fit to fly. He gently pointed out that she needed to eat regularly and Alison promised that she would.

As Alison settled into her seat in business class, she was relieved to find that the plane was only half full. Alison closed her eyes and relaxed before she was catapulted back into her mother's manic world. She missed Rosie already but maybe a change of scene would be a good thing and at least Alison would be able to explore the delights of New York City. That's if she had time before the launch of The New Store. Roz seemed to be working on the launch twenty four - seven and insisted it was the only way Alison would be able to gain the experience she needed for her new role. Just think of the clothes, the glamour and the bagels. Alison smiled and looked out of the tiny window as the plane descended; she got her first glimpse of the fabulous New York skyline.

Chapter Twenty Four

Roz breezed into her luxurious apartment followed by Alison. Roz had talked incessantly since she had picked her up from the airport and she was exhausted already. Roz's brown stiletto boots clattered on the cherry wood floor as she waltzed down the hallway and threw open the double doors to a large bedroom in theatrical manner, turned around, threw her arms out and asked.

'Here we are – home sweet home - what do you think?'

'Wow – it's fabulous Mum,' Alison breathed as she looked around her room. The Manhattan skyline stretched out before her in its all its glory. Even though it was January the sun shone and bounced off the floor to ceiling windows in her bedroom, temporarily blinding her. She put up her hand to shield her eyes from the glare, and focused on her surroundings. Her walls were painted a winter white with a beautiful chrome king size bed taking the centre of the room. Above the bed was a print of *The Kiss,* by her favourite artist, *Gustav Klimt.* At the bottom of the bed was a modern oak chest with a fat round vase on top of it shaped like a goldfish bowl with a weird looking flower in it or was it a leaf? Alison's eyes were drawn to the magazine on the chrome bedside table - the latest magazines including the one on the top featuring Roz on the front cover; the headline read Just Roz or Just Fabulous? Britain's new Queen of Style hits New York with a vengeance. She looked absolutely stunning, her straight blond hair coiled around her strong jaw line. Her satin raspberry blouse moulded around her pert breasts that any woman twenty years younger would envy. Her topaz eyes shone with triumph as if she was going to conquer the world. Alison looked up to see Roz beaming at her, her heart swelled with pride that her mother had achieved so much. Living in New York suited Roz and Alison had to admit she'd worked like a woman possessed so had earned every moment of her success.

'I thought we'd stay in and order pizza New York style tonight, the concierge will bring it up. I don't want you getting over tired because we don't have much free time. I hope that's alright?'

'Yes – its sounds like fun. It's been a very long day and I'd like a bath and an early night to be honest.' Alison said flopping onto the bed.

'Well that's settled then – as soon as I saw that picture hanging on the wall. I decided this would be your room. Before you unpack I'll show you the rest of the apartment and then I'm going back to the office for a little while. You can come with me or stay here – it's up to you darling,' Roz offered, hoping that Alison would stay behind; she would work twice as fast if she wasn't there.

'I'd like to stay here – unpack and have a nap, if you don't mind,' Alison stifled a yawn. Her head was starting to hurt again and she began to feel nauseous. She blinked rapidly whilst she listened to Roz.

'Good – make the most of your spare time because once we get you started, you won't have time to nap,' Roz mused as she stood hovering in the doorway.

Alison just stared at her in astonishment and fumed silently. Hello? Where have you been for the past few months? Can't you see that I'm still not myself, that I'm absolutely shattered or are you blind? Alison tried to calm down but anger rose in her throat and she gritted her teeth as she listened to Roz talk about her day. If it wasn't for Rosie complaining good- naturedly that Roz telephoned her three times a day for a progress report on Alison's recovery, Alison would have thought her beloved mother didn't know anything about her condition. Either she hadn't listened to Rosie's advice at all or hadn't realised that Alison needed a nap from time to time. It was as if her accident had never happened and the memory of it had been hastily brushed under the carpet.

Alison lay on top of the bed, not moving and looked up at the modern lights on the ceiling; they were beautiful but lacked a homely touch. She closed her eyes and drifted off to sleep, not hearing her mother dash out the door, her ear glued to the phone barking orders at some poor minion on the other end. 'Why can't you get me a seat? Then I'll have to fly first class. I have to make that meeting or they'll have my guts for garters....'

When Alison woke up, she wondered where she was at first. The apartment was shrouded in darkness and eerily silent. The light on her mobile winked at her, two text messages and one missed call. She picked it up and squinted at it. One each from Rosie and Tom and her mother's number was listed.

With a heavy sigh she staggered to the bathroom and ran herself a luxurious bubble bath. Roz had left the coffee machine on; Alison poured herself a cup and walked back to her bedroom. I bet she's going to be late. Looks like I'm going to have to order my own pizza. Her mobile went off, Alison picked it up. Roz's voice boomed down the line and she had to hold away from her ear. Why does that woman have to shout, I'm not deaf!

'Darling – I'll be back in an hour. Just help yourself to coffee in the kitchen and there's some cookies in the cupboard to the left of the fridge. Have you had a nice nap?'

'I'm just going to get into the bath so that's cool Mum. You don't have to rush home.'

'I've got a couple of emails to send and then I'm free for the rest of the evening. By the way darling, I'm going to Edinburgh the day after tomorrow. I've got a meeting with the bank that I can't get out of. I'll only be a couple of days but I've got Lucy helping you out till I get back,' Alison felt a wave of relief wash over her and felt guilty because Roz was trying so hard to make her feel at home.

'Okay Mum, no problem. I'll see you when you get back.'

Oh Lord – what have I let myself in for? I wish I'd stayed in Sandwich. Life seemed so much easier there. I don't even know what I'm going to wear, Alison thought miserably.

***

Whilst Alison struggled to get to grips with her new job in New York, Roz flew back to Edinburgh for her meeting with the bank to discuss her various cash flow problems. She wasn't looking forward to it.

It had always struck her as soon as she walked into the offices how ornate the ceiling was. The Bank of Scotland in St Andrew's square is famous worldwide for its beautiful architecture and plush interior. As Roz waited she took in her surroundings. The large circular entrance of the bank where all the transactions took place reminded her of a large indoor coliseum and it was as silent as a library.

The brown marble floor shone, even the customers talked in hushed tones as if they were intimidated by the austere atmosphere. The domed ceiling was painted in gold leaf paint, royal blues and warm yellows. Roz wondered if the architect had drawn his inspiration from the Sistine Chapel or an over-iced wedding cake. A young efficient looking woman in a navy suit approached her and said.

'Mrs McIntyre – Mr Patterson will see you now – sorry to have kept you waiting.'

'Not at all.' Being polite came naturally to Roz even though she was fuming, she couldn't afford to be kept waiting. Her mobile phone buzzed continually in her pocket but she ignored it.

Roz was led into Mr Patterson's office; he was a tall man in his fifties with a mop of unruly white hair and piercing blue eyes. He ushered Roz to a beautiful ornate French chair. The mahogany desk was enormous and the rest of the room was filled with precious antiques.

God, I must be in the wrong business, Roz thought as she took out her figures for the last six months from her briefcase.

'Good afternoon Bill – how are you? I trust you and your family are well.'

'Fine thank you – would you like anything to drink before we get started?'

'No thank you,' Roz smiled but inside her heart was hammering ten to the dozen. Bill sat down behind his enormous desk and opened up a large file.

'I've looked over the figures from the last tax year and I'm really concerned that the gross profit we predicted for this year is nowhere near what you are achieving at present.'

Roz swallowed hard. She didn't like the stern tone of Bill's voice.

'I'm in the middle of negotiating another site for the New York store. So the overheads will go down, sales are well above our targets and it's not even spring yet...' Bill was losing patience and interrupted in an exasperated tone.

'Roz – it's not the New York store that concerns us. You are not making enough profit to make the repayments on the loans we've given you. I can't hold off the board any longer. If you don't come up with some cash soon – the bank will have no alternative but to foreclose on all the overseas stores. My advice to you is to cut back and do it now. You may be able to save the UK stores but you must get some capital and get it quickly.'

'I've been with this bank for twenty years! You can't do this to me, this is ridiculous. All large retail companies go through bad patches and my company is no exception. I have over 5,000 staff to consider, some of them have worked for me for years. If I don't have a business to run I've nothing. I thought you of all people would understand that!'

Roz couldn't believe what she was hearing and she wasn't prepared for Bill's answer: the man she had been dealing with for all those years was turning his back on her too.

'Roz – we've been in partnership for a long time and I've tried to use my influence because you are my oldest client and friend. My hands are tied. I've done everything in my power to stop this happening but you refuse to take my advice. I can't hold the board of directors off any longer, I'm near retirement age and I can't afford to make any mistakes now. You must understand, this is business, take my advice; cut and run while you can.'

Oh my God, this can't be happening not when I am so close to securing a huge deal in New York that could bring in celebrity clients. With Hollywood stars wearing my clothes I'll have no problem securing capital. What about the loyal staff that have stuck with me for all those years? What am I going to tell them? The press will have a field day and my competitors will circle around me like bloody vultures. Well, failure is not an option – I'll show them. Roz looked down at her figures and tears pricked the back of her eyes. Don't you dare cry – not here – hold it together.

'Roz are you alright? – you're very pale.'

Roz cleared her throat. 'I'm fine. Look can't you give me till the end of the month to sort something out? I'll report straight back to you and then we'll have a meeting to discuss downsizing. Just stick with me until the end of the month and I'll come up with the cash. I'm meeting a major investor in New York – he has the capital that I need and is very interested in Just Roz.' Bill watched her intently and her insides twisted like a writhing ball of worms. He sighed and clasped his hands together.

> 'Okay, but mark my words if you don't get some capital by the end of the month, we will shut the overseas operation down, whether you want to or not.'

Roz didn't flinch and smiled magnanimously.

> 'I understand your position and I'll be in touch at the end of the month once I've met my investor. Thanks Bill, once again for your assistance. I do appreciate it.'
>
> 'I'm sorry it wasn't a happier outcome for you but you've been struggling for a while.'
>
> 'I'll be in touch,' Roz shook his large manicured hands and walked out the door in shock.

Bill watched her go and sighed, it was a shame. He liked her; she was shrewd, hard- working and beautiful but he knew her time was up and he felt sorry for her. Roz marched down the stairs, she felt sick and light-headed and had to get out of the building as quickly as possible.

Her mobile started to buzz angrily but Roz just switched it off. I don't know what I'm going to do this time. I've got nothing left except debt and despair. Why does this have to happen now when I'm so close to opening my dream store New York? Sod's bloody law, that's what it is. I can't fail now – I'll just have to wing it somehow. Even if I sell all my shares and remortgage the houses in Edinburgh and France – I still won't have enough but it will keep my American creditors happy till this deal goes through.

Roz sat behind the wheel of the car and she brushed away her tears. Come on girl – you'll survive – you always have.

Adam Wilkes was the only one that was willing to give her the money she desperately needed. The trouble with Adam was that he wanted a large share of her company but it dawned on her she had no choice. She'd have to agree to whatever terms he wanted or go belly up. She re-applied her make up when she got into her car and drove back to her office; her face was as grey as granite but she had to make the best of a bad situation.

Chapter Twenty Five

Alison had only been in New York for 24 hours before Roz informed her that she'd have to manage on her own for a bit. She felt as if she'd been thrown into a pit of crazy, snarling dogs. Her head throbbed with a dull ache that wouldn't leave her and to top it all the rehearsals for the fashion show wasn't going to plan.

'Surely we don't have to do this again,' A tall model shrieked from the catwalk. She flicked back her shiny raven hair and glared at the director, a little bald man in black. Katya Petroski was New York's most famous model with a notorious temper to match her dark, cat shaped eyes. Alison and Lucy, Roz's PA, watched in dismay as she stormed off the catwalk in a cloud of silk and chiffon ruffles.

'That's it – that's a wrap for today,' Alison yelled and closed her eyes in exasperation. They're all mental – and it's doing my head in! She thought what the hell am I doing here, it's all so pointless.

'Alison – you can't do that. Your mother will have a fit,' Lucy's voice squeaked and it reminded Alison of a whining child.

'She isn't here and I say four hour's practice is enough. If they don't know the sequences now they never will. Can't you see these girls and boys are exhausted? Enough is enough – don't you agree?'

The bald headed man shook his head vigorously, and Alison tried not to laugh, he reminded her of a nodding cartoon dog. As the rest of the models slunk off, Alison left to go back to her mother's office. Lucy stared at her open mouthed. Alison was her mother's daughter alright and she'd sworn Alison was different when she first met her; now she wasn't so sure.

Why did I agree to come here? I must've lost the plot. I hate it, the supermodels behave like toddlers and everyone's going over the top about how wonderful they look. They look like walking skeletons but what do I know? Not a damn thing. Alison thought as she wandered down the lobby. What is that dreadful sound? Someone was being sick. Yuk!

She could hear them retching their guts up and it came from a nearby toilet. Alison pushed the door gently and was surprised to see it was Katya. Her dark hair fell over her shoulders. The milky stench of puke permeated the claustrophobic air of the toilet cubicle making Alison feel nauseous herself.

'Go away,' Katya growled.

'I heard you from the lobby. What's the matter? You should've said you weren't well; I'd have given you the day off.'

Alison knelt down and started to rub Katya's back and was horrified to feel her ribs poking out underneath her thin dressing gown. The girl was too weak to protest and hot tears slid down her face.

'It's a bug – I'll be okay in a minute.'

Alison noticed that her fingers on her left hand were wet, and guessed what she'd just done.

'It's not a stomach bug is it? You make yourself sick to keep your weight down. How often do you do this?'

Katya ignored Alison and so she pressed on.

'Is it worth it? Is it worth risking your health for a few minutes of glory? You can't keep doing this to your body – you'll collapse one day and then where will you be?"

"You don't understand the pressure I'm under. I have to stay on top or they'll just find someone younger and prettier. It's none of your damn business anyway.'

'I do understand more than you realise. I'm only twenty-one and I nearly lost everything, my family, my life and more importantly, my childhood memories. I had a car crash and when I woke up I couldn't recall anything for months.'

Alison whispered fiercely surprised that she told this strange girl so much about herself. The girl looked at her in amazement, no one had dared to talk to her so frankly before so Alison continued.

'There is more to life than modelling. I heard a rumour that you're really good at art. Why don't you start living instead of just existing? Ok, so you're famous and it's addictive but you have money as well. You're young enough to start a new career, a more fulfilling one. If this is the life you want then fine but my advice would be to leave this crazy world of fashion behind before it robs you of the chance to have a normal life, a future. Think about it – please. Not for my sake but for your own.'

Kayta just nodded and Alison helped her to her feet.

'Who are you? I've never seen you before.'

'I'm Alison – Roz's McIntyre's daughter. I'm overseeing this show till she gets back. Look I've got to go – are you okay now?' Alison looked genuinely concerned so Katya decided not to rant at her for giving unwanted advice whilst her head was down the toilet.

'Yeah – well we'll see.'

'I'm sorry I don't know what's wrong with me today. I'll leave you to it.'

Alison felt foolish and left before she threw up, the smell was so overpowering. That's it – I'm going to call Rosie tonight. I've had enough; she's the one person that'll tell me the truth. I don't trust my own judgment anymore.

Lord – I'm so exhausted I can hardly think straight.

Alison leant on the wall for a few moments and when she looked up she froze. A tall man came towards her, she blinked and swallowed, her chest felt really tight like someone had an elastic band around her heart. He was over six foot two and had blond hair and blue eyes; he broke into a cheeky grin, his eyes roaming all over her body. Alison went cold.

'Excuse me Mam – do you know where the dressing rooms are?'

'Down the lobby on the left,' Alison was transported back in a nano-second to the night of the rape. His aftershave smelt familiar and there was something else.

'Cheers babe,' he was just about to slope down the hall, when finally, Alison found her voice and asked tentatively.

'Excuse me – can I ask you what aftershave are you wearing?'

'CK One – why?' He stopped dead in his tracks and turned to face Alison, who was rooted to the spot, and he noted that her face was a mask of fear. She looked like a ghost with luminous green eyes.

'Oh nothing just wondering that's all – I've got to go. See ya.'

'Hey are you okay babe – you've gone really white?'

'Yes – I'm fine – I was just curious that's all. I've got to go Bye…'

'Crazy chick,' He muttered under his breath and started to whistle as he sauntered down the corridor.

Alison raced down the hall desperate to put as much distance between them as she could. Oh my God, I remember his face cold, calm and calculating. Her mind was a whirlpool of jumbled thoughts. The pictures of her rape suddenly flashed through her head like rubbish that bubbled up to the surface after lying in the depths of a murky pond for a long time.

It was all too real and the memories of that night were as sharp as paper cuts, each memory becoming more vivid and painful than the last one.

She remembered laughing at his jokes at a party. He was over confident and arrogant as if he was used to women falling at his feet all the time. He kept trying to touch her and Alison kept dodging his advances. What she couldn't work out was why she spent so much time humouring him? Was he somebody important?

By the time Alison got to the safety of the office she broke down, gulping for air and collapsed on the leather chair; it squealed in protest. Oh heavens almighty – I remember his face leering at me, those cold blue eyes, high forehead and a slightly hooked nose. He wore the same aftershave as that guy and was probably the same height as that model I've just bumped into. He's a similar build to the man who attacked me but only he's much older. I must ring Tom she thought but before Alison got to the phone, her stomach lurched and heaved, she just managed to grab the waste paper bin and was violently sick. Oh God, I'm going to faint as she sank down onto the chair by the desk and picked up her mobile. Alison shook so much; she could hardly press the buttons on her phone. Tom had called earlier to say that he was on his way to New York but his flight had been delayed due to the bad weather in Boston.

> 'Tom – thank god! She croaked and continued. Where are you? I'm okay. Can I meet you at the airport? There's something I have to tell you, I can give you a description of the man who raped me. Yes – I've just remembered him now. I'm so scared Tom, no I'll call Rosie. Mum's in Edinburgh at the moment. See you in an hour.'

She hung up before Tom had the chance to ask her any question and then tried Rosie's number but all she got was the answering machine.

'Rosie – it's Alison can you ring me on my mobile as soon as you get this message.'

Alison put her head on the desk and tried to empty her mind. Tears had made a puddle on the desk, her nose was running but she didn't care.

She'd never felt so frightened and alone in all her life. She had to control her emotions for the sake of her recovery. An hour had passed before she was calm enough to get out a pad of lined paper from the bottom drawer in Roz's desk and wrote down a detailed description of her assailant.

Alison was in such a hurry to go home that she left the pad on Roz's desk picking up the stinking bin where she had vomited on her way out before dumping it in the trash as she made her way out of the building. The memory of his face was emblazoned on her mind and she couldn't forget it, as hard as she tried. She had to keep calm and concentrate for Tom's sake as much as her own. She didn't want to have another seizure and her headaches were becoming more frequent and severe as each day passed.

Alison was determined to get the man who raped her and she'd fight him all the way through the courts if she had to. She had to stop this guy from doing it again to some other poor woman. If I see you again – I'll rip your fucking head off, she thought. A blinding rage pulsed through her body. Never again will anyone do that to me – ever. She jumped into her car, turned the engine on, put her foot down on the accelerator and her Audi TT roared down the multi storey car park startling two passers by.

Chapter Twenty Six

As soon as Tom touched down at JFK, he tried Alison's mobile again. It went straight to voicemail. He fought his way through the throng of passengers and waited anxiously in arrivals for Alison. He scanned the crowd for her. As soon as she saw him her face lit up. She looked stunning in a paisley jersey dress and a black winter coat that was unbuttoned. The dress clung to her in all the right places showing off her gorgeous curves.

'Oh Tom. Thank God you're here.' Alison ran over to him and surprised him by giving him a tight hug. He wrapped his arms around her slender waist and took in her scented hair. It felt so right being here with her and the crowds just melted away as if they were alone together.

'Are you alright – I've been so worried about you,' Tom stared into her emerald green eyes and his heart missed a beat.

'Yes – I'm so glad your here Tom. I've missed you,' Alison replied softly. She was so close to his face, he had to fight the urge to kiss her soft, full lips. Reluctantly, Tom let her go but Alison held onto his arm and continued.

'Let's go for a coffee – it's just round the corner from Mum's office, they do bagels and coffee to die for and then I'll tell you what I've remembered because I can't get it out of my head. I can't stop seeing that awful face and I'm so scared. I don't want to be on my own at the moment. I know I'm being irrational but I think he's just going to re-appear and rape me again. Is that insane or what?' Alison raked her hands through her hair and her agitated state really worried Tom.

'Alison calm down,' Tom replied gently. 'Take deep breaths and take your time – I'll go to the hotel afterwards.'

As they spoke, Alison realised that she really liked Tom. She had developed strong feelings for him that went beyond friendship, she felt safe with Tom.

Rosie had been right, Tom was the only man for her and he had been under her nose all along. The only fly in the ointment was what if he didn't feel the same way? She'd texted Rosie on the way to the airport but she hadn't answered. Alison presumed that she was busy at work. Once they'd settled down with steaming hot coffee and delicious bagels, Tom spoke first.

'Alison – I want you to relax and try and remember as much as you can about the man who attacked you. Are you ready to do this?'
A dark scowl settled on Alison's face and Tom reached out and squeezed her hand.

'It came to me so suddenly, one minute I was walking down the corridor going back to my office. Then I saw this guy coming towards me and I thought for one insane moment, it was him but he was a model that mum had booked for the fashion show. He asked me a question and as he got closer I realised he looked like the man who raped me,' Alison burst into tears and covered her face; she struggled to contain her emotions that swirled around like a whirly gig. Tom said more gently.
'Tell me what he looked like? It's okay – just take your time. We have all the time in the world,' His blue eyes bored into hers and it sent a warm shiver down her spine.

'He was tall, about six foot two. He had such cold eyes: pale blue eyes, short blond hair and a high forehead. He was broad and muscular and had a hooked nose.'

'Great Alison – that's a really good description. Can you remember what he was wearing?'

Alison wiped her tears with the napkin that came with their bagels, she struggled to compose herself.

'A suit, a grey suit – I think but I'm not sure. I remember his aftershave; it was overpowering and distinctive. I remember following him down a corridor, we were chatting. We were at a party I think; he's very arrogant and cocky obviously the kind of man who's used to getting his own way with women.'

'Would you recognise him if you saw him again? Could you pick him out in an identity parade if you had too?' Tom asked, his pencil poised over his notebook.

"Yes – I would. Alison answered tearfully, Tom asked a difficult question.

'Alison do you think you know this man?'

'I think so but not intimately, I don't think he was my boyfriend or anything. I'm sorry Tom but I can't remember anything else. Do you think you have enough of a description to carry on with the investigation?'

'Yes – you've done really well and we've still got the numbers from your phone to go through,' Tom pushed an A4 piece of paper in front of Alison to look at.

'I've printed out a sheet with all the numbers that were stored on that phone. Do you recognise any of them?'

Alison shook her head, and asked. 'Do you want me to start ringing them to see if I recognise their voices?'

'No but I think Roz will be able to help. She may be able to work out which ones are clients and which ones are your friends. Do you know when she'll be back? I can only stay for a couple of days.'

Alison nodded thoughtfully and said. 'She flies back later on tonight – around nine but we're free first thing tomorrow as I need to brief her on what's been going on since she left.' Alison hoped her mother would be pleased with what she'd done so far but she wasn't holding her breath as Roz was almost impossible to please.

'Okay – I'll come to your office first thing. If that's convenient?'

'Of course – I'll let Mum know as soon as she arrives home.'

'Alison – it'll be alright. We'll get this guy and tackle this together, one step at a time. I have to get to my hotel and then I'll ring Harry, we maybe able to get some mugshots of guys with previous convictions,' Tom felt he was finally getting somewhere and was anxious to start looking for this man. He hated upsetting Alison but it was necessary to get to the truth.

'Would you like to meet me later for dinner?" Alison asked, hoping that he'd say yes. Tom looked up from his notepad which he was still scribbling in. He could hardly contain his delight at her sudden interest in him and grinned.

'Sorry – I can't I'm swamped with work, by the time I get back to the hotel and speak to Harry, it'll be quite late.'

Alison's face fell and she looked dejected so Tom added quickly.

'Maybe another time when we're both free? You know you can call me anytime you like   don't you?' Tom said and Alison reached out for his hand and looked into his gorgeous blue eyes.

'I know and I really appreciate it Tom,' she said gently.

This time, it was Tom who struggled to compose himself or was Alison just imagining it?

God I want to kiss you so badly, but I can't and it's killing me, Tom thought as he tore himself away from Alison to go to the hotel. They said their goodbyes and hugged each other again outside the Deli and Alison decided to walk back to the office, lost in her own thoughts.

***

Once Tom was settled in his room, he picked up the phone and dialled Harry's number, who was in charge of Alison's case.

> 'Harry – it's Tom. I've got a really good description of Alison McIntyre's attacker. She can't remember his name but what she does remember is going willingly with him from party to an office or industrial building. I'm going to interview Alison and her mother tomorrow morning. As soon as I'm finished – I'll report back to you. Thanks Harry.'

Tom tried not to think of Alison as he got ready for bed. He lay between the cool sheets for a long time, staring at the ceiling. He needed to be focused on the case instead of Alison herself. Despite that, he was looking forward to meeting her in the morning. He went to sleep dreaming of her and it warmed his heart knowing that she still needed him.

Chapter Twenty Seven

Roz managed to catch an earlier flight and she'd just dropped into her office to check on Alison. To her surprise, Alison wasn't there and she'd locked the office door but hadn't tidied up her papers. This irritated Roz and when she picked up various folders Alison had been working on the previous day, she spied what Alison had written on the pad. The man she described reminded her of someone but she dismissed it.

That's interesting – I wonder if she's phoned Tom Bernstein. Roz thought and then put the folders back in the sleek filing cabinets that were adjacent to her desk. Jetlag began to set in. Roz decided to go straight to her apartment; hopefully Alison would be there and then she would find out how she had fared in her absence. She was in a grim mood; she'd arranged a meeting with Adam Wilkes for tomorrow afternoon. Roz knew that she needed Adam more than he needed her. She hated being dependent on someone else for cash. It wouldn't be her company anymore as he wanted fifty per cent share. Mind you – if the bank has their way – they'll close me down, Roz thought sorrowfully. I've no choice but to accept Adam's proposal, I'd rather go into partnership instead of receivership. I'm so close to my dream – I can almost taste it.

On the other side of town, Alison was on the phone to Rosie. They'd not been in touch for over a week so it was good to catch up. Not that Rosie had much to say for herself, she'd been working overtime at the surgery and hadn't had time to phone her parents let alone anyone else.

'Rosie will you be able to get time off to visit me in New York?' Alison asked and crossed her fingers, she badly needed some support. She missed her friend and longed to have leisurely coffees and cosy chats.

'Yes, I should be able to make it. I'm due to take some days off so I'd thought I would come in time for the launch of the store. You sound like you've had your hands full these last few days. Have you had the chance to rest? It's still very important to your recovery,' Rosie was concerned because Alison sounded so flat.

"I've only managed it today and that's because Tom was here. He was really encouraged that I'd given such a detailed description. You were right about Tom you know. I really like him Rosie, I hugged him when we met at the airport and it felt right."

Rosie grinned and thought Tom and Alison would make a great couple if they ever got it together.

'Have you kissed him yet?' Rosie enquired, trying not to be nosey.

'No – not yet but I did ask him out to dinner. He said no.'

'He did what?' Rosie couldn't hide the surprise in her voice; she knew Tom would jump at the chance. There had to be another reason.

'Well, that's not strictly true, he didn't say no straight out but he said we could meet up when we're both free.'

'Alison – the next time you're with Tom and the opportunity presents itself – *kiss* him.'

'I'm not doing that!' Alison said in mock horror, laughing. Rosie was unbelievable; Tom should make the move not her. Before Rosie could say anymore, Alison heard Roz calling out to her.

'Darling – I'm home. Are you here?'

'I've got to go – that's Mum and she'll want a blow-by-blow account of what I've been up to."

'I'll call you tomorrow night Alison. Say hi to Tom for me and good luck'

'Thanks. I think I'm going to need it.'

Alison hung up and walked into the large living space that incorporated the open plan kitchen, to find Roz lounging on the corner sofa. She smiled at her daughter.

'Who was that on the phone?'

'Just Rosie – how was your trip by the way. Did everything go to plan?' Alison asked as casually as she could.

'Exhausting – be a love and make me a cup of tea please? I'm parched: I popped into the office before I came home. Alison I wish you would tidy up after you leave. It's not good business practice to leave stuff lying around,' Alison walked over to the kettle and switched it on. She turned and faced her mother.

'Sorry – I forgot. I left in a bit of a hurry. Mum – I've been to see Tom today. I remembered the man who attacked me. I've given Tom a description and he's coming to the office to interview us both, first thing tomorrow morning....'

'What? Alison I don't have time. Why didn't you check with me first? I've got a very important meeting with Adam Wilkes who is a major investor in the company. We're going into partnership together and...' Roz 's voice trailed off when she saw the steely glint in Alison's eyes. The colour rose up her neck and she slammed the mug down on the counter so hard it broke.

Alison snapped; she couldn't believe her mother could callously put aside her feelings in favour of the business.

'Mum can't you see this is important to me? We're talking about the man who beat me and left me for dead for Christ sake! Or are you too wrapped up in your beloved company to see that?

Tom has come all the way from Boston to interview us and all he's asking is a few minutes of your precious time.' Alison raged and continued unable to stop herself from blurting out what really happened to her.

'Well, I'm not cancelling it. It's too important.'

'I was raped Mum, he raped me, beat me and I had a horrific car accident that nearly killed me. I nearly lost *everything*. You know what - make your own bloody tea – I'm going out for a walk! I cannot believe you are taking this couldn't give a damn attitude. I'm going out before we both start saying things we'll regret later,' Roz stood rooted to the spot as Alison stormed out of the kitchen and threw her a murderous look.

'Alison – come back. I'm so sorry – you didn't tell me you'd been raped. Please come back!

Roz got up to go after Alison but she was too slow. She sank back onto the sofa and squeezed her eyes shut and tried to digest the information she'd just heard. She was in shock and felt terrible for not being more sympathetic. Am I such a bad mother that my own daughter couldn't tell me about the rape? They were like strangers and Alison was so different to herself in every aspect. I must make it up to her somehow, I just don't know how but I must try.

Alison grabbed her coat and walked out of the apartment leaving Roz wondering what to do next. She couldn't cope with being on the receiving end of Alison's angry outburst. It was the last thing Roz wanted, especially now when she required Alison's co-operation more than ever. Roz tried to ring Alison's mobile but it went straight to voicemail.

Alison spent two hours drinking hot chocolate in the late night Deli down the road; the bitterly cold January air calmed her down.

She spent most of the time talking to Rosie; she desperately wanted to ring Tom but decided it was too late as she didn't want to impose on him. When she arrived home, she was relieved to find her mum had gone to bed and had left a note by her bed.

I'm so sorry Darling – please forgive me. I DO care and of course I'll see Tom tomorrow.

Lots of love

Mumxxxxxxx

Alison sighed and rubbed her eyes. As hard as she tried she couldn't get his face out of her head. She hoped that she wouldn't have nightmares tonight. Suddenly, a wave of sadness swept over her, she felt so drained. She slipped off her clothes and climbed into bed, too tired even to brush her teeth. She went out like a light.

Roz woke up with a start at 6am, it was still dark and she hauled her weary body out of bed. She dressed quickly and was ready to leave by 7am; before Roz left she checked that Alison was in her room. She felt reassured when she saw Alison's dark hair spread across the pillow, snoring softly. I hope she's calmed down – I'll call her later to apologise. Maybe she's right – all I think about is the business.

I have to and she's not the only one who's going to lose everything. I've got 5,000 mouths to feed, bills to pay and I don't know how I'm going to hold it together but I have to, for everyone's sake, Roz thought as she drove to her plush New York store.

***

Tom arrived just after nine to a scene of chaos and carefully stepped through the mountain of plastic bags and cardboard boxes of Just Roz merchandise ready to be demonstrated in store. Various outfits were randomly thrown over mannequins' heads which added to the bedlam. Before Tom had the chance to ask where Roz McIntyre was, he heard a piercing shriek from the back of room.

'No – don't put that there, I want that belt with the purple jacket not on the pink dress!' Roz grabbed the offending belt and marched towards to the cowering window assistant when she stopped in her tracks. Roz reminded Tom of the cartoon character Cruella De Vil, only she was much scarier.

>'Tom – I'm sorry I didn't see you there. My apologies for the pandemonium here but I have to get every little detail right for the fashion critics. It's a big moment for Just Roz. Would you like to step this way and we'll start our meeting in my office,' Roz beamed, her voice as smooth as syrup.

>'Hmm – I won't take up much of your time – is Alison here?' Tom asked as they crossed the floor to her private office.

>'Yes – I left her in the office doing some admin.'

What Roz didn't tell him was they'd hardly said two words to each other since their argument the night before. It was unlike Alison to be so unforgiving; Roz just put it down to the stress of her job and the recollection of her attack.

What Roz didn't realise that she added to Alison's distress by refusing to discuss the issue. Tom's heart missed a beat when Alison looked up and beamed at him.

>'Tom – thanks for coming so promptly.'

Roz couldn't fail to notice the electric spark between them and watched bemused at the normally cool Tom blush.

>'That's okay – I don't have much time so I'd like to get started as soon as possible.'

>'Alison – you sit next to Tom and I'll sit behind my desk.'

Alison moved from the desk and sat next to him on the luxury leather sofa. Once Roz settled herself at her desk, she clasped her manicured fingers ready to face the interrogation.

The quicker we get this over with the better, she thought, and smiled at the two young love birds magnanimously. She had to admit Tom and Alison made a handsome couple but Alison could do much better than a lowly detective. She just needed the confidence to realise that, Roz thought. Now Alison and Adam Wilkes would make a fantastic couple. He had a weakness for beautiful woman and Alison was a stunning girl. Now that *would* be a match made in heaven. Tom cut through Roz's wistful thoughts.

'Alison have you had the chance to go over the phone numbers I gave you?'

'Yes – but I only know a few.'

'What telephone numbers?' Roz asked suspiciously.

'We found Alison's mobile phone at the scene of the accident, it was found further down the ravine where she hit that boulder. That's why I'm here, I'm hoping that you'll be able to tell me which ones are business associates and which ones are her friends,' Tom interjected; his dark blue eyes bored right into Roz making her feel ill at ease. He gave her the numbers watching her intently as her eyes scanned the page.

'Yes I can tell you most of them but I'll need at least 24 hours as I cannot recall all of them from the top of my head,' Roz cleared her throat because she recognised one of the numbers; it jumped right out at her like an angry red boil and she shifted nervously in her seat.

'Can you tell me the ones you know then?' Tom said looking straight at her but Roz didn't answer, she just stared at Tom but without really seeing him. *That's* Adam Wilkes number, how does he know Alison? They don't know each other. Oh my God – someone must have introduced them at that drinks party in Boston for Chloe, they must have swapped numbers…

'Mum – you're not listening,' Alison said impatiently.

Roz looked up and said apologetically.

'Sorry Tom what did you say?'

'Are there any business associates on the page that you may recognise?'

'No – none of them look that familiar. As you imagine I'm constantly on the phone and I can't be expected to remember every single number I dial every day as that would be impossible,'

Roz admitted innocently, praying that Tom would back off.

Tom changed tack and asked other probing questions and Roz answered each one as calmly as she could.

Alison watched her mother with growing irritation; she seemed distant and sometimes obstructive. Or was it her imagination? Alison felt sick with worry. Once Tom had got all the information he could, he left, keen to follow up the leads he did have.

He was aware that Roz hadn't been entirely helpful. She was hiding something and he would find out eventually what it was. He could have sworn she knew one of the numbers because her body language had changed and she was clearly flustered. He would ring Alison later to see if she was alright. He wouldn't have time to see her before he caught the flight back to Boston.

Roz made her excuses to Alison and left the office. She was due to meet Adam Wilkes in an hour and had to prepare for the most important meeting of her life. The future of her company was at stake and she'd have to be on the ball if she was going to succeed.

Chapter Twenty Eight

Roz made her way to meet Adam Wilkes at one of the hippest hotels in Manhattan on the trendy Upper West side. She was too nervous to marvel at the fabulous views of Central Park. As she walked into the ultra modern lobby, Adam greeted her in his usual laid-back style.

'Roz – you're looking as stunning as ever,' Roz couldn't help blushing as Adam looked particularly handsome in his Armani suit and crisp cornflower blue shirt. It set off his grey-blue eyes to perfection.

'Thank you Darling – you look pretty good yourself,' she said as he stood up and gave her the customary greeting of a kiss on each cheek. Roz took in the scent of his aftershave and tried not to sneeze, it overpowered her senses.

'Shall we head to the bar?' He placed his hand on the small of her back, as if it was the most natural thing to do. Roz nodded. This is it, there's no going back now.

'Sure – I could murder a skinny latte,' she admitted gaily, even though her stomach flipped over at the thought.

'I was impressed with your business plan for Just Roz and I'm pretty confident that we can do business together. There are a couple of things I would like to discuss with you before I draw up a contact.' Adam looked at her pinched face and continued. 'Don't worry Roz – it's all good and I'm sure you'll be happy with what I'm proposing.'

Once they'd sat down with their lattes, relief flooded through Roz but she sensed Adam wanted more than a pound of flesh, so she braced herself.

'I'm glad to hear that Adam, I do need the shirt on my back after all,' she spoke evenly with a mischievous glint in her eyes and Adam roared with laughter.

'And a very pretty shirt it is too,' he said eyeing up her pretty white silk shirt that moulded her lovely breasts – hmm very nice he thought and continued. 'I propose that we go into partnership, I'm prepared to give you 3.5 million dollars in cash for Just Roz. However I want 50 per cent of the gross profit and a seat on the Board of Directors. I will leave the day to day running of the business in your capable hands. The company will still be called Just Roz – I've no plans to add my name to it – just my backing." This is going better than I thought. I still have control of the business but 50 per cent of the profit – ouch. Roz smiled sweetly and replied.

'50 per cent is a lot of money Adam wouldn't you consider 35 per cent? I do have two children to take care of and Alex hasn't started university yet. I need money to live on and that doesn't leave me with much room for manoeuvre."

Adam leaned back in his chair and studied her for a moment. His eyes narrowed in concentration, he sensed the desperation in her voice and knew he'd won. Roz leaned forward, her café latte untouched, aware that she was holding her breath. Finally after a few seconds that seemed like hours to Roz, Adam replied.

"I'm afraid those are my terms – I know how passionate you are about your business. I've had my accountants study the figures and to put this in amount cash I want 50 per cent. I also think Just Roz would do exceptionally well in LA. Have you considered opening a shop in LA?"

Roz stared at Adam opened mouthed; she'd dismissed the idea because the money just wasn't there. She quickly recovered and pointed out.

'I'd never considered it but how will we find the cash?'

'The profits from the New York store will fund it. I'm confident that you'll do very well.'

Roz felt a surge of excitement and let herself relax for the first time in months. Her hands shook as she sipped her latte and said.

'Thank you for your vote of confidence. Adam I don't even need to think about this. You have a deal, I'll get my people to organise another meeting with your people and we'll take it from there.'

'Excellent – let's have some bubbly to celebrate.'

'Hmm – that's a super idea.'

Roz radiated a confidence that she didn't feel. She'd lost complete control of her company; however, the thought of success in LA overshadowed her loss. Maybe it won't be so bad; at least I'll have Adam to share the burden of the running of the company. I won't feel so alone and I won't have to struggle so much. Oh my God – LA here I come!

Roz was so engrossed in making plans with Adam, she completely forgot to ask how he'd got Alison's phone number and why he'd not mentioned it before? Adam was pleased that she'd accepted his terms and it meant that he'd spend lots of time with Roz and he'd get to meet the lovely Alison again. He knew from his well-placed sources, that Alison had a car crash recently and remembered nothing of her past. That suited Adam just fine, and as the bottle of Vintage Bollinger arrived, they toasted the future success of Just Roz. The fashion show was in twenty four hours and she couldn't wait to bask in the glory of her success.

***

Tom's phone went off as he walked back to his car, fresh from interviewing a witness regarding a mugging that had taken place on

Boston Common. He'd flown back from New York the night before and had got up very early to pursue the leads Alison and Roz had given him. The long hours were catching up with him and he suppressed a yawn.

It'd been a long day and he'd finally managed to track down and taken statements from all of Alison's friends and business associates that were on her mobile phone, except one. The phone buzzed again and he couldn't ignore it.

'This is Tom Bernstein – yep – really? That's very interesting, do we have this guy's address? Send a car over right away to pick him up. We'll see if he has any previous convictions – great work Matt. Call me when you bring him in.' Tom hung up and hurried over to his car.

'What's up?' asked Harry who was sitting in Tom's car eating a hot dog with all the trimmings. The smell of onions and mustard permeated the confined space, making Tom feel hungry.

'That was Matt – one of Alison's business associates is refusing to answer any of our calls. We've tried his home number several times and can't get a reply.'

'Do we have a name?'

'Adam Wilkes.'

'That name sounds familiar, I'm sure I've interviewed him before. Right – you go back to the station and look this guy up and I'll contact Roz to see if she knows how to get hold of this Adam Wilkes. Call me if there are any further developments.'

'Sure Harry – Um is your phone switched on?' Tom asked sheepishly waiting for his boss's reaction.

'Damn it man – of course it is!' He checked his pocket and switched it on.

Tom drove down the highway, hoping that Harry was right. He would love to nail the bastard that had raped and tried to murder Alison. However, Tom would like to dish out his own form of justice but he dismissed those thoughts as he rushed back to the station.

He hoped that the description that Alison gave them matched with Adam Wilkes. They desperately needed a result. He was almost certain the perpetrator had done this sort of thing before and wouldn't hesitate to do this again to some other unsuspecting victim. The profiler's report was sure that they were dealing with a confident, deceitful and cunning man. He had to be good looking, charming and maybe linked to a high powered profession. Tom hoped he would become over-confident and make a mistake then he would be able to catch him and put him away for a very long time. He would do everything in his power to protect Alison at all costs and Tom wouldn't rest until he'd caught him.

Chapter Twenty Nine

Alison returned to the apartment for an afternoon nap, she was dreaming again.

Alison was running through the thick fog, she kept looking behind her as a silhouette of man ran after her. He kept calling after her to stop but the closer he got the faster she ran. She kept stumbling over rocks and landing on soft ground, she grazed her knees and they bled. She continued to run up some rough grass and then she realised she was on a beach with large sand dunes. The grass was coarse and the sand was wet and sticky like heavy clay.

'Alison – come back – its okay! You're not in trouble. We know you didn't mean to hurt your brother. Come back here, you'll get lost in this fog – Alison!'

'Daddy - is that you? Where are you? I can't find you, don't leave me Daddy.'

'It's alright sweetheart I'm over here, just stay where you are and I'll find you.'

Alison stopped dead in her tracks and waited for the fog to clear, she shivered with the cold. Then she saw the tall, dark figure of a man coming towards her. As the fog cleared she saw his face, he had short grey/blond hair and gentle blue eyes. His face broke into a huge smile; Alison relaxed and ran to him, her arms open wide to hug him.

'Come here, you little horror –what am I going to do with you?' Her father chuckled scooping her up into his arms and tickling her.

Alison woke up with a start to find that Roz had rushed into the room. Roz heard Alison shouting in her sleep as she came into the apartment, still tipsy from her meeting with Adam. Through her alcoholic haze, Roz noted that on this occasion Alison wasn't distressed, in fact she grinned from ear to ear. She tried to steady herself by leaning on the door, Roz wasn't used to drinking so the champagne had gone straight to her head.

'Are you alright Darling – I heard you shouting in your shleep? Look I know things have been difficult for the last couple of days but, Darling, I'm genuinely sorry for not supporting you enough. I truly am – can you forgive me? I do love you, I know you think I don't but I really do and will do anything I can to help,' Roz slurred, trying to appear sober.

Alison suppressed a giggle; she'd never seen her mother drunk before so she must have had a good afternoon. 'Okay Mum – let's forget about what happened. I hope you will support me after the fashion show is out of the way. I want us to get along. I really do but I find it difficult to talk to you because you are always so wrapped up in the business.'

'Okay – I'll make more of an effort and that's a promise. Tell me about this dream you had.' Roz stumbled over to the bed and plonked herself down on Alison's bed. She reached out and squeezed Alison's hand. Alison grinned she quite liked Roz in this state, she seemed more approachable somehow.

'I dreamt about a beach and I was lost. I think I was dreaming about dad. Mum, I think I've remembered my dad but I'm not sure.'

'I'll get your journal out. What did he look like? Can you remember?' Roz asked as she rummaged around the bedside drawer for Alison's journal. She located it under a pile of Alison's knickers and yanked it out and started scribbling with exaggerated concentration. Alison tried to keep a straight face and continued, 'It was so vivid. It was really foggy and I was on a beach, he ran after me calling out my name. He was as tall as you and had short grey/blond hair. He wore a blue jumper and he had warm and kind eyes. He found me and I felt safe with him, I called him Daddy. Isn't that great, I remember my dad. Mum, I'm starting to remember more.' Alison smiled and hugged her mother, who didn't flinch this time when she hugged her and said 'I can't wait to ring and tell Rosie what I've remembered, she'll be thrilled.'

'Why don't you wait till tomorrow? I've got shhome pretty exciting news myshelf. The description you've given me is your father and I think I remember that day on the beach. That's wonderful darling – it really is,' Roz suppressed a burp and Alison chuckled good naturedly. 'It looks like you've a great time. It's not like you to knock back the booze mum.'

'Well as I said – we have plenty to celebrate I got the capital I needed for the business and we might be opening a shop in LA!!! Can you believe it? – your mother's going to have celebrities buying her clothes but before I say any more I think I'll have a nice long hot bath.' Roz said defensively, slightly rattled by Alison's observation on her alcohol intake. Alison wasn't prying, she genuinely was pleased to see her mum relax and enjoy herself for a change.

'Okay Mum – I'll get up. What do you want to do for dinner tonight?'

'Shall we be really naughty and order Chinese? I don't think I can be bothered to cook.'

'Fine by me – we've not had a night in to pig out for ages. I'll pop out and get some ice cream.' Alison suggested. She was glad that she wouldn't be dragged out for yet another business dinner. There'd been too many of those lately.

'Okay Darling – there's money in my bag just help yourself.'

Roz had staggered to the bathroom and was already running a bath, she'd managed to light candles and the smell of vanilla and lavender wafted from the bathroom.

'Do you need any cashhh Darling?' Roz shouted again forgetting she'd just Alison the same question.

'No – I'll see you in a little while,' Alison replied as she hauled her jeans on and grabbed her coat to go out the door.

As soon as she was outside she texted Rosie to say that she'd finally recalled who her dad was. Her phone buzzed with a reply from Rosie to say that she'd booked a flight to New York and would be with Alison tomorrow. Alison looked forward to spending an evening with her Mum for a change and was delighted that her old friend was coming to visit. Unfortunately, Stuart and Jane Rosie's parents couldn't make it due to work commitments. Life was pretty good at the moment, she thought happily as she bought her favourite ice cream, Raspberry Pavlova for her, and Belgium Chocolate for Roz.

***

Whilst Alison was in New York buying ice cream, Tom was still in his office going through all the mugshots of men with previous convictions for rape and assault. He squeezed his eyes shut, opened them and took a sip of water then a face just jumped right out at him. It was the tanned blond face of Adam Wilkes. Tom scanned the report. He'd been charged with attempted rape of an eighteen-year-old model but the charges were quashed by the District Attorney due to lack of evidence.

Alison's description of the man that had attacked her was spot on; also he refused to take any calls. Tom was convinced Roz knew who he was; he had a major suspect at last.

'Bingo!' Tom muttered and called Harry.

'Harry – you were right. Adam Wilkes was charged with attempted rape a few years ago but the case was dropped by the DA due to lack of evidence. I'll pick up Matt on the way to his apartment. Yes – I'll make sure we've got a warrant to search his flat and his offices. Don't worry everything will be done by the book,' Tom assured Harry but one question dominated his mind, where was Adam now?

Adam called Roz whilst Alison was out and informed her that he was in Cape Cod doing a fashion shoot.

He apologised to Roz saying that he wouldn't be able to make the fashion show but would meet her at the after show party. Roz hid her disappointment well but Adam assured her that he'd have the contracts ready for her to sign within the next couple of weeks. By the time Alison came back Roz was out of the bath and looked eager to fill Alison in on the latest developments.

'Who rang whilst I was out? Brad Pitt? Or Johnny Depp?' Alison laughed watching her Mum jump about like a scalded cat. It was really funny to see her mum so animated. The normally cool and sophisticated woman she had seen over the last few months seemed to have vanished and Alison preferred the new Roz.

'Ha bloody ha. No Adam just rang – he can't make the fashion show but he'll come by with the contracts at the after show party. This is it Alison – we're really going to hit the big time. You'll love Adam, he's rich, charming and gorgeous,' Roz waltzed down the hall to the bedroom to put some clothes on.

'I'm going to be rich and famous – Woo hoo!' Roz squealed.

Alison's blood ran cold. Adam. Wasn't he on her mobile phone list? Maybe there were two men called Adam but that was just too much of a coincidence. She couldn't remember the names Tom had mentioned off the top of her head but for some reason that was the one name that rang alarm bells in her head.

She made a mental note to ring Tom later. Alison got really wound-up when she couldn't even remember simple things like names, times, anything that might piece together her recent past. She just needed to put it to the back of her mind and enjoy the one and only precious evening that she had with her mum.

The next few days were going to be full-on and Alison felt overwrought already. One thing that cheered her up, she'd remembered her father at last and that alone was worth celebrating.

Maybe Roz wouldn't mind if she took a step back from the business now this new partner had joined. She had a glimmer of hope; she might have the chance to go back to her other life in Cape Cod. She wanted to walk along the beautiful beaches again and gain a degree of control over her own destiny. At the moment, it looked like an impossible dream.

Chapter Thirty

It was late in the afternoon before Tom and Matt turned up at Adam Wilkes's huge offices on the Upper East Side with a warrant to search the building. Another team of officers had gone to see if Adam was at home. However, they were informed by his housekeeper that he was away on business until tomorrow night. Tom knew from Alison's vague description that she had been attacked underground. So he started with the basement.

It took Tom Bernstein and his team a further five hours to find out what part of the building Alison had been attacked in. There were traces of blood everywhere as he and Matt walked along the grim corridor. Tom's heart beat faster, he mulled over what Alison must have gone through. He marvelled at how strong she was to survive such an ordeal and he loved her all for the more for it. Matt interrupted his thoughts and looked at him quizzically.

'Tom - Are you listening? You seemed pretty preoccupied at the moment. It's not like you buddy.'

'Sorry Matt – I was thinking about Alison and how I'm going to tell her that the man who *allegedly* raped her is a business associate of Just Roz. He matches her description perfectly, I'm sure he's our guy. Her mother must have recognised his number on that list, but she said nothing. We need to do more digging into her background but we don't have much time.' The launch of the biggest party in New York is tomorrow night and I've a got a hunch if Adam is involved with Roz McIntyre's business, he'll be there. Do you know how long he's out of town for?' Tom asked.

'No – the housekeeper was one fierce lady and it took us all our time to get out of her where Adam was,' Matt admitted.

'I'll try and contact Alison myself but first we need to collect all the evidence before the night is out'

'When are you going to see Alison?'

'First thing tomorrow,' Tom muttered, but he'd try and text Alison later on.

'Do you want me to come with you to the launch party tomorrow night?' Matt asked.

'No – if Adam is there – we don't want to spook him. I want to question him and Roz McIntyre myself. She's hiding something – I know she is. It will be a good opportunity to catch her off guard when the champagne is flowing. Alison's arranged for me to see her straight after the press conference. She won't be able to fob me off this time.'

'If Harry finds out – he won't be pleased.'

'Relax I'll do everything by the book and inform Harry later.'

'That's a helluva risk Tom. I can't back you up this time buddy.'

'I know – just trust me. I'll get a result. I just need to bend the rules a bit.'

Matt and Tom lifted up the yellow police tape in the bowels of the building. The forensics team hadn't arrived to gather evidence, so they'd cordoned off the area that needed to be searched. Nothing had prepared them for the dark and dingy room that met their eyes. The grey walls were wet with damp and the room stank of stale sweat and dried blood. The single light bulb swung back and forth in the breeze that was coming from corridor. It added to the sickening ambience of the room, as if a modern artist had flicked blood all over the walls to try and make some grotesque statement.

'Hell's teeth – look at this place. That evil bastard! How could he do that to Alison?'

Tom muttered angrily and before Matt could reply, Tom punched the wall with his fist. He took gloves off and stormed out the room and was promptly sick all over the floor.

Matt was shocked at Tom's angry outburst; in all the years that he'd worked with Tom he'd never seen him so agitated. They'd joined the force and trained at the same time. Even though they had attended some pretty unpleasant scenes in the past, Tom's extreme reaction troubled Matt. Was Tom becoming obsessed with this case or could it be the girl? Word had got around that she was beautiful but Matt had never had the privilege of meeting her. Matt popped out of the room and asked. 'Hey buddy, are you alright?'

'Yeah – I think I'm coming down with a stomach bug. I'll be okay in a minute. You go ahead and I'll go and get some water. '

Matt's phone went. 'Hi Harry – what's up – really? We'll be on our way.'

'What is it?' Tom asked, still leaning on the wall with a tissue over his mouth. He cursed himself for losing it in front of Matt. He was mortified.

'We've got to go back to the station,' Matt said cautiously.

'Why?'

'They've found some documents that may help us with the investigation in his apartment. It's a contract to give Just Roz 3.5 million dollars in cash. It looks like Alison's mother has struck a deal with this guy.'

'Do we have enough evidence to arrest them both?' Tom asked.

'No. Harry says he wants to see the documentation first because Adam Wilkes is a rich and powerful man. This has to be absolutely watertight. Before we can arrest either of them, we need one hundred per cent proof. Otherwise, both Adam Wilkes and Roz McIntyre could sue our asses and Harry's had enough bad publicity to contend after the Danvers case in 2006. Remember?' Matt pointed out trying to reason with Tom.

'But Alison could be in danger. We can't afford to wait.'

'If Adam is involved and we don't know that for certain. He wouldn't attack Alison in such a public place. Think about it, she could lead us straight to him,' Matt added

'You can't use her as bait – that's crazy,' Tom protested his mind in turmoil.

'Tom – calm down buddy. Harry will take you off this case if he finds out you're getting too involved, use your head. You'll be no use to Alison if you're suspended. Don't mess with Harry Fox coz' you'll come unstuck. He's not a man to be trifled with.'

'I guess you're right. Look can you keep quiet about the fact I lost it back there. I'm in enough trouble with Harry as it is and I want to see this thing through.' Matt didn't answer right away and stood with his hands on his hips looking at Tom. 'Matt? Can you keep quiet – just this once?' Tom sighed as he ran his fingers through his dark hair in frustration. Matt shook his head and said.

'I won't tell Harry this time – but if you lose it again Tom, I'm gonna have to report it. It's my duty and I want to keep my job and keep you out of trouble. Please listen to me you're a good cop – think about what you are throwing away here.'

'Yeah I know buddy. Thanks – I appreciate it.'

Tom had been pacing up in and down the corridor the whole time Matt was trying to persuade Tom to think logically. Matt felt sorry for him. He could see how much Tom loved Alison and it wasn't good for his career to get so emotionally involved. Tom needed a vacation; he'd been working flat out on this case for too long. Everyone knew that except Tom and he was as stubborn as Harry.

**

On the other side of town Alison and Roz had polished off the last of their indulgent meal. They'd had a good evening watching a girly movie and were blissfully unaware of the danger Alison was in.

'I love that movie. It's so long since I've watched anything so funny,' Alison said wistfully and Roz's heart went out to her. The guilt weighed down on her when she thought of Adam and the possibility that he may have attacked her daughter. She told herself repeatedly, she had no other choice but to accept Adam's investment and it could be just a weird coincidence.

Once the cash was in her account, then she'd go to the police with her suspicions. She prayed that Alison wouldn't recognise Adam; if she did then Roz would have to come up with another plan. Adam looked like Alison's attacker but Roz told herself not to be ridiculous. The champagne and excitement has just gone to her head. The stress of running the business was just making her irrational. There are lots of tall blond men in New York. I can't possibly be expected to remember everyone's phone number. After all, a little white lie won't hurt anyone would it? she thought to herself.

'Mum – you're miles away, are you alright?' Alison enquired kindly.

'Yes Darling – I was just thinking about the party tomorrow. There's still so much to do,' Roz said in a faraway voice, her thoughts swirling around in her head like a whirlpool.

'You've done a fabulous job, it'll be a huge success and now you've got the financial backing you desperately needed. Everything will go smoothly,' Alison replied reassuringly.

Roz smiled back at her daughter and said.

'I'm bushed and we've got a mega busy day tomorrow so I'm off to bed.'

'I won't be far behind you,' Alison chuckled. Her phone sprung into life. It was a text from Rosie. *Call me please.* Alison pressed speed dial and Rosie answered.

'Alison – I'd thought I'd try and catch you before you went to bed. I've managed to get an earlier flight so I was wondering if you're free tomorrow afternoon before the show. I was hoping we could pig out on New York's finest cuisine and have a good chat at the same time.'

'Sounds great Rosie, call me at the office when you arrive downtown. I'll meet you round the corner at that Deli I told you about. I've got so much to tell you, Mum and I had a huge argument the other day but we've cleared the air. She's on top form at the moment.'

'That makes a change,' Rosie retorted grimly. She didn't did trust Roz as far as she could spit.

'Yeah – I know, look I'll see you tomorrow. Tom came to see us as well, but I'll tell you about that when I see you,' Alison said stifling a yawn.

'Alison?'

'Yes?'

'I've really missed you Honey – the place is too quiet without you.'

'I've missed you too Rosie. It looks like Mum's got the cash for the business that she desperately needed and she's talking about opening a store in LA. Can you imagine – Hollywood here we come. She's been dancing around like an over-excited toddler all evening. It's really funny to watch.'

'I'll bet – where's she getting the money from? I thought she was broke? Rosie asked.

'Some really big shot in the fashion world has just given her a cool 3.5 million pounds in cash. Can you believe that?'

'Yeah – just make sure you introduce him to me coz' I sure could do with some more funding for my research.'

'Well – he'll be at the after show-party so you may get your wish. Apparently, he's not only rich but gorgeous as well according to Mum and she has pretty good taste in men usually.'

'Knowing my luck he's probably gay or he won't fancy me anyway. It's the story of my life. I bet he's gay.'

'Rosie – you're unbelievable. I don't think he's gay but I didn't bother to ask.' Alison giggled.

'That doesn't surprise me – maybe I'll fall in love with him and we could get married in Vegas by next Tuesday,' Rosie giggled.

'After me you are first in the queue okay?'

'What about the lovely Tom? He'll be heartbroken – you fickle woman,' Rosie scolded.

'I'm not sure he fancies me you know – he hasn't made a move on me yet.'

'Don't be absurd Alison – I'm telling you – he's crazy about you but he can't get personally involved until he stops working on your case. Alison – think about it. I'm not the only one who's noticed the way he looks at you. Utter adoration. I can put money on it that he'll keep in touch with you after this is all over.'

'I hope you're right Rosie Shaw or I'm going to make the biggest fool out of myself.'

'Oh crap! Honey – that's my pager – see you tomorrow and try and get a good night's sleep eh?'

'Yes Ma!'

'Watch it – take care. I'll text you when I'm at the airport,'

Rosie hung up.

Alison sighed wistfully and cradled her phone lost in thought; she hardly spoke to her old friend these days since her mother had started monopolising her time.

Even Lisa, her old room mate from the head injuries hospital had stopped calling her as Alison never had time to call her back for a chat. Alison felt guilty because she and Lisa were really good friends for a long time. I must send her an email before I go to bed and arrange to meet her when I get back to the Cape. It was a shame Lisa couldn't make the fashion show but she'd just started a new job in as a special needs teacher in a school for children with learning difficulties and being disabled herself, Alison reckoned Lisa had a long and brilliant career ahead of her.

On the way to her room, she noticed Roz's door was closed. The lights were out and the apartment was eerily silent. Alison stared out at the city skyline and suddenly felt homesick for the windswept beaches and quaint little towns of Cape Cod. In her heart Alison felt she belonged there, this mad metropolis would never feel like home.

Unbeknown to Alison, Tom had tried to ring her whilst she was chatting to Rosie and when he tried the apartment phone, all he got was an engaged tone. Roz had switched it off so that none of her staff could disturb her. She wanted to look her best for the party and needed as much sleep as she could get.

Chapter Thirty One

Rosie got off a packed plane and was relieved to land in New York. She'd sat next to a harassed mother with a grumpy toddler the whole time and now her head throbbed. Terrific, now I've got to fight my way through the terminal to get a taxi. Rosie thought but cheered up at the thought of seeing Alison again. She was dying to hear all about Alison's new job and she'd been working six days a week on a new research project. Rosie also taught two evenings a week at local university. She just couldn't say no and Alison scolded her for not taking more time to relax.

Alison had been in the office since 8am, overseeing the caterers and making sure the band knew where to set up. All the models had arrived for the show. Roz was particularly stressed and Alison had borne the brunt of her wrath on several occasions. This added to her anxiety leading Alison to question why she was here. She was surrounded by Divas, the fashion director and the party organiser who drove her to distraction by having tantrums at the slightest provocation. The press would be arriving later in the afternoon and Roz had gone back to the apartment to prepare for the launch. Alison couldn't wait to escape the pandemonium and have a girly chat with Rosie. There was nothing more she could do, it was sink or swim, and by the amount of work Roz had put into the show it was going to a roaring success. The store looked fabulous, set out in typical New York style, all sparkling chrome and glass. Just as Alison was about to check the changing rooms for the third time her phone went off.

'Rosie, how was your flight? Oh dear – well I'll see you in ten minutes. Can you order me a cappuccino and the biggest blueberry muffin you can find? I'm going to need it after the antics of certain individuals I've had to put up with this morning. You have no idea what it's like here, it's mental! See you in a mo,' Alison giggled.

When they'd settled into a cosy booth in the corner, Rosie was pleased to see that Alison looked well despite the stress of living with her mother and coping with the pressure of a new job. Her green eyes sparkled and her skin glowed, life in New York suited her or so Rosie thought.

'How much time do you have off before you go back home, Rosie?'

'Three days, I've got an extra day booked after I get back from the launch. Anyway, I'm doing pretty well. How's life with Mommy dearest?' Rosie asked with a wicked glint in her eye. Alison rolled her eyes and laughed.

'She's been alright actually; we had a nice time last night. We stayed in, stuffed our faces with ice cream and watched a girly movie. We did have a massive argument the night before though.'

'Oh – what was it about?' Rosie asked quizzically.

'Tom had come to see us about some stuff and Mum wasn't exactly helpful. He'd found my mobile phone at the scene of the crash and gave us a list of numbers that they'd retrieved. Of course, I didn't recognise any of them and Mum could only pick out a few that were familiar to her,' Alison continued, thinking aloud.

'It's a bit strange because Mum's pretty on the ball with phone numbers, especially when they're connected with the business,'

Alison added wistfully, wishing she didn't have to talk about what had happened.

Rosie looked at her sceptically; Alison had a wounded expression that settled across her face every time she mentioned Roz. Alison always managed to make excuses for her mother's selfish behaviour and it irked Rosie, who would love to tell Roz a few home truths about where her priorities should lie.

'What did she say?'

'Well, she couldn't be expected to remember everything and she had enough to think about with the launch and everything. She's had a lot of worry regarding the company finances and had to fly back to Edinburgh for a meeting with the bank. When she said that, I just lost it and stormed out,' Alison choked back the tears and shook her head.

Rosie reached over the table and squeezed her friend's hand and said.

'Good for you Alison, she can be a very selfish woman. I don't know how you put up with her. I would've strangled her with my bare hands by now.' Rosie swallowed hard trying to control her anger. How could a mother behave like this towards her daughter? She couldn't understand it. Alison smiled sadly and said.

'I don't think she realised how important it is to me but she does now. She apologised and she's trying harder to make an effort and offer support but I really don't know if I'm cut out for this kind of life. I'm really homesick for Cape Cod; life seemed less complicated when I was working in the coffee shop. I miss it Rosie and I miss the people I worked with.'

Rosie had been keen to discuss an idea she'd had whilst Alison was away in New York so she seized the moment.

'I did have an idea about what you could do instead but I've not had the chance to talk to you about it until now.'

'Really – what's that?' Alison perked up, intrigued by what Rosie had to say.

'You know you have a real empathy for people and you are great at giving advice. Well, have you ever thought of going into counselling or psychotherapy? Alison, you are a natural, people open up to you and because of what you've been through yourself. You have a depth of understanding that no other professional will have.

'Think about it, you were giving me advice when I first met you in hospital and you were my patient,' Rosie smiled, reminiscing.

'Gosh – I'd not given it a thought. Do you think I could do it?'

'Alison Honey – you'd be great and you could practise anywhere. You could go back to the café if you wanted and study part time. It would take longer to get qualified but it'd be worth it. If that's what you really want, you could always study in Edinburgh, either way. It's up to you.'

Alison smiled at her friend; Rosie was the closest thing she had to a sister. Her mind was in overdrive, thinking about all the possibilities. Rosie sipped her cappuccino and waited patiently for Alison to answer. A huge grin spread across Alison's face, she could stay here with Rosie and maybe she'd be able to see Tom.

'You know that sounds just the thing I'd love to do. I've always been into psychology. Only what do I tell Mum? She's going to be so disappointed that I'm not following in her footsteps,' Alison said biting her lip.

'Alison – you can't live your life to please someone else. You have to do what's right for you. You've only got one life Alison; you've got to go for it. If being a counsellor is what you really want to do, then think about it carefully before you make any decisions. I don't want to push you into something that you're not comfortable with. I just want you to be happy, that's all,' Rosie leant back in her chair and watched her friend intently.

'Oh Rosie – you are the only person who really understands me. I didn't realise how unhappy I've been until now. I'll think about it and have a word with Mum once the launch is over.'

'I'll leave it up to you because I don't want her to think I've put you up to this.'

'No – you're right I need to tackle this myself and tactfully. The more I think about it, the more it makes sense,' Alison said thoughtfully.

'How's Tom? Have you heard from him recently?' Rosie asked changing tack.

'Yes – what are you like?'

'Well – it's my job as your best friend to be curious?' Rosie protested innocently.

Alison roared with laughter but before she had the chance to tell Rosie how she felt, her phone buzzed loudly. It was Roz, who'd been trying to get hold of Alison for the last half hour. 'Oh bugger, its Mum!' Alison put the phone to her ear but held it away from her head, Roz's voice was so loud even Rosie could hear her. 'Sorry Mum – I'd just popped out for a quick coffee. Sure – I'll be there in 10 minutes.' Alison stuttered and went bright red.

Rosie didn't like the way she spoke to Alison but kept quiet. What a way to speak to your daughter – that woman is obsessed and it's not healthy. God help poor Alison when she gets back. Rosie thought and smiled at Alison sympathetically whilst she placated her mother.

'I've got to go. I'd love to stay for longer but you know how it is.' Alison said sheepishly, getting up from the table.

'I'll make my way to the hotel – don't worry and I'll see you at the launch. Try and take it easy – I don't want you having another seizure.'

'Yeah – I will. See you later and thanks for coming.' Alison shouted over her shoulder as she flew out the door, nearly colliding with a customer who was on the way in. Rosie shook her head sadly; the quicker Alison left New York, the better. Well I guess I'd better go and figure out what on earth I'm going to wear? Rosie thought grimly.

By the time Alison got back to the apartment, Roz was incandescent with rage.

'Where the hell have you been? How could you swan off like that at a time like this? You are so selfish Alison!' Roz spat. Alison just stared at her open-mouthed.

Despite her fury, Roz looked absolutely stunning in a Grecian style silk halter neck gown. The dark blue colour suited her creamy completion and wavy blond hair to perfection.

'I'm sorry – I'll get ready now.' There was nothing Alison could say and she felt her Mum was being unfair when she'd accused Alison of being selfish. She'd worked just as hard but supposed maybe sneaking out to meet Rosie wasn't such a good idea after all.

Alison changed into a strapless olive green gown; the colour brought out her lovely eyes and complimented her long chestnut hair. Roz had arranged for a make-up artist and hairdresser to come to the apartment. Alison stood silently as they set to work on her. Once they'd finished, her hair was pinned up into a simple French knot with little ringlets around her cheekbones. Alison studied herself in the mirror, she had to admit that the gown was beautiful but the make-up was a bit on the heavy side. Roz insisted that she needed heavier make-up for the harsh light of the cameras. Alison didn't have the heart to argue with her, she was more at home in a pair of jeans and t-shirt.

'Alison – you look gorgeous,' Roz exclaimed and Alison just smiled and said quietly.

'So do you Mum. This is your moment so enjoy it.'

'Thank you Darling and I'm sorry about losing it earlier. It's just…'

'It's okay Mum, you were stressed,' Alison cut in wanting to forget the whole thing; she was nervous enough.

'Oh hell's teeth, the limo's arrived. Are you ready? You don't have to say a thing, just smile at the press and I'll do all the talking.' Roz explained linking her arm through her daughter's as they walked out to face the world. Alison gulped as her mother lead her down the corridor to the lift. She'd rather be anywhere else than here.

Chapter Thirty Two

As soon as they stepped out the limo, the press went mad. Alison couldn't see a thing except flashing lights as bright as the sun; it blinded her temporarily. She blinked rapidly. She felt disorientated and couldn't concentrate on what her mother was saying to the waiting journalists because her head was spinning. Roz, on the other hand, loved the attention and smiled waving to the crowd of onlookers who'd gathered to spot their favourite celebrity. Roz worked the red carpet like a pro and Alison had to admire her for it.

'Smile Darling and say Hello to anyone who shoves a TV camera in your face. And stay behind me!' Roz hissed in her ear.

Alison felt like a goldfish out of water, she smiled and waved on cue. She felt sick and dizzy and this was only the start of the evening. Finally, Roz led her through the throng of VIPs to a seat tucked behind the stage and slumped onto the nearest chair. Her heart was pounding and she was breathing heavily. She closed her eyes for a moment and tried to visualise the gentle shores of Cape Cod. Eventually, her heart slowed down, she felt calmer and opened her eyes and stood up ready to enjoy the show she and Roz had worked so hard on.

Alison watched her mum work the room; she remembered everyone's name and Alison marvelled at how sharp her memory was. She'd picked up a glass of Champagne from a passing waitress and sipped it. Alison was too nervous to eat any of the tempting canapés that were on offer, in case it spoiled her make-up. Lord, it was going to be a long night. She'd scanned the room trying to spot Rosie but she couldn't see her. I hope she got here in time, knowing what Rosie's like she'll be at the back somewhere. I'll try and find her after the fashion show. She hurried back to her seat to sit by Roz who was beckoning her.

Alison jumped out of her skin and sat upright when the music started; the models slunk by in single file in an array of fabulous clothes.

The music pumped out the speakers so loudly, the vibrations hit Alison's chest and her ears ached. The circus had begun and Alison prayed that it would go smoothly. The crowd gasped and Alison noted that the fashion journalists were scribbling on their pads at a furious pace.

Roz was also in the front row, watching their every move intently. Her face impassive, anyone looking at her would think she was relaxed but Alison knew that wasn't the case. She didn't know how Roz could be so composed and professional. Alison struggled to concentrate, her mind kept drifting back to the conversation she'd had with Rosie earlier in the day as she tried to concentrate on the show.

There was a roar of applause when Roz appeared on the stage. Surrounded by models and her design team, she could give any of them a run for their money.

> 'Thank you so much for coming to the launch of Just Roz, it means so much to me that so many of you could make it here this evening,' Roz gushed.

More clapping and whooping from the crowd so Roz continued, thanking everyone in true Hollywood style. Alison felt whoozie; terrified she was going to faint. Whilst her mother delivered her speech, she crept out and hurried down to the office that she shared with her mother. The corridors were quiet, as everyone was out the front. I'm sure I left an apple in my drawer so I'll eat that and have a glass of water. Maybe I'll feel better then. She thought.

As Alison enjoyed a quiet moment and collapsed on the sofa not caring whether it creased her dress, Rosie fought her way to the front of the stage. She couldn't see Alison, but to her surprise she saw Tom Bernstein at the back of the front row. He was with two other plain clothes men. He looked harassed and Rosie was instantly suspicious. What was he doing here? Rosie picked her way carefully through the crowd and greeted him. Roz had finished her speech and the guests were free to mingle and enjoy the party.

'Tom this is a surprise. What are you doing here? I didn't think this was your thing.'

'Rosie have you seen Alison?' His voice was low and urgent ignoring her questions.

'No Tom – What's up? I've just arrived the traffic was murder. Alison insisted that I get a taxi. It would have been quicker to walk.'

'Alison's in danger, we found the room where she was raped in. It belongs to Adam Wilkes. He's an associate of Roz's and is supposed to be here. I've checked the guest list, but I've not seen him yet.'

'Oh my God, that's awful.' Rosie cried. 'She could be anywhere. I'll try the restrooms and her office is at the back of the stage, if I see her first I'll call you.' Rosie said hurrying off to the back of the stage.

'Okay – I think I can see Roz – I want to have a quiet word with her as well.' Tom said grimly and Rosie winced. She wouldn't like to get on the wrong side of Tom as she watched him go striding off towards Roz.

'Alison - Are you in here?' Rosie pushed through the gaggle of gossiping women and they glared at her. There was no reply. Rosie rushed down the corridor but unbeknown to her, Adam Wilkes had passed her on the way to Roz's office. He'd gone around the back to avoid the press. Although he loved putting on a good show, he was not in the mood tonight. The business trip hadn't gone well and he was in a foul mood.

He'd not seen Roz yet. He checked his watch impatiently. He knew she'd be on time as the contract he had in his briefcase was ready to sign. The money would be transferred into her account by noon tomorrow. He'd called her earlier that morning and she promised him that she'd be in her office by nine. It was almost nine now.

He knocked on the door and walked right in. Alison sat bolt upright and nearly choked on the remains of her apple. There in front of her was the man who raped her.

She recognised him instantly, her throat contracted and she couldn't breathe. The colour drained from her face and she just gaped at him rooted in her chair.

'Oh I'm sorry I thought this was Roz's office. I'll come back.' Adam said quickly realising that Alison had recognised him by the look of sheer terror on her face. As he stepped outside and closed the door behind him, Roz appeared in a cloud of blue silk and held her arms out.

'Adam darling – I so glad you made it. Have you been waiting long?' but before she could reach him, the door flew open and Alison stood in the frame of the doorway with an angry look in her eyes. She pointed at Adam and growled 'It was you!' Adam's handsome face stared innocently back at her with his hands up.

'Who is this woman Roz? Is she drunk? Or just insane?'

'I'm not drunk or insane. You raped me! You bastard!' Alison growled, her legs were like jelly and she struggled to stay on her feet. Her mind flashed back to the night she was raped, his face contorted with hate as she pleaded with him to stop. It was too much, fear pumped through her veins and her blood turned to ice and she stepped slowly back into the office, not taking her eyes off Adam. Before Adam could say another word Roz cut in. She noticed he had gone very pale under his tan. 'What are you talking about Alison? This is Adam Wilkes our primary investor. Are you sure you're not drunk or having a seizure before you make ridiculous accusations. I'm sorry Adam – I think Alison is confused.' Roz snapped. 'It's him– that's the man that raped me and left me for dead. Why don't you believe me? Why do you *always* take every one's else's side except mine? For once in your life will you listen to me and *fight for me for a change!*' Alison's voice trembled, her fists were curled up and she had a murderous look on her face.

Her hair had fallen down and she looked wild. Rosie had heard Alison's high pitched voice and came hurtling down the corridor just in time to witness the ugly scene unfolding before her. 'It can't be Darling? Are you *sure*? Just think about what you are saying for a mmoment.' Roz stuttered.

'The woman is insane I've never seen her before in my life. Look lady – you're confused. I've never met you before…' Alison cut through Adam's voice. 'Of course I'm bloody sure!' Alison spat and stepped further back into the room trying to put as much distance between Adam Wilkes and herself. He was smirking and it made Alison madder. Alison felt she had been punched in the chest and there was an elastic band wrapped around her heart.

She searched around her mother's desk for something to protect herself with and picked up a sharp silver letter opener that lay on the desk. She pointed it at Adam. 'You stay away from me or I swear to God I'll kill you! Rosie, thank God you're here they're trying to convince me I'm crazy or drunk and I'm not. I've never been so sure of something in my life.'

Rosie moved slowly towards Alison and stood by her. 'It's okay no one's going to hurt you whilst I'm here.' Rosie said gently, standing next to her and facing a disbelieving Roz who thought that her daughter had lost her mind.

'I'm telling you! It's him Rosie – I'm not going to let him hurt me again. No bloody way!' Alison waved the letter opener in front of Adam. 'Put the letter opener down Alison – *I swear I won't let anyone hurt you.*' Rosie said approaching Alison slowly. Alison continued to rant, 'Tell them Adam, you raped me and beat me. Admit it. Tell the truth!'' It was Adam who spoke this time, he was rooted to the spot as he had to come up with an excuse to leave and fast. 'This is ridiculous – she's obviously crazy – I'm leaving and you can forget the deal Roz,' He blustered as he pushed his way past a startled Roz and bumped straight into Tom Bernstein.

'Adam Wilkes. I'm arresting you for the rape and attempted murder of Alison Jane McIntyre. You have the right to an attorney...' Tom grabbed Adam and threw him none too gently against the wall. He continued to read Adam his rights, cuffed him and let him away.

'You can't do this – you've no proof. Don't you realise who I am?' protested Adam but Tom was in no mood to reply and before he led Adam away, he said. 'It'll be okay – Alison I promise you,' Alison dropped the letter opener and it bounced off the ground. She sobbed in Rosie's arms. Roz just stood there dumbstruck she couldn't take any of this in. Her whole world had come crashing down like a row of dominoes. She stared at her sobbing daughter, who was being comforted by Rosie and croaked.

'I'm so sorry darling – I didn't realise. Let me take you home.' Alison stopped crying and looked directly at her mother as if seeing her for the first time.

Roz's voice shook and her stomach was in knots. Alison collapsed onto the sofa and Rosie was at her side. Alison was in shock and couldn't stop shaking but before she could open her mouth Roz spoke hesitantly.

'Okay Alison – there's something you need to know and I was hoping that this day was never going to come.'

'Please Mum just tell me what the big secret is? Why are you dealing with scum like him?' Alison pleaded.

'I knew something wasn't right about Adam but I had no proof, I would've understood the situation better if I had known. The company is in serious trouble, the bank is going to foreclose on all the loans and I desperately needed Adam's money. I thought it was odd that his number was listed on your mobile but I *never* imagined for a moment that he was the one who raped you. Honestly, you've got to believe me,'

Alison looked up and spoke harshly.

'You're a liar. Tom asked you if you recognized those numbers and you said no. I'm your daughter, you're supposed to love and protect me. How could you stand there and lie to me? I'm your own flesh and blood. How *could* you? Alison asked incredulously.

'I'm sorry Alison. I had a very difficult time giving birth to you. I tried my best to take care of you but you were very difficult and wilful as a child. Not only that, you're the spitting image of your father, I felt shut out. You and your father were always so close. I've got 5,000 mouths to feed. Staff that have been with me for over twenty years will lose their jobs, maybe their homes…'

'Bullshit! That's no excuse to treat me the way you did! I'm so angry with you I can't even bear to look at you right now. You don't love me or anyone, its Just Roz you love. You'd probably sell your own mother to keep your precious business going. You make me *sick*.' Alison spat and continued. 'Please tell me – why didn't you say anything before?'

Alison's voice quivered, she knew deep down in her heart she'd never know the answer as to why her mother put her business first before her and it broke her heart.

Roz sat on the sofa and tried to hug Alison but she shrugged her off none too gently. Roz put her head in her hands and started to cry uncontrollably.

'Come on, Alison you're flying home with me tonight.' Rosie said quietly and led Alison away.

'I hope you're satisfied.' Rosie said through clenched teeth at Roz as she walked past.

Roz bowed her head and looked at the floor wishing that the ground would just swallow her up. She couldn't look into those green eyes full of anguish. Roz couldn't speak and sank deeper onto the sofa and sobbed. Roz had lost her business.

Despite the roaring success of the fashion show, she was finished. Even that didn't matter because she realized Alison would never forgive her for putting her business first and she'd lost her daughter for the second time too. Everything she had worked for lay in front of her in tatters.

Chapter Thirty Three

With Adam in custody, Tom rang Alison. The image of her tear-stained face haunted him and he was desperate to know that she was okay, so he kept ringing her mobile until he got an answer. Eventually, she answered the phone at his fourth attempt.

'Alison – I need to talk to you. It's not about the case, it's about us,' Tom said holding his breath waiting for her answer.

'Tom I can't – I'm leaving New York tonight with Rosie. It's just too complicated right now and I don't know what's going to happen.'

'It won't take long, I've been meaning to…'

'No Tom – not now. It's too difficult and I can't cope. Please understand,' Alison said sadly.

'Please stay in touch and if there's anything I can do. Just let me know.'

'Goodbye Tom.' Alison hung up and collected the last of her things. Rosie stood in the doorway.

'Are you ready to go?' Rosie asked softly.

'Yes,' Alison replied taking one last look around her room. She realised she had never belonged here, and she couldn't wait to go back home to the safety of Cape Cod, to normality, to the friends who genuinely cared about her.

***

Adam's lawyer had tried to get him bail but due to the seriousness of the charges against him, he remained in the cells. Harry and Matt had interviewed him yesterday but Matt was called away on another case. It was Tom and Harry who were ready to question him today. They'd finally received all the evidence, including the DNA on Alison's tattered dress. It matched Adam's DNA.

Tom hoped that Adam would confess to save Alison the ordeal of going to court as they walked down the corridor to the interview room that Adam was incarcerated in. He had a gnawing pain in the pit of his stomach that Adam was going to be as difficult and evasive as possible. He was one slimy son of a bitch.

Tom needed every ounce of self-restraint to stop him from beating this creep to a pulp. *I must do everything by the book so that we have a strong case, there's no way he's going to worm his way out of this one.* Tom thought.

Harry watched Tom out of the corner of his eye. He sensed that Tom was wound up and that troubled him. However, he had decided to give Tom the benefit of the doubt by letting Tom interview Adam Wilkes. Harry was going to suggest to Tom again that he needed time off. He'd been working on this case for too long. Tom looked tired and pale but it wasn't from work, unbeknown to Harry, Tom had let Alison slip through his fingers again. He would go after her once he'd proved Adam had attacked Alison and all the other poor women, that would hopefully come forward once the news was made public. Tom was utterly convinced Adam had done this many times before. The press were circling the station already and Tom was looking forward to being at the press conference when Harry would make a statement.

'Tom - Are you listening to me?' Harry said impatiently.
'Yes?'
'What room is he in twelve or fifteen?' Harry asked.
'Um – room twelve.'

Harry was glad they had caught Adam and all they needed to do was collect the rest of the evidence to link him with the other rapes. He'd done this before, Harry was certain of it.

'It's fifteen.' As they opened the door Adam was sitting there with his lawyer.

Adam looked tired and scruffy because he'd spent the night in the cells. He sat slumped on his chair moving his coffee cup from left to right. When he saw Harry and Tom walk in he smirked. His lawyer, a small grey-haired man who had a face like a weasel, Tom thought. Harry sat across from Adam and Tom switched on the interview tape and sat down beside Harry. Tom stared at Adam intently. Adam glared at Tom defiantly.

'Well, Mr Wilkes, we're going to continue questioning you from yesterday. This is Tom Bernstein my partner who has collected a lot of the evidence from the crime scene,' Harry said carefully.

'Oh really? I don't know what you are talking about,' Adam said contemptuously staring at his manicured nails.

'Oh come on Mr Wilkes. I think you do. You drugged Alison and dragged her down to the basement to rape her. Did you not? You planned this attack, like you planned the others. There are three new witnesses that have come forward and they will testify against you. Including a nurse called Benjamin John James from Ashvale Mental Hospital. I believe he supplied you with the drugs you needed to keep your victims quiet. We've done some digging into your past and found out the two of you went to the same High School. Not only that, we intercepted some very interesting texts and emails…'

'I think I need another word with my client.' The lawyer interrupted. Adam said nothing and his expression changed, his eyes narrowed. There was no escaping justice this time. Tom smiled with satisfaction; so he tried a different tack to persuade Adam to confess. He'd saved the best piece of evidence they had until last.

'I am showing Mr Wilkes exhibit H142, the blood stains on Alison McIntyre's dress match blood stains in the room, bed and the corridor. The same blood stain is mixed with your blood, Mr Wilkes – how do you explain that? Your DNA was found under her fingernails when she tried to fight you off. You drugged, raped and beat Alison McIntyre with the intention of killing her. Admit it!' The tone of Tom's voice rose slightly and Adam picked up on it right away.

The poor sap was in love with Alison, he could see it in his eyes. This is an ideal opportunity to wind him up, thought Adam vindictively. After all I have nothing to lose; they can only get me on one charge. He grinned at Tom and hissed.

'Yes Okay I admit we did have a bit of rough sex, but I didn't intend to kill her. She was the best, she put up one hell of a fight and I loved every minute of it!' Adam smirked and Tom's face reddened.

'Adam – be quiet! I want a recess to talk to my client please,' the grey lawyer said nervously putting his glasses down and grabbing Adam by the arm.

'Let him continue for the tape,' Harry said calmly whilst giving Tom a hard nudge.

'I loved putting that mouthy bitch in her place and a good slap never hurt anyone.' Adam sneered leaning back on his chair. Tom snapped and abandoned all self-control.

'You filthy little bastard!'

'Tom – stop it!' Harry yelled and stopped the tape, it was too late.

Tom leapt over the table with lightning speed and rugby tackled Adam onto the ground punching him so hard, he screamed. He tried to thump him again but he was pulled off by Harry and two other officers who had ran into the room when they heard the commotion.

'Tom! Stop it! You bloody fool! – Get out now and I'll see you in my office!' Harry roared pushing Tom in the direction of the door. Tom stormed out of the room and rushed down the corridor to get some fresh air.

'Well, that's police brutality for a start – I'm going to sue you bastards for that.' Adam said spitting out the blood from his split lip and glaring at Harry.

'I'm sorry I'll suspend him right away. Get Dr Tomlinson to have a look at his injuries.' Harry barked and added 'Interview suspended.'

'You won't get away with this; I'll sue you for assaulting me, won't I?' Adam whined, still spitting blood onto the floor and looking at his lawyer but the grey man said.

'Assault? What assault? – you provoked the officer and in my opinion he used reasonable force to restrain you – don't you think so Mr Fox?'

Harry stopped and turned around, his jaw dropped. In all the years he had dealt with Mr Sayers, he'd never done them a favour, not once. He must really dislike his client and Harry tried not to smile when he saw the horrified look on Adam's face.

'I think you might be right Mr Sayers, we will look at the CCTV and I will give you a full report within 24 hours.'

'What? You can't do this – I want someone else to represent me? Do you hear me?'

'We'll discuss this later when you have calmed down Mr Wilkes.' I am retiring at the end of the month and I've arranged for my colleague to take over your case as I'm getting too old for this,' Mr Sayers finished soothingly.

As two large policemen dragged Adam down the stairs he was still screaming and shouting. Adam had finally cracked when he realised that he was not going to get away with attacking Alison, like he had with all the others. Harry was furious with Tom and strode down the corridor to his office. Everyone jumped out the way when they saw the sour look on his face. He was shocked at Tom's behaviour; he had to suspend Tom as he couldn't protect him from his superiors. Tom was off the case permanently. Thankfully because of his impeccable record to date, he would keep his job and not end up doing traffic duty for the rest of his career. He threw open the door, it almost came off its hinges. Tom sat with his head in his hands and didn't look up. Harry stood over Tom with his hands on his hips.

'What the hell were you doing in there? Do you realise the trouble you are in Tom? You bloody idiot! I've no option but to suspend you with immediate effect – give me your badge and gun! You attacked a prisoner – what were you playing at? You'll be lucky you won't end up doing traffic duty for the rest of your life! What have I told you? If you feel that you're getting wound up – leave the room! I'll have to launch a full internal investigation now! That's if Adam Wilkes doesn't sue your ass first! I am so disappointed in you.'

'I know - I'm so sorry I let you down Harry. This case has been getting to me for a while now,' Tom said as he looked up at Harry, his face was pale and his eyes were full of anguish. When Harry saw how distressed Tom was, he put his hand through his hair, walked over to his desk and sat down.

'Look – go home and I'll be in touch in a couple of days. I'll speak to you when I've calmed down. I'll figure out something.' Harry muttered.

'I'm sorry Harry.'

'Save it Tom – get out of my sight!'

After Tom left, Harry took a small silver flask out of his drawer and took a gulp. He shook his head as he watched Tom walk down the office. No one dared to speak to Tom, they knew what had happened.

Harry was gutted as he watched one of his best officers leave the department. What a day, the phone sprung to life; it was John Bloomfield, his superior officer. His heart sank, news travels fast he thought as he tried to explain Tom's actions.

Tom got into his car and punched the steering wheel several times in sheer frustration. He'd lost his cool, maybe Harry was right? He needed time off and with a bit of luck, he could go and see Alison to update her on the case; it would give him an excuse to see her in Sandwich. He was sure she'd go back to her little apartment above the coffee shop. It was a risk worth taking, now he was off the case. He had to tell her how he felt. If she rejected him again then he would walk out of her life for good and that thought terrified him but he had to tell her that he loved her. He was sure she felt the same as Tom felt that the chemistry between them in New York had been so strong. However, Tom wasn't going to count his chickens just yet. He rubbed his eyes and sighed. Suddenly, he felt shattered. He started the engine and drove home. He needed to get a couple of days rest before he headed back to the Cape again.

Chapter Thirty Four

Two weeks had passed since Alison and Rosie had left New York. Alison got her old job back working in the coffee shop. Joe and Andy the shop's owners were only too pleased to hire her again. She'd kept her apartment above the shop and began to rebuild her new life. She threw herself into her job to forget her mother's betrayal but Adam's face still haunted her dreams at night. Alison wondered if the nightmares would ever stop but Rosie had reassured her that only time would help her to forget and just to take a day at a time. Some days were harder than others and the pain and emptiness she felt was overwhelming at times.

Roz had tried to contact Alison on many occasions but she'd found out since that Roz faced charges for denying that she knew Adam and obstructing the police in their investigation. Alison had asked the DA in Boston and the Scottish Police to drop the charges against her mother, the fact that her company had gone into administration was punishment enough. She'd been deported back to Edinburgh.

***

She hadn't heard from Harry Fox or Tom Bernstein for days, they seemed to have quite forgotten her. Alison didn't have time to call them either because she'd a counselling course to organise. She often wondered if her father would have been pleased with the choice she'd made. She needed stability in her life more than anything else; Rosie had been fantastic but Alison couldn't rely on her forever. She stood with an empty coffee pot in her hand with a dazed look in her eyes when Andy said.

'Oh she's off again – will you stop daydreaming and fill that coffee pot!'

'Great – how many cups has she broken this week?' asked Andy shaking his head looking at Joe who rolled his eyes.

'Just two,' Alison grinned sheepishly.

'Alison –Honey – Get a move on or I'll fire you again if you're not careful!' Andy chuckled.

'Don't you dare fire that girl or you'll have me to deal with!' snorted ninety year old Doctor Pascolo who glared at the two men waving his walking stick in a menacing manner.

'Don't worry Doctor Pascolo – they're only joking. I'm not going anywhere, anyway how are you today?"

Alison continued to chat to the old man who came in for lunch every day. His wife of fifty years had just died and Alison chatted away to him like she did to all the other customers. She knew everyone in the little community; she was respected and well liked.

Rosie still worked long hours but had joined an art class. She saw Alison every day when she popped in for a bite to eat. Tom hadn't been in touch and Alison felt bad that she'd been so off hand, she guessed that he'd given up on their friendship and she didn't blame him. Alison served the last customer and it was getting dark, she'd washed the last of the table tops when the door opened. 'We're closed,' she said without turning around to see who it was.

'I know – it's you I've come to see.' A familiar voice said; she turned around to see Tom standing in the doorway with a pensive look on his face. A smile spread across her face and she dropped the cloth on the table and hurried over to him. Her heart started to beat that little bit faster. He looked gorgeous in faded jeans, a black t-shirt and leather jacket. 'Tom what are you doing here? – it's so good to see you.' Before Tom had time to reply she held out her arms and wrapped them around his neck. He returned her embrace. They held each other tightly for a long time. Tom could feel her soft body leaning against him and took in the familiar scent of her hair. Time seemed to stop.

'Oh Tom – I'm sorry I treated you so badly. I've missed you.' Alison said softly, it felt so good to be in his arms again and as she leant against his lean body, a thrill of desire pulsed through her body for the first time.

'I thought you weren't interested in staying friends. So I thought I'd back off for a bit. You know – give you some space to settle in.' Tom lifted her chin and kissed her passionately, she returned his kiss and the room spun crazily around him.

'Wow – that was some kiss.' Alison said when they'd finally paused for breath, looking at Tom's grinning face and continued.

'You could have called me anytime. It was a crazy time back in New York. I couldn't think straight,' Alison tried to break away from his embrace but Tom wouldn't let her go.

'Alison – I wanted to tell you how I felt so many times but I couldn't. You were so vulnerable and I didn't know if you felt the same.' Tom added.

'I think I always cared for you but I've had so much to cope with that I've only realised how I felt since I came back home. I started thinking about you and wondering how you were getting on.' Tom grinned, he couldn't believe what he was hearing. He kissed her lightly and replied.

'I wanted to keep in touch with you but I couldn't because of my job. It's been hell. I thought I lost you. You seemed so distant when you left that night. I wasn't sure you felt the same but the chemistry between us seemed so strong at the time. I've wanted to tell you this for months. It was on the tip of my tongue so many times but there never seemed to be the right moment and I didn't want to upset you further. You've been through so much I didn't want to tip you over the edge. So I kept quiet. Alison - Do you want to go out for dinner tonight, nothing heavy – just a pizza?'

'Well you haven't lost me. I need to finish up here but I'd love to Tom. I need to finish clearing up and then we have the rest of the evening to talk properly. If that's okay?'

'Sure – take your time.' Tom kissed Alison again and she reluctantly pulled away from him. Tom sat down and grinned, Alison finished cleaning the rest of the tables and they chatted happily, as if they'd never been away from each other.

They walked arm in arm down the road to the local pizza like they'd been together for a long time. When they'd ordered pizza and drinks Tom said reluctantly.

'Alison – I hate to mention this but there's something I need to tell you about the case. There's been a development and I wanted to tell you first before anyone else.'

Alison stopped drinking her diet coke and looked at Tom anxiously. Her blood ran cold and she shivered because she could see the anguish in Tom's eyes. Tom took her hands in his.

'What is it?'

'I've been suspended from my job that's why I had the time to visit. Adam Wilkes confessed to raping you. So you won't have to go to court.' Tom stared at the floor, embarrassed and blurted out.

'I'm so sorry Alison – I lost it and punched him several times. Harry and the guys had to haul me off him. He was laughing; you know, boasting about what he'd done and, Oh God, Alison I couldn't help it.'

Tom let her hands go, leant on the table and put his head in his hands, he couldn't look at her. Alison felt a sudden surge of love for this man, the love of her life had been right under her nose all along.

He'd fought so hard for her; there was no doubt in her mind that Tom was all she ever wanted.

'Tom – look at me.'

Tom looked up and to his surprise Alison wasn't angry, she smiled sadly and said.

'You did that for me?'

'Yes.'

'Tom you could have lost your job. What's going to happen? I mean, will you have a job to go back to?' Alison asked anxiously, she couldn't believe what she was hearing. Tom shook his head and admitted.

'I don't know. I've let you down and…' Alison interrupted him.

'No you haven't. I'm glad you hit him. He'll get what he deserves when they sentence him in court but Tom you could have lost *everything*.'

Alison reached across the table and took his brown hands in hers. At that moment, she had so much love for this man, who'd not only stayed with her through the tough times but had risked his job for her too. She could see the anguish in his lovely blue eyes and she said.

'Tom – you're upset. Let's go back to the apartment and we can talk properly there.'

'Are you sure?'

'Yes – I'll make you some coffee coz' we can't really talk here.'

As they walked back to her apartment, they pasted the little park bench where Tom had sat months before in despair thinking he'd lost Alison. He couldn't believe that Alison was by his side. Alison led him by the hand up the narrow wooden stairs and let them both in.

Tom's heart was hammering in his ribs; as he watched Alison make the coffee and handed him a cup. He stood over Alison and said. It's now or never, he thought.

'Alison – there's something else I've been meaning to tell you. I love you. I've loved you since the first day I set eyes on you. I know it's a bit soon to tell you but I can't risk losing you again…' Tom put the coffee cup down and reached out, took her in his arms and kissed her again, the desire for her rising.

He let her go, waiting with bated breath and was about to say something else but Alison put her finger on his lips to silence him, she moved closer to him and stroked his cheek looking into his cornflower blue eyes.

'Shh- I love you too Tom. I think I always have. I can't imagine not being with you. Oh Tom – you're so lovely.' She said softly, her eyes were bright with tears. He kissed her face, her cheeks and her full lips, she groaned with pleasure. Alison surprised Tom by kissing him back with equal passion and it took his breath away. As they stood in the little kitchen and for the first time Alison knew without a doubt; her life was here with Tom on the Cape.

They spent the night in her little apartment making love in her bed and talking to the small hours. Alison hadn't been with a man since she'd been raped. She was worried she would have flashbacks but with Tom, it was so utterly different from any other man she'd been with. He was a gentle and a considerate lover. He touched her in a way no man had touched her before even though she hadn't had much experience with men. She sighed with pleasure and snuggled into the crook of Tom's arm. They stayed in each other's arms, as naked as babies till dawn.

Alison knew that she now lived the life she wanted. She'd lived Some Other Life in New York and Edinburgh, it wasn't the life she'd planned but at last she could be herself again and with Tom by her side, she could face a bright future.

Epilogue

Alison settled into her psychology course and her life on Cape Cod. Her friendship with Rosie grew and they remained very close. Tom managed to hang onto his job and got a transfer from Boston to a bigger town near Sandwich on Cape Cod. Although Tom wasn't as busy as he was in Boston he was content just to be with Alison. They were pretty serious and were in the process of finding a bigger apartment to move into.

Rosie started dating Matt, Tom's old work colleague from Boston. He'd helped Tom move down to the Cape and they'd hit it off instantly. Tom and Alison were delighted that they were accidental matchmakers.

Roz McIntyre was charged with wasting police time, even though Alison had tried to intervene but escaped a prison sentence and got 12 months community service. Her company had been taken over by a rival firm so Just Roz lived to fight another day. She'd tried to write to Alison and contact by her phone repeatedly. Alison couldn't bring herself to contact her mother just yet. Alison would forgive her someday because she knew only too well that life is too short to be angry at the mother forever. For the moment, the memories of her mother's betrayal were still too fresh, too raw.

Alison's father and her brother Alex had visited them during the summer and they'd all got on well. It was as if Alison had never left them. Alison's father, David, had hit it off with Tom. Alison was relieved because they were planning a wedding in the autumn of the following year. What had happened in the past just wasn't important anymore. It was the future that mattered to her now. Alison had lived some other life. It was not the life she'd wanted or hoped for. She was a survivor, a strong and independent woman. The most important people in her life were her family and her amazing friends, Rosie, Tom and Lisa who had helped her through her darkest days.

Lightning Source UK Ltd.
Milton Keynes UK
04 December 2010

163879UK00002B/169/P